Praise for *A Hover of Trout*

A warm hug of a book; a literary mug of cocoa with a dash of murder for spice. Jinny Alexander once again captures village life with her quirky cast of characters. I'm already looking forward to Jess O'Malley and the gang's next outing.

AMANDA GEARD
The Midnight House, The Moon Gate

A Hover of Trout is an excellent second book in the Jess O'Malley Mystery series [...] as well-written as the first, with intriguing characters, plenty of suspects, and some interesting character dynamics.

KELLY YOUNG,
The Travel Writer Cozy Mystery Series

A Hover of Trout, the second in the Jess O'Malley Mystery series, is an absolute joy for those who love classic detective mysteries. Sprinkled with a little romance along with the comfort and familiarity of Jess's rural Irish village, this expertly-crafted page-turner of a whodunnit had me guessing until the end. An excellent addition to the series!

ALISON WEATHERBY,
The Secrets Act

Fabulous characters and witty dialogue as more mysteries are revealed and solved by Jinny Alexander. I guarantee you will go back and read Book 1 in this charming mystery series.

MIKE MARTIN,
Award Winning Author of the Best Selling Sgt. Windflower Mystery series

The story is satisfyingly twisty with plenty of red herrings, coupled with likeable, believable characters. There's plenty of fun, and a lot of heart. The Jess O'Malley series deserves to become a firm favourite with mysteries lovers everywhere.

GERALDINE MOORKENS BYRNE
The Caroline Jordan Mystery series and *On the Fiddle! The Music Shop Mysteries*

Lyrical, atmospheric, Alexander's words lure you alongside amateur sleuth Jess O'Malley into the tangled webs of Ballyfortnum village. Very soon, you're too caught up to leave, nor do you want to. If you need a cosy weekend escape read, this is your ticket.

DAMYANTI BISWAS,
The Blue Mumbai series

This, the second in Alexander's Jess O'Malley series, is an incredibly satisfying read.

Jess O'Malley is the perfect companion on a wintery evening with the curtains drawn and a steaming mug of hot chocolate! A frothy mystery sprinkled with just the right amount of intrigue and a healthy dollop of romance, what's not to love?

MAIRI CHONG,
The Dr. Cathy Moreland Mysteries

Praise for *A Diet of Death*

This is a light-hearted cosy that will delight fans of M C Beaton's Agatha Raisin. […] Highly recommend it to those looking for a frothy, enjoyable read that is low on violence and high on feel-good entertainment!

MAIRI CHONG,
The Dr. Cathy Moreland Mysteries

Well-written and intriguing, this mystery revolving around members of a weight-loss group is one that will keep you turning the pages until the very end.

KELLY YOUNG,
The Travel Writer Cozy Mystery Series

A classic British style whodunnit.
With an engaging and believable heroine - Jess O'Malley - and set in rural Ireland, this is a fun mystery with lots of heart. An enjoyable read leading to a satisfying solution, already looking forward to the next book.

GERALDINE MOORKENS BYRNE
The Caroline Jordan Mystery series and *On the Fiddle! The Music Shop Mysteries*

The whole book was a warm, comforting read for anyone who loves mysteries. Highly suggested for fans of *The Thursday Murder Club*.

ALISON WEATHERBY,
The Secrets Act

Jinny Alexander's outstanding cosy mystery *A Diet Of Death* is a real treat. (And not the kind with calories!)

J. IVANEL JOHNSON,
The JUST (e)STATE Cozy Mysteries

This tale is a homage to those much loved classic detective authors, and is perfect for escaping the worries and stresses of the world.

LOUISE MORRISH,
Operation Moonlight

Jinny Alexander embeds her murder mystery with the satisfying atmosphere of rural Ireland. […] Cozy mystery readers who enjoy stories of friendships and murder possibilities will find *A Diet of Death* unusually strong in its atmosphere, which does equal justice to both the murder mystery component and the entwined lives of a small village […]

MIDWEST BOOK REVIEW

A HOVER OF TROUT

The Second Jess O'Malley Mystery

JINNY ALEXANDER

Copyright © Jinny Alexander 2023

Jinny Alexander has asserted her right to be identified as the author of this Work in accordance with the Copyright, Designs and Patents Act 1988

All rights reserved.

No part of this publication may be reproduced, distributed, or transmitted in any form or by any means, including photocopying, recording, or other electronic or mechanical methods, without the prior written permission of the publisher, except as permitted by copyright law.

This story is a product of the author's imagination and as such, all characters, settings, and events are fictitious. Any resemblance to real persons, living or dead, is purely coincidental.

ISBN Paperback: 978-1-916814-02-8

ISBN ebook: 978-1-916814-03-5

Cover Design: Wicked Good Book Covers

Map of Ballyfortnum: Jinny Alexander and Dewi Hargreaves

Visit www.jinnyalexander.com

www.OverSpilledInk.com

This book is dedicated to all the people who came together to contribute to the idea for this book, when I asked on Facebook a million years ago. I wonder if you remember?

A note to my American-English readers

I'm so glad you're here! I'm a British author, living in the Republic of Ireland, and all my books are set in Ireland or the UK. As such, I use British English in my writing so you'll notice a few extra letters – **U**s after **O**s, for instance, and **L**s that come in pairs. I make up for these extras by using fewer **Z**s…

I hope you'll enjoy my natural English voice and immerse yourselves fully into my UK and Irish settings and characters, but if you're still not convinced, I recommend a nice cup of tea.

Over here, a nice cup of tea fixes *almost* everything.

Love, Jinny xx

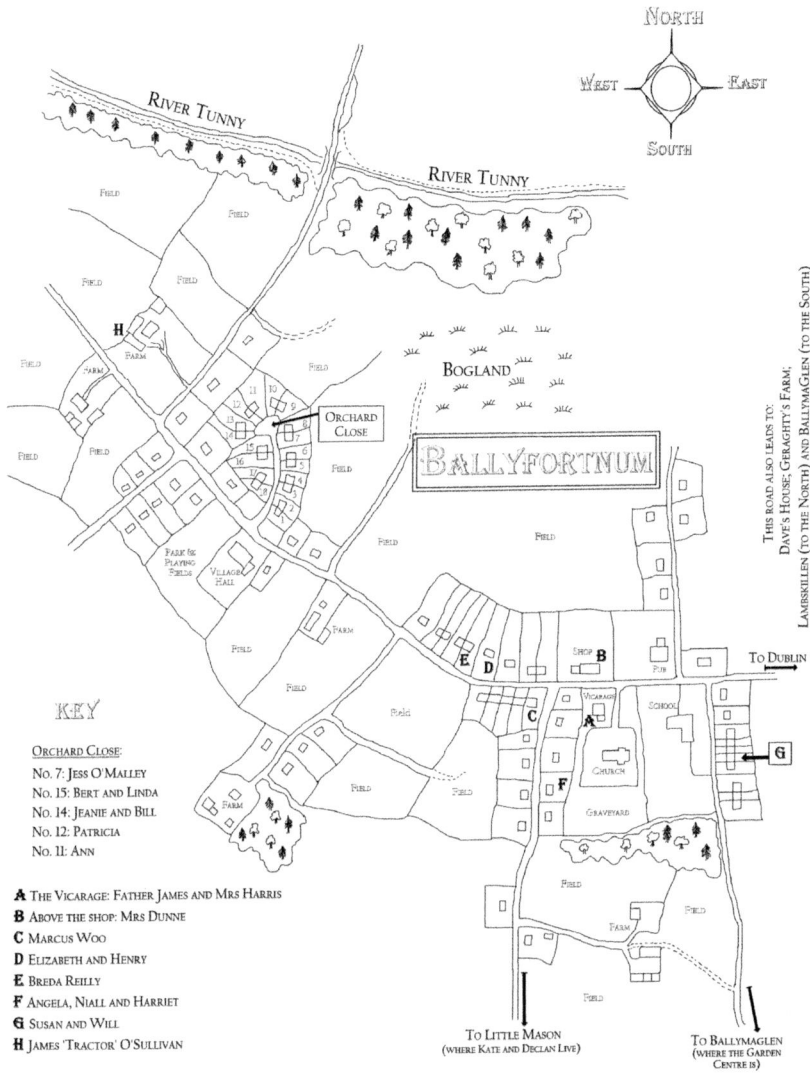

Chapter One

T he dead man had not gone far.

An upturned green canvas folding stool lay on the grassy bank. A fishing rod dangled hopefully over the river's edge, its neon float bobbing in the current. The top of a holding net emerged from the river, the length of it disappearing into the murky depths below.

As Jess passed by, a flash of silver glimmered in the water as a trout hovered briefly just below the surface, captive in the long, green net.

"Looking for a way out, huh, Fletch?" Jess bent to ruffle her Labrador's black-velvet ears, clipping on his lead so he wouldn't disturb the fisherman's setup or startle the fish. "Guess he's nipped off for a pee. Or a stretch of his legs."

It was not uncommon for there to be fishermen along the banks down here by the Tunny, and Jess recognised many of their faces to nod a hello or exchange brief pleasantries. Today though, this site was the first they'd passed. It was almost dusk, and she guessed most of the fishers would be packed up for the night by now. Chances were this fellow would be just around the next bend, chatting with a mate: "Will we head off now, or give it another half hour?" Jess could imagine them saying, one holding out his cigarette for the other to get a light, or offering a last beer before they quit.

She was half right.

As they rounded the bend, Fletcher barked frantically, tugging at the lead with such excitement it was all Jess could do to hold him back. Her cheeks warmed with embarrassment. Fletch's barking would scatter the fish as fast as it had destroyed the silence. She yanked the lead, swearing at the dog in a low angry hiss.

"Fletch, shut it! Shut up." Jess glared down at him, wrapping the lead tightly around her hand to rein him in close, before looking around to see what he was barking at. There was no one in sight. No fisherman, no dog walkers; not even a swan. A ripple suggested a passing school of fish, but otherwise, the river was calm and still, the reflection of the wooded bank as finely drawn as that of the treeline above the water. Without even the softest breeze, the reeds and bullrushes stood almost motionless, yellow-green and stiffened after several weeks of unusually dry weather.

Fletcher strained towards the water's edge, emitting a low growl that occasionally erupted into a suppressed bark when he couldn't hold it in any longer.

"Okay, okay." Giving in, she allowed the frantic dog to drag her forward.

They edged closer to the water, Jess still restraining Fletcher, but increasingly curious as to what had caught his attention.

And there he was. The fisherman.

He lay face down, his head almost hidden amongst the reeds. His checked jacket billowed, swollen by the water puffing it out like an inadequate life vest. His legs twisted awkwardly, pulled downstream by the current but tethered by the rest of his body, presumably snagged on something Jess couldn't see.

Hand to mouth, she muffled a scream and started towards the body, dropping Fletcher's lead to slither down the bank. Her trainers had little grip on the loose, dry soil, and she grabbed wildly at a broken fence post as she slipped towards the water. Too steep. Too dry. If she continued, the earth would landslide her into the river, and she would end up alongside the fisherman, unable to climb back out. It would be madness to try to reach him. She scanned the ground, swinging her gaze this way and that. There must be a branch, a stick—anything, *something*—with which she could reach the man.

Fletcher nudged her leg with his nose, threatening to unbalance her.

She let go of the post, flailing her arms, wobbling dangerously towards the river. "You idiot!" Her voice was shrill in the quiet air. She grabbed onto the fence post again, shoving Fletcher away with her free hand. "Go away. Go back. Sit!"

He turned to her with mournful eyes, but dropped onto his front paws, and lay on the grass.

Jess returned her attention to the man, and the fence post. She grasped it firmly in both hands and shook it, but although it moved fractionally, the old wooden post was sturdier than it appeared, rooted too deep for her to pull free. She clambered back up to the grassy track, grabbed Fletcher's lead, and dragged him, protesting, across the beaten-earth path, where she looped the lead around a thin silver birch.

The Labrador whined but sank to his haunches and sat, a doleful expression in his chocolatey eyes.

"Wait." Jess put a hand out towards him, palm out-facing in a 'stop' gesture. "Wait there, Fletch, I need to find something to help him." Her voice rose a little and she glanced around wildly, willing someone, anyone, to appear on the empty track.

No one did.

"Hang on, I'm coming," she said, barely louder than a whisper and not sure who she was telling. Herself? Fletcher? Not the immersed fisherman, several feet away, head still tangled in the reeds, anyway. Jess ducked under the low branches of the first row of trees: a straggly line of silver birches edging the regimented rows of cultivated pines beyond. Below the trees lay the odd twiggy branch, each one thinner than her finger, and brittle from the long dry summer.

Useless.

Further in, the pines were covered in velvety green moss, their branches laden with spiky needles that scratched her arms. Here beneath the thick canopy, the ground was damper, darker, shaded from the long days of August sun. Jess's feet sank into the mossy earth and she grabbed at a branch to steady herself before surveying the ground for something she could use. Anything. There has to be something. *Come on Jess, think.*

She heaved at a length of broken branch almost as fat as her arm, and long enough, *please*, to reach the man. With an angry scrape, it pulled free from the tangle of interlocking pine branches, showering a fresh flurry of dead, browned pine needles across the woodland floor and Jess's arms. A twig snapped back from beneath a larger branch, whipping her across the cheek. Her hand flew to her face, brushing at debris, dirt, and tears. From beyond the pines, Fletcher whined softly.

"I'm coming, Fletch, I'm coming." She grabbed the branch with both hands, biting her lip as the gnarled bark grazed her palms, and dragged it back to the riverbank.

Positioning the branch as close to the man as she could without it falling into the water, she gripped the solitary fencepost once more for support and eased down the bank as far as she dared. She wedged her heels against a grassy clump, one foot sideways against the ridge of grass, knee bent, her weight back towards the higher ground. Balance secure, she released her grasp on the post and hoisted the branch in both hands, praying silently that the dry ground would support her weight and not send her sliding into the river below. Slowly,

slowly, she eased the branch, heavy and unwieldy, towards the man. Almost there. Just a little more. She tipped her body forwards, keeping her weight low over her bent leg, just about keeping her balance, and stretched out to prod the body with the branch.

It bobbed under the water, throwing a rainbow of ripples out across the river, glistening and shimmering in the glow of the dying sun. The body floated to the surface again, rocking gently as it settled back into position. Bubbles rose with an arm.

"Dammit!" she shouted, loud and echoing in the still air. "Dammit! I can't reach him. I can't reach him, Fletch." She dropped the branch and sank onto her bottom, watching the body rise and fall as it found its floating level. "Feck it!" Still watching the man, she slithered backwards up the bank towards her dog.

Fletcher wagged his tail morosely, sweeping it once, twice, across the crumbly soil below the birches.

Jess knelt beside him and buried her face into his velvet-black fur as a sob escaped her.

He licked her arm and nudged her with his nose.

"Okay, okay." She pulled her phone out of her pocket, forgetting momentarily that she would get no signal here. "Shite!" She glared at her phone, then at Fletcher, back to the man in the river, and then back at the phone screen. "I don't know what to do."

Jess stood helpless on the track for a moment, panic threatening to overwhelm her. "Breathe, Jess. Breathe," she told herself. She smoothed back the curls that had broken free in the exertion of trying to reach the man, and retied her ponytail in a quick, untidy bundle. Hair out of her eyes, she stood up straight, took a deep breath, another one, another one, and made a decision.

"Okay, Fletch," she told her dog as she unhooked his lead from the tree. "He's stuck fast and I am pretty sure he is dead, so he's not going anywhere... We'll walk back towards the road until we pick up signal, and then we'll call Marcus? Okay?" She looked at Fletcher for reassurance, and he obligingly wagged his tail, eager to resume his walk.

Chapter Two

Back at the road and still clutching her phone, Jess leaned onto the padlocked gate and scrolled to Marcus's name in her contact list. "Please answer, please answer, please answer," she whispered as she listened to the distant ringing. He'd be home, she knew, having finished his night shift this morning and now heading into a couple of days off, but would he be sleeping? Surely not—he usually tried to catch a few hours in the morning, then get up for the afternoon and force himself to stay awake until 'proper bedtime' as he laughingly called it.

"Come on, damn you, answer it." She shouted at the phone, just as he picked up.

"Jess?"

At the sound of his voice, Jess burst into tears.

As she stood on the roadside, the sun almost gone and shadows creeping menacingly across the tarmac, Fletcher whined at his sobbing mistress. He nuzzled her leg with his nose, and she ducked to wrap an arm around his neck, grateful for the solid warmth of his body. She took a deep breath, sniffed loudly, and spoke again. This time, the words flowed out in a rush, tumbling over one another as if they too, were caught up in the undertow of the river.

Marcus listened without interrupting, bar mumbling encouraging "mmhm" noises whenever Jess paused for breath.

Finally spent, she stopped.

"Jess," Marcus said, using what she had come to know as his firm, no-nonsense, policeman voice, "since it's almost dark, I presume you drove down there?" He paused long enough for her to confirm that, yes, she had driven the twenty-minute walk from her house to the river. "Go and get into your car, lock the doors, turn on the engine and the radio and the heater, and wait. I'm on the way." Even as he spoke, she could hear him moving through his cottage.

She pictured him grabbing a jacket, snatching his keys off the hook in the kitchen, giving Snowflake a distracted pat...

"Stay there, Snow, I'll be back soon," he said, slightly muffled as he turned away from the phone, and reinforcing her image of him saying goodbye to his little Westie and shutting the door between them on his way out to his car. "I'm on the way, I'll stay on the phone until you are in your car, but then I have to hang up to drive. Go now."

Reassured by his calm voice, she did as she was told, crossing the road, and walking the short distance to the layby where her little red car waited for her beside the open stretch of commercially-farmed peat bog.

"Okay, I'm in the car."

"There in five, sit tight." He disconnected the call.

Jess took his advice and turned on both the heater and the radio. Only now did she realise she was, in fact, shivering violently. He'd have known that, of course. Marcus Woo, high-ranking Garda, neighbour, and friend, was used to dealing with people in shock. And this was not the first time he had had to deal with Jess in a state of shock. Only a few months ago, the two of them had outed a neighbour as the killer of two members of the village slimming group, and the attempted murderer of one other. Since then, Jess and Marcus had become increasingly close friends, and Jess looked after Marcus's dog while he worked, whenever she was able.

Jess turned the radio up loud and leaned her head against the headrest. She closed her eyes, but the bloated, floating horror of the dead man instantly filled her mind. With a shudder, she opened her eyes again.

"Come here, Fletch." She patted the empty passenger seat, encouraging him to jump across from his usual spot on the back seat. Uncertain, he cocked a questioning ear, but needed only one more pat of the seat to persuade him. Jess pulled him down to lie partly across her lap, straddling the handbrake awkwardly with his back legs still on the passenger seat. She hugged him to her, needing comfort, but with one brief meeting of his wet nose and her chin in an apologetic doggy kiss, he pulled away, turned around twice on the passenger seat, settled into a curled-up bundle, and went to sleep.

As the last ribbons of orange sunset gave way to deepening blues, darkness threatened to engulf the bog, the woodland, and the stretch of winding river in between. Jess glanced at the neon numbers on the dashboard clock, willing Marcus and his Gardai colleagues to hurry. *They'd better be here soon or it will be too dark to see anything.* Scant moments later, the bright lights of a car bounced into view, brightening both the darkening landscape and Jess's spirits. The car slowed as it passed, then swung around in a U to pull up beside her in the layby. Marcus. Jess scrubbed fresh tears away with the back of her wrist and pulled on the car door handle to release the central locking.

"Stay there," he said. "I'll get in. We have to wait for lights and backup anyway. They're on the way." He peered in the window, as Fletch clambered across Jess's lap to greet him. "Will I get in the back then?" He pulled open the door behind Jess's driving seat. Rather than sliding in, he called Fletch through the gap between the two front seats, told the dog to stay, and jogged around the car to slide into the newly vacated passenger seat. Only now did he reach across to Jess and pull her into a clumsy hug, awkward in the cramped space.

"You okay?"

She sniffled into his shoulder, pulled away, offered a watery smile, and nodded.

He patted her leg gently as he withdrew to look at her properly. "Now, tell me what you've found."

By the time Jess had described how she had tried unsuccessfully to reach the man to pull him free from the water, the sky was inky blue and the sun gone.

Marcus retrieved a hastily-made flask of tea from his car, but before he could slip back into Jess's car, the colours of the sky changed again: strobing lights cast blue-black-blue-black-blue-black shadows across the horizon, then across the trees at the roadside, then the road itself, and finally over the old iron railings of the bridge. Marcus passed the flask in through Jess's window, talking rapidly into his phone as he did so. He cut off the call, turned on the phone's flashlight, and stepped out into the road to guide first a police car and then an ambulance to a halt alongside the gate that Jess had climbed over nearly forty minutes ago.

Chapter Three

Unable to answer any questions beyond roughly where to find the dead man, and on Marcus's assurance to his colleagues that Jess was not a 'person of interest', she was now curled up on her sofa in her home at Number 7, Orchard Close, sipping hot chocolate, with a fleecy blanket around her shoulders and Fletcher asleep on her legs.

Her elderly neighbour and dear friend, Linda, perched on the other sofa; two empty plates and a drained mug on the low table between them.

Marcus, unable to leave the river until the area had been sealed and preserved, had suggested that the young, uniformed Garda who had arrived in the patrol car should run her home, but Jess had insisted she could manage. As a compromise, Marcus had called Linda before allowing Jess to return to her car, to ask the older woman if she would sit with Jess for a while in case of shock.

"You're making a habit of this, Jess love," the widow said with a wry smile, referring to the evening less than four months previously when Marcus had called on her for similar baby-sitting duties, after Jess had been both instrumental in, and present for, the arrest of a fellow villager for murder.

"I'm okay though," Jess insisted, realising as she said it that it was almost true. Before being permitted to leave the area, she had walked along the torchlit riverbank with the police and the paramedics, to bring them back to the scene, although, as she had told them, they would have found it just as easily without her. Dark by then, bar the moonlight and clear, star-filled sky, she couldn't say for certain which bend in the river would reveal the upturned stool and abandoned fishing paraphernalia, nor exactly in which clump of reeds the fisherman's body bobbed.

The sombre group had simply walked, sweeping flashlights across the grassy path, until Fletcher pulled excitedly on the lead, and the metal legs of the stool glinted in the torchlight.

"Around the next bend then," Jess had said unnecessarily, as Fletcher strained towards the riverbank.

Having established the location, Marcus had called Linda, promised to call Jess later, and instructed his uniformed colleague to escort her to her car along the rough earth of the river path. Jess recognized this young Garda from that night back in the springtime when she'd helped ensure the arrest and conviction of that Ballyfortnum neighbour, but the two walked along in thoughtful silence aside from an odd "Mind your step" until at last, he shone his torch onto Jess's car door, lighting the keyhole for her.

"You sure you're okay to drive?" he said. "It's not a bother to run you back."

"I'll be grand," she'd said, unsure as to whether she meant it or not. She slipped into the driver seat, and the Garda closed the door behind her, stepped aside, and waved her off before setting back across the road and through the gate, towards the dead man.

By the time Jess had swung her car into the little driveway of her semi-detached house in Orchard Close, Linda had the lights on, tea brewing, and a plate of apricot-flecked cookies ready on a plate. She engulfed Jess in a warm hug as soon as the latter had kicked off her boots and dropped Fletcher's lead on top of them. Jess let her head rest onto Linda's shoulder for a long moment, before gesturing her elderly neighbour back into the living room.

"I can stay, if you like?" Linda offered, pointing down at a bag-for-life on the floor beside the sofa. "I brought my nightie over, in case you wanted company all night."

Emotion thumped in Jess's chest. She reached across to squeeze Linda's hand. Her elderly neighbour was finally getting used to sleeping alone in her own house, which stood facing Jess's on the other side of Orchard Close, following the death of her husband, Bert, in February. The two women had been close since Jess had first moved into Orchard Close to care for her sick father a little over two years ago, but since first George O'Malley's death and then Bert's, they had become even closer. Jess relied on Linda in a way she'd not been able to rely on her own mother in years. Linda, in return, treated Jess as another daughter—one she saw far more often than either of her real daughters.

Now though, Linda's face was etched with tired lines so Jess sent her home, watching from the doorway of her house at Number 7 until Linda was safely inside Number 15 with the door closed behind her. Jess waited, watching as the lights came on to show Linda's passage through the hall then plotted Linda's path upstairs to bed. Only once the downstairs of Number 15 was plunged back into darkness did Jess retreat into her own house and close the door, for once ensuring the bolt was across and the safety chain attached.

She let Fletcher out into the back garden for one last pee, then dragged her weary body up the stairs to bed. Leaning back against her pillows, Jess picked up her current book and gazed unseeingly at the jumble of words, her thoughts drifting back to the unfortunate fisherman.

It was a long time since Jess had been fishing.

Way back before their parents had decided to up sticks and move out to Ballyfortnum, Jess's father would often bring her and her brother Eric out to the midlands for a day trip to the countryside. George O'Malley was a keen fisherman, enjoying the relaxation of countless Sunday afternoons beside the river, or settled with a picnic, a thermos, and his fishing tackle on the shores of any of the many lakes lying across the midlands. It was the fishing that had been one of the main lures for Jess's father, George, in deciding where to move to when he and Doreen had retired.

Jess's older sister, Alice, aloof and problematic, had never joined those fishing trips. It was only in the last few months that Jess was beginning to rebuild a solid, happy relationship with her sister. Now, as she thought of her, Jess smiled; a mix of relief that Alice finally seemed well, and genuine delight as she replayed some of the happy times the sisters had spent together this summer.

However, despite Alice jostling with Eric for space in Jess's thoughts, it was not her older sister who Jess texted now, as she lay awake playing out possible scenarios of the fisherman's last moments through her mind. Instead of Alice, she texted Eric, who still fished on occasional Sunday afternoons or twilight summer evenings, after his daughters were tucked up in bed for the night. Eric, now living down south with his wife and children, enjoyed the calm of fishing to balance his busy work and family life. In their childhood, it was Eric who had been Jess's closest ally and co-player in their endless games of mystery and sleuthing. It was Eric who shared her love of mystery books, and thus it was to Eric that she now instinctively turned, as she sat up in bed unable to sleep. She tucked the phone under her chin and shuffled against her pillows as she listened to the sound of ringing, far away in her brother's house. She tugged the bedcovers up around her shoulders, sending an indignant Fletcher sprawling across her legs, as the phone went to voicemail. She disconnected it with a sigh.

How're you? she texted instead, briefly courteous before getting to the point: *How'd you kill a fisherman and why?* She hit SEND, then followed the text immediately with a second message: *I found a dead one. Another fine mystery for the Lollipop Club.* She added a laughing emoji, a lollipop emoji, and a thinking-face emoji, smiling wryly as she lightened the recollection of her discovery with a humour she didn't yet feel.

Although still a bit creeped-out by the dead man, part of her revelled in the confusion her text would cause her brother. She pictured him squinting at his iPhone; wrinkling his brow and rubbing his freckled face, puzzling over her message before chuckling in inevitable amusement as he, too, recalled their childhood detective club. He wouldn't see her message until morning, but she felt better for having shared her thoughts. Besides, remembering the decades-ago adventures of the Lollipop Club always brought a smile to her face and a flutter of determination to her belly.

Now she had put *Why* and *How* into the visible words of the text message, they grew larger in her own mind, and she could imagine the letters floating around in her thoughts as pulsing, bold, old-fashioned typewriter font, demanding that she grab them and act upon them. With a sigh that caused Fletcher to cock an ear and shift his weight, she threw back the duvet again and got out of bed. Padding downstairs, she found her notebook tucked beside the kettle, which she automatically flicked on. Waiting for it to boil, she rooted in the junk drawer for a pencil. She made tea, then carried the steaming mug, notebook, pencil, and another of Linda's cookies back upstairs to the bedroom.

"Well Fletch," she said to the unimpressed dog, as she got into bed again and yanked the covers back up around her chin.

He opened one eye, got up, turned around, then plonked himself firmly back onto her feet.

Her dog clearly unwilling to listen to her, she muttered to herself instead as she wrote.

WHO? *(ask Marcus, obv) Newspaper, radio, RIP.ie, if he won't tell*

WHEN? *Not long before I found him, I reckon*

WHY? *Presume not an accident? Murder then...?*

WHAT WITH? HOW? *(How to find out... Marcus? Will he tell???)*

WHY?

She scrawled the word for a second time, this time underlining it with a violent jabbing stroke of the pencil that poked a hole in the paper. She underlined it again, with a little less force, and drew a curling arrow back up to its partner above, going back and forth over the line with the pencil to darken it.

"Why, why, why, Fletch? Why is he dead?" Jess chewed the end of the pencil and realised that she knew nothing. Knowing she should try to sleep, and wait until morning, she texted Marcus anyway: *Can't sleep. Did ya find out who he was?* Was Marcus still at the police station? Or even still at the river? Or had he handed over to his on-duty colleagues and gone home? Jess guessed he would still be working, otherwise he'd have called to see how she was ... unless, unlike her, he had decided it was too late to contact anyone and was mistakenly thinking he would disturb her sleep ... Jess doodled squiggles, lines, and childlike fish across the page and around the margins. Stifling a yawn, she made a bullet-point plan of action:

1. *Call Marcus (if he hasn't answered)*

2. *Check the radio obits in morn — what time are they on — ask Linda...*

She'd never quite got used to this country habit of reading out obituaries three times a day on the local news, and never deliberately listened to them. She caught them accidentally the odd time she tuned in for the local radio station's '80s hour, when the death news often ran on so long that 'hour' could easily be reduced to only a handful of '80s songs, squeezed into just thirty minutes and punctuated by adverts and DJ commentary.

She crossed out the number 2 and replaced it with 3, then added a new number 2 squished into the space between her original two lines:

2. *Ask Linda about obit times.*

Below the new 3 on the list, she added another item to be checked off:

4. *Take Fletch to river for walk.*

Plans committed to paper, she drained the mug of tea, reached out to snap off the light, shoved her feet under the warm bulk of Fletcher's gently-snuffling body, and allowed sleep to take over.

Chapter Four

As it happened, Jess neither needed Marcus nor the local media to tell her who the mystery fisherman was. In her state of aftershock, she had overlooked that, on waking after her restless night, the morning would bring with it a new Wednesday. It was not a text from Marcus that woke her, but one from Linda.

I'll pick you up, you will be too tired to drive.

Jess gazed blankly at the phone for a moment, trying to piece together the foggy pieces of the text. Linda. Pick her up. Oh. Wednesday ... Gardening course day.

Jess and Linda had embarked on a gardening course in the neighbouring village of Ballymaglen a few months ago. Jess's father had been a keen gardener, and had become good friends with his opposite neighbour, Linda's recently deceased husband Bert. Together, Bert and George had kept Orchard Close blooming, and worked tirelessly to help Ballyfortnum maintain its Tidy Village status for several consecutive years. Now, with both Bert and George gone, Jess and Linda had decided that they should learn how to maintain their respective gardens and honour the memory of their loved ones. So, back in the spring, just as the clocks went forward to usher in Summer Time, Jess had enrolled them on a new course at the garden centre. Together, they had attended every Wednesday from mid-March to June and then extended the initial planned duration to continue throughout the summer. It was just coming to an end, as the summer holidays neared their climax, and Jess knew already that she would miss those Wednesday mornings. She had become friendly with the course facilitator, Shay, and under his encouragement had enrolled for a more intensive gardening course at college. It was due to start in a few weeks' time. Meanwhile, she was also, again encouraged by Shay, working two afternoons a week at the garden centre, and loving it.

Caught unawares by this particular Wednesday, Jess swore loudly, nudged Fletcher off her feet, and swung herself out of bed. "Dammit Fletch, I'm not ready!" She rooted in the wardrobe for clothes and fired a text to Linda.

Running late. Overslept, forgot. 15 min? In underwear and T-shirt, she raced down the stairs, threw open the French doors for Fletcher to go out and pee, and was shimmying into her jeans just as the kettle rumbled to its boil. A welcome packet of *pain au chocolat* lay open on the worktop, and she released two from their cello wrapper, dumping one on the worktop and biting straight into the other, not bothering to find a plate.

Ten minutes later, after a quick wash and hasty tug of a brush through her unruly dark curls, she was just about ready when Linda beeped her car horn from the road between their houses. Jess waved her trainers at the window, held up a finger to signify she'd be out in a minute, called Fletch back in and shut the French doors. Jamming her feet into unlaced trainers, she shuffled out of the door and slid gratefully into the passenger seat of Linda's car.

"I forgot, sorry," she said, and rested her head against the headrest, her eyes closed. "Sorry. I made it though!" She opened her eyes again and smiled triumphantly at her neighbour. "Blimey, Linda, I haven't moved so fast in ages. Let's go." The course had been originally scheduled to run for only twelve weeks, and finish in June, but the group had enjoyed it so much they'd cajoled Shay into extending its duration. Despite his initial protests that there would be less practical learning they could do through the height of summer, he had given in to the persuasion, with the caveat that these extra weeks would include a lot more theory and 'classroom' learning. They'd taken an enforced break for two weeks in June, since he was already booked for a fortnight in the sun. However, once he returned, bronzed and refreshed after an exotic-sounding trip to Marrakech, he willingly opened up the makeshift classroom again, and most of their little group agreed to converge for another eight weeks until the end of the summer.

"Good practice for your real course," Shay had said with a wide smile as Jess paid the extra fees. "Here; these'll keep you busy." He'd scooped an armful of gardening books from the over-laden desk and dumped them into her arms, to borrow in preparation for college. Although she'd groaned in mock pretence under the weight, she'd been steadily working her way through them in the long summer evenings alone at her patio table, or in her sunny yellow kitchen as the real sun went down over the distant hills, out of sight to the westerly-facing front of her house.

Only a few minutes late after Jess's frantic dash to be ready in time, but not the only late arrivals, Linda neatly reversed into a parking space as another of their course-mates pulled up alongside them.

Mike walked across the car park with them, holding open the door to the larger of the garden centre's two portacabins for them to enter ahead of him.

As they crossed the threshold, it was apparent that the group were not, as Jess would have expected, already making notes about plant diseases, or best planting conditions, or species that grow best in the heavy clay soil or peaty loam typical of the locality. Instead, there was a murmur of subdued excitement, and the hiss of a newly-filled kettle slowly coming to the boil.

"What's up?" Jess asked, squinting around the little group of people who had become her friends over the last few months.

"Didn't you hear?" Moira didn't wait for an answer. "Viktor Dąbrowski was found dead yesterday. Mila's brother."

Jess scanned the stuffy portacabin, searching for Mila. She wasn't there.

Mila Dąbrowska, an immigrant arrived into the area from Poland some years ago, was initially shy with the group but had grown with the seedlings they'd nurtured from week to week. As the herbs they had sown into little plastic pots had developed first shoots, then leaves, then, finally fragrance, Mila had shyly matched them. She reminded Jess of coriander—demure blossom with a delicate scent and hint of something exotic. Despite her underlying timidity, as Mila had become more comfortable within the group, she had shown an endearing sense of humour and a gentle manner, and Jess liked her very much.

At Moira's words, a chill prickled Jess's spine, raising goosebumps on her bare arms that were at odds with the August heat. Even before she asked her next question, Jess was certain she already knew what the answer would be.

"What ... what happened to him?"

Words rushed together and jostled for space. "Died …" "Yesterday …" "Distraught …" The voices merged and blurred until they became a pounding in Jess's ears. The chill from moments earlier turned to a blaze of heat. Her knees buckled, and she groped wildly for an out-of-reach table. Too far … too far away …

Mike grabbed her arm, pushing her forward.

Jess sank into a padded, metal folding chair, shaking off Mike's grip as the seat became solid beneath her.

In the corner of the room, the kettle burbled to its noisy boil. The click as it turned itself off reverberated in the silence of the room.

"Jess. Jess. Are you alright, love?"

"She's gone awful pale…"

"Put her head between her knees!"

"Jess…?"

A chipped Bart Simpson mug was pushed into her hands, steaming and swirling as she wrapped her hands around it, ignoring the scalding heat of the china.

"Fishing?" she eventually managed. "Did you say fishing?" Tea slopped into her lap as she looked around the room at the worried faces, searching for the one who might have uttered those telltale words. She placed the mug onto the table with trembling hands as Linda's voice ebbed and flowed like the water lapping at the edge of the riverbank.

"She found him," Linda explained. "It was our Jess who found him."

Jess heard the chatter in waves—a badly tuned radio drifting in and out of her focus—as the vision of the floating, billowing man bobbed up and down, up and down, in her mind.

"Drink," someone said, lifting the mug and pressing it back into Jess's hand.

She took several large swigs, the hot liquid scalding her tongue. The burning cleared the fuzziness from her head, and with a determined shake to dislodge the image of the fisherman, she forced herself to focus on the concerned faces around her.

"Mila's brother? Our Mila? Oh no! How is she? Who ...? I mean ..." Jess tailed off, unable to make the questions she wanted to ask form into any coherence. "Wow." She drained her tea and got up, crossing the room to refill her mug.

Once the burble of excitement died down, some of the group left. Others volunteered to busy themselves with potting on plants in one of the polytunnels. The rest of the morning passed in a blur of tea, biscuits, and speculation, but for Jess, very little gardening of either the practical or the theory kind.

Shay, solicitous and concerned, made sure the kettle was continually refilled and, averting a potential mini-crisis, popped out to the nearby supermarket to restock the rapidly-decreasing supply of biscuits.

"You okay Jess?" he murmured every time he passed near to her, patting her arm, or stroking her back in comforting sympathy.

Despite the subdued buzz running through the group after discovering such drama in their midst, no one knew any real information. Moira, being a neighbour of Mila, had heard the news as she had called to Mila, as was their usual routine on a Wednesday morning, to walk the short distance to the garden centre together from the estate where they both lived. Mila, Moira relayed, had insisted that she would be fine, and that Moira must go on to the class and make her apologies for Mila not showing up for the course today. Aside from telling Moira that her brother had died, and had been found in the river the previous evening, she hadn't said more, but been pulled back into the dim hall of her house by unseen relations.

"I'll call in to her later," Moira told Jess, "but I won't intrude."

"Of course not," Jess agreed. "Give her our love. Tell her we are thinking of her."

Moira gave Jess a quick hug as the group broke up and went their separate ways.

"Well," Shay said, waylaying Jess on her way out, "we didn't get much done today. Sorry. Are you okay? Will you still be coming tomorrow?" Thursdays and Fridays, being the garden centre's busier weekdays, were the afternoons Jess spent helping out and learning the ropes. "It's no problem if you want to take the next couple of days off?"

Jess shrugged. "I'll be fine. It'll take my mind off it. I just keep seeing him, you know ... floating there in the water." She shuddered at the recollection.

Shay put an arm around her shoulders and she let herself be pulled close to him for a moment, faintly aware of the rich, earthy scent of his T-shirt.

Chapter Five

Jess sat back in the passenger seat and sighed. In the relative silence of Linda's car, she leaned her pounding head against the headrest and closed her eyes, then opened them and groped in her pocket, squirming on the seat as she searched for her phone. Had Marcus called with an update? "Oh," she said, "I left it at home."

Linda shot her a glance, a question on her brow, but turned her attention immediately back to the road.

"My phone. I just realised I hadn't heard from Marcus, but I left my phone at home, so…" Jess shrugged. "Ah well. I guess we found out as much as he would have been able to tell me anyway—maybe more!"

"Mmhm." Linda, concentrating on driving, paid little attention. She held the wheel firmly at ten-to-two, her knuckles white with the effort of attentiveness.

Jess, undaunted by her friend's lack of response, continued to talk. "Do you think someone killed him? I guess it's likely he just fell in … I don't know, trying to get something … watching an unusual fish … that sounds a bit mad, don't you think? But something like that. Tripped, maybe? Do you think I should go and see Mila?"

Linda flicked her eyes towards Jess without turning her head. "I don't know, pet, maybe in a day or two. We could pop over together. I'll bake a nice cake. Not yet though, love; they won't want strangers popping in just yet." Linda returned her full attention to driving, and Jess switched on the radio.

"I guess you're right. Mind if I try to find news?"

Home, Jess kicked off her shoes and padded barefoot into the garden. The patio slabs were warm from the mid-August sun, and the metal of the garden table hot to touch. She put down her notebook, a glass of water, and her phone, and leaned back with her face to the sun and her eyes closed, basking for a moment as she considered the information she had learned.

She'd met Mila's brother once. He'd collected Mila after the course one Wednesday lunchtime, back at the start of the summer—their mother's birthday, she'd said, waving her hands to encompass the group as she made vague "my brother" introductions before grabbing her bag from the bench in the corner of the polytunnel and leaving with him. Jess couldn't remember what he'd looked like though, and couldn't equate him with the sodden, bloating, face-down fisherman she'd found in the river only yesterday.

"Only yesterday, Fletch, seems like so long ago already."

Fletcher paused briefly in his sniffing of the borders, and glanced up at her. Seeing nothing to interest him, he resumed his investigation into a particularly aromatic patch of earth, scrabbling with his paws.

Jess yawned and picked up her phone to read the text from Marcus she had found waiting for her:

How are you? No real news. Treating as suspicious. May need to take another statement from you later. Just leaving now, need some sleep. You Ok?

He'd sent it only moments after the text from Linda that had spurred her out of bed in such a rush that morning. He'd be awake now, she guessed, as she typed out the response: *Turns out I met him once - brother of someone I know. Weird, huh? You still sleeping?*

His answer came instantly: *Oh? That's a coincidence. How did you know him? Just up now. You still OK to have Snowflake later?*

Sure, come for dinner if you like? Nothing fancy, I'm wrecked too—pizza ok?

Jess often looked after Marcus's little West Highland terrier while he worked, since he'd voiced his concerns that his long work hours meant he may not be able to keep the little dog his daughter, Lily, had loved so much. Marcus didn't see his young daughter often since her mother had taken off to America with one of Marcus's colleagues a year or so ago. The Westie was no trouble to Jess, and in truth, she had quickly grown to look forward to Marcus's company and friendship. In the mornings, he would usually drop or collect Snowflake without stopping, but in the afternoons when he came down before a nightshift to drop Snowflake off, or when he came to collect the little dog in an evening after a day shift finished, he would sometimes loiter for a while. After so long living alone, most of her neighbours elderly and retired, Jess hadn't realized how lonely she had become. She couldn't quite decide exactly how she felt about the policeman, but they had fallen easily and quickly into a companionable and comfortable friendship.

That would be perfect, if you're sure? His answer, again, was immediate, and a flutter of pleasure rose through Jess's chest.

"Stop that," she hissed to herself, putting the phone down on the patio table and strolling across the parched lawn to her new-this-year vegetable plot. Smug with her new-found gardening expertise, Jess selected an assortment of salad leaves and plucked a handful of cherry tomatoes from the small lean-to greenhouse she'd installed against the fence. "Hah, Fletcher! Salad from the garden, look!"

Fletcher lay stretched out on his back with his belly turned to the sun, and ignored her.

The garden had been her dad's thing. It had become his hobby and his main pastime since his wife—Jess's mother—had run off to Spain with a younger man not long after they had moved to Ballyfortnum. George O'Malley had weeded and hoed and dug through his grief, and come out of it with a solid cluster of new friends around him in the form of his neighbours in Orchard Close. He'd exchanged gardening knowledge for home baking, and by the time Jess moved in to nurse him through those final difficult months of his illness, he'd become a valued and ingrained member of the community.

After his death, Linda's husband had taken over, maintaining George's neat garden for Jess. Only after Bert's sudden death in February had Jess discovered that she had inherited her father's passion and green fingers. On the very first day of the gardening course, back in March, she'd been amazed to feel an instant emotional pull—a desire to learn how to work the same magic on the land that first her dad and then Bert had demonstrated. Looking around her garden now, she felt a surge of pride.

The borders hummed with a vibrant mix of cottage garden flowers and an enchanting collection of herbs. The air was abuzz with insect activity, and the flower borders stretched away down the garden where they segued into a neat vegetable plot offering up carrots, spinach, and assorted salad greens. Not bad for the first season. Not bad at all. By next year, the herbs would have spread, filling some of the bare earth, the perennials would be settled in and the ground cover plants would be ... well, covering more ground. Yes, she definitely felt proud. Her dad would be proud too, she knew. With that thought, she pulled a foam kneeling pad and a trowel from the little shed, and spent the next half hour weeding, her mind wondering as she dug at those stubborn buttercups that spread like wildfire.

Viktor... Her dead fisherman now had a name. *Viktor...* floating face down, pinioned by unseen weed, just waiting to be discovered. If he hadn't got caught up in the reeds, he could have been swept along in the current and ended up ... well anywhere, Jess supposed, as she pulled another rogue buttercup out from between a straggly young lavender plant and a fragrant clump of thyme.

She had been allowed to leave before the body was pulled from the river, so hadn't had to see the poor man's face, but she could picture the checked shirt, stained dark from the water and fading daylight. By the time the young Garda escorted back to her car, the rest of the police crew were already busy erecting floodlights and police tape. They would enclose the area around the body, and back along the path, to create a cordon around the fallen stool and abandoned fishing lines, the Garda had explained as they walked.

As an earwig scurried up her trowel, she remembered that brief flash of silver as a fish had flapped in the holding net. That ripple of water as it breached the surface for a second, just before Fletcher had dragged her on; onwards around the bend to find the body of the fish's unfortunate captor. She sat back onto her heels and grimaced at the irony of the fisherman becoming the prey. *Eugh.* With a shudder, she shook away the unbidden image of fish nibbling at a dead man's toes, and stabbed her trowel into the baked earth once more. Perhaps an animal rights activist had tipped the man into the water?

Some people didn't agree with fishing ... She stretched her back, easing out the kinks, then clambered to her feet.

Discarding the trowel on the hot metal patio table, she stepped into the cool shade of the kitchen in search of her notebook and pen.

With no space left on the page on which she had already doodled notes during the night, she turned to a fresh sheet and wrote a heading in neat capitals, underlining the unfamiliar spelling for emphasis:

<u>VIKTOR DĄBROWSKI</u>

Below this, she added *fisherman*. An arrow, branching down and left led to his address—a little vague, as she only knew he lived on the same estate as his sister Mila, possibly in the same house, but either way, he'd lived on a road she didn't know the name of, at a house she didn't know the number of.

She drew another arrow, this one neatly vertical from Viktor's name, passing beyond the address and onward to about halfway down the page. At its point, she wrote **WHY** in large capitals, circled it twice, and added her first idea in another branch of the web: *Animal rights/fishing protest?*

It was a start, at least. Marcus would be here soon, and she would be able to press him for more information.

Chapter Six

Marcus didn't have much to divulge. "You know I'm not allowed to tell you anything about an ongoing investigation, Jess." He tore off another slice of pizza and took a large bite.

"But you already told me it's being treated as suspicious? And you said you may need to interview me some more, so you can tell me what about, can't you?" She picked at the salad bowl, hunting for pieces of cucumber under the lettuce leaves.

He laughed. "No, not really. You'll get an official call if you're needed. Nice try."

She waved a piece of lettuce at him. "Okay, okay, but tell me, why do you think it was suspicious? I mean, does that mean he didn't just fall in? How do you know? Was he hurt?"

"Oh Jess ..." He shook his head slowly, his eyes creased with amusement as she interrupted him again, holding up her fingers to emphasize her words.

"One. I found him. You wouldn't even know he was there yet if I hadn't found him." Arguable, perhaps, but he let it go. "Two. Turns out I know his sister. I thought I'd call around to her tomorrow; see how she is ... I'll get Linda to bake something nice for the family ..."

Marcus pretended to glare at her, his mock annoyance betrayed by a twitching of his mouth as he tried not to laugh.

"Three ..." She held up the third finger.

He caught her hand in his and pinned it to the table, holding up his other hand in a 'stop' gesture. "Jess, you are *not* going to call around and start quizzing the family of a murder victim the day after his body is found. You are simply not."

But the damage was done. "Murder? Murder is it now? Ha!" She stabbed a cherry tomato with her fork and held it aloft like a well-won trophy. "So, go on, tell me how you know it's murder, or I get the last slice of pizza."

Marcus was silent. He looked at the pizza. He looked at Jess. He looked at the pizza again and sighed. "Jessica O'Malley, I swear you will cost me my job one of these days. We won't know for certain until we get the results of the postmortem. Can you not keep out of trouble for five minutes and leave this one to the police? Just because you proved who killed Dave and Angela, that does not give you the right to know everything about every other suspicious death in the county, you know?" His dark eyes held hers, unblinking and stern, but the twitch of his mouth belied his amusement. "And how in the world did it happen to be *you* who stumbled on this poor man, and how, just *how*, does it turn out that you *knew* him?" Taking advantage of her distraction, he grabbed the last pizza slice, folded it in half, and took a large bite.

After Marcus collected Snowflake on Thursday morning—yawning and red-eyed, he hadn't come in—Jess shoved her feet into her walking boots and held open the back door of her car for Fletcher to leap in.

"River, huh, boyo?" She pushed the door shut and slid into the driving seat. A day behind in pursuing the plans she'd scrawled in her notebook the day before, she wondered aloud whether the police cordon would still be in place. The river was only a five-minute drive, and whilst Jess generally preferred to avoid the incongruity of driving the car to go for a walk, she loved the peace and tranquillity of the river; the silence, and the wildlife. On days with oodles of spare time, she enjoyed the twenty-minute walk there and back, but today she'd need to be home in time to get out to the garden centre for the afternoon shift, and besides, it was still too hot to walk for miles.

In the winter, the riverbank path would become saturated and boggy, making walking impossible, but from late spring to mid-autumn it was a favourite place for a leisurely stroll.

Fletcher loved it at the river, too, and even before Jess had parked in the same little lay-by as on Tuesday evening, he had his front paws up against the window, tongue lolling and tail wagging in gleeful anticipation. Here, he could run off-lead along the grassy bank or in and out of the trees, unhindered by livestock or roads. It was only when approaching unfamiliar dogs, or fishermen, that Jess needed to restrain him.

As it had been on Tuesday evening, the water was calm and the surface as still as glass. A pair of swans drifted by on the far side of the river, hissing towards Fletcher as he ran down the bank to bark at them. Gentle ripples indicated fish in the shady shallows under a weeping birch tree but otherwise, the river was silent. There had been another car in the lay-by, newer and cleaner than the usual tatty vans or old estate cars that Jess associated with anglers or dog walkers. Police, maybe?

She walked in the same direction as she had on Tuesday, and as they rounded a bend, the hum of low conversation drifted towards her. Up ahead, two men stood on the riverbank, one gesticulating and the other nodding in agreement, both too well-dressed to be casual walkers. Beyond them, a ribbon of blue and white plastic tape fluttered weakly in a momentary breath of air, but dropped immediately to hang limp alongside the post it was tied to.

Still a crime scene, then.

Jess called Fletcher to her and clipped on his lead. She pulled him close—"Heel, Fletch."—and approached the men.

Neither was familiar and neither was in uniform, but she guessed from their smart clothing and official manner as she walked towards them that they were policemen. She wrapped Fletcher's lead around her hand to stop him jumping up at them, and held out her other hand in greeting.

"Jessica O'Malley. I found him. Did you find anything?" Even as she said the words, she wished she could bite them back. Would they have told her more if she had pretended to be a casual passer-by instead of someone returning to a crime scene? Too late now ...

The shorter of the two men, greying, stockier, and in need of a shave, spoke first. "We're just packing up. We've finished." He gestured around the scene. The stool was still in the same place it had been on Tuesday, but now collapsed and leaning against the tackle box. The fishing rod had been pulled in, and the long keepnet lay in a flat circle on the grass.

"You released the fish?"

The man nodded.

"I'm glad," Jess said. "I was thinking about them trapped there—they kept me awake more than the man you know? Is that weird? Sorry, I'm rambling." She flapped a hand as if to dismiss her words, but hoped her prattle would get them talking.

The taller man turned away, busying himself with winding the blue and white tape into a coil around his hand, but the one who had spoken was friendlier, and acknowledged her worries about the fish with a kind smile.

"Sometimes it's easier to worry about the little things," he said. "Takes your mind off the bigger things. You're Jessica O'Malley, you say? You're a friend of Marcus Woo, I believe?"

She nodded. "Do you know who the man was? Or what happened to him? Was it an accident, do you think? I guess you don't tape—" She waved her arm to encompass the riverbank, the trees, the path. "—er... this ... just for an accident though? Did someone kill him then?" She decided not to mention that she already knew the name of the dead man, or that Marcus had already let slip that they were treating the death as suspicious. "I suppose I just wanted to come down here, sooner rather than later, you know, not let it build into a sinister memory that would stop me walking here again—I love it down here ..." She tailed off, acknowledging her prattling with another wave of her hand and a self-conscious laugh, but the man nodded in agreement.

"I do know," he assured her, his smile sympathetic and kind. "Things build in your mind. Better to face them head on, I always think."

Behind him, the taller man huffed, screwed the rolled tape into his pocket, and picked up the tackle box and fishing rod. "You gonna talk all day or give us a hand here, John? Be nice to get out of here sometime today."

John shrugged at Jess, arms outstretched and palms upwards—*what can you do, there's work to be done*—and said, "You carry on, Jessica. Enjoy your walk. All's quiet."

Jess nodded. "Still, I'm glad it's bright and sunny. It would be spooky if it were dull or foggy."

John laughed, gave a small wave, and gathered up the rest of the fisherman's belongings in an untidy and awkward bundle.

"What'll happen to his things?" Jess asked.

"Family." The taller man grunted over his shoulder and strode off down the path back towards the road.

The friendlier one—John—gave an apologetic shrug. "He doesn't like sunshine," he said with a grimace. "This poor man—" John nodded down at the fishing gear spilling from his arms. "—has family nearby. Over in Ballymaglen. Local enough, so. Someone'll take it to them. Not like he's going to need it anytime soon."

"S'pose not," Jess agreed. "Who was he?"

To her surprise, the Garda answered her question, giving the name she already knew. "Viktor Dąbrowski. Polish. Been here about six years. It'll be in the papers. No secret, not now the family are informed." John turned to follow his colleague down the path, but Jess had one more question.

"Wait. What happened to him?"

John turned back to meet her gaze and shrugged again. "Dunno yet. I'd say it was no accident though. You're fine now, with us around, and that big dog. And broad daylight. But maybe stay away later in the evenings, after dark, or without the dog, for a while, until we know a bit more, right?"

Although the sun was blazing down on the river, Jess shivered, as if the day had suddenly clouded over. She sensed movement at the periphery of her vision. Had the trees suddenly taken a collective step forward to cast a shadow over the riverbank? She shuddered again. *Don't be silly, Jess. It's just the breeze.* "Actually," she said aloud, "maybe I won't go any further today after all. Mind if I walk with you back to my car?"

Chapter Seven

Driving home, and remembering her determination to not let the incident scare her away from one of her favourite walks, a wave of annoyance crept over Jess. How easily she had succumbed to fear and left the river.

By the time she'd grabbed a quick sandwich for lunch, shut Fletcher in the house, and was on her way to the garden centre for her afternoon work shift, she was thoroughly bad tempered. She pulled out across the main road, causing an oncoming van to swerve and honk its horn angrily as she veered into the hard shoulder to allow it to pass. The driver waved a furious hand in a gesture she recognised more by its accompanying beeping, flashing of headlights, and the driver's turn of head rather than the fingers themselves as the van overtook her. She swore at him, flipped on the radio, and swerved back into the main carriageway. A speed camera van parked by the bridge caused her to slam on her brakes again, causing another barrage of angry beeping, this time from the car behind her.

"Dammit!" she yelled at the irate driver. Making an abrupt decision to get off the road for a moment, she knocked on the indicator and swerved into a field gateway. Safely out of the traffic, she cut the engine, her knuckles pale as she clenched the steering wheel.

She sighed loudly and relinquished the grip, folded her arms across the steering wheel, lay her head on her wrists, closed her eyes, and took a couple of slow, deep breaths.

"Come on Jess, get a grip before you kill someone." She sat there for a moment, counting her breaths to calm herself. *In, out, in, out. One. Two. Three. Four. One. Two. Three. Four.*

Her phone lay on the passenger seat, staring up at her. She stared back, considering. Would he think her completely insane? If not him, who else though? She straightened in her seat, picked it up, typed, deleted, typed again.

Marcus, don't laugh at me ... I need a favour. Will you and Snow come for a walk by the river with me? Sat, maybe, when you're off? I got freaked along there earlier. She added a sad face emoji and hit SEND.

As soon as she'd sent it, heat rushed to her face. A glance in the rear-view mirror confirmed her embarrassment. She'd thought it would help, but just felt even more stupid. She thumped the steering wheel. "Dammit, dammit, dammit." Tears prickled her eyes. She rubbed roughly at them with balled-up fists. "Whatever's wrong with me today?" she grumbled into the unresponsive pigeonhole as she rooted for a tissue. Finding only a paper napkin with a coffee shop logo, she wiped her eyes, blew her nose, and tried to pull herself together.

Having a shite day, I'm going to be late, she texted to Shay. *On the way now, there in ten.*

She stared blankly at the screen for a moment, then squared her shoulders, took a deep breath in, let it out slowly, sniffed loudly, and turned the key in the ignition. She checked the mirrors for traffic, signalled, and pulled out onto the now empty road, at a speed as sedate and sensible as that of any geriatric Sunday afternoon driver.

By the time she pulled into the car park and tucked her little car into a shady corner by the recycling bins, she had recovered her composure, although her mood was still grim. She slammed the car door shut and strode purposefully across the tarmac to the gateway leading into the garden centre's yard.

Shay, obviously on the lookout for her, met her before she reached the nearest polytunnel. "You look like you need a cuppa? What's up?" He didn't wait for her to answer, just waved a pointing hand towards the tunnel furthest from the public spaces—the one where seedlings were started and specialist plants were nurtured. Behind it, in a cluttered scrubby area, pots were cleaned and dead flowers hidden in a heap behind a pile of pallets, well out of sight of customers and clients. "Go on over there and get potting. I'll bring you tea." He reached out and gave her shoulder a gentle rub, then lifted his hand to push her hair out of her eyes. "Go on, I'll be with you in a minute."

Jess offered a feeble smile without meeting his eyes, and did as he suggested. As soon as she stepped into the humid polythene tunnel, with its hot, damp air and the earthy smell of wet compost, her shoulders loosened, her head rose, and her spirits lifted. She grabbed a pile of small black pots and set to work.

When Shay found her ten minutes later, two stained mugs steaming in his hands, she had already worked through several trays of plants, having neatly stacked the discarded seed trays at one end of the workbench, and set the potted-on cyclamens out in neat rows.

"Good timing, I'm just finished with those. What next?" She took one of the mugs from his outstretched hand, sighed softly, and leaned back against the trestle bench. "Thanks, I'm ready for this."

"D'ya wanna talk about it?" he asked, raising an eyebrow quizzically. "Mila's brother, I presume? It must have been quite a shock to find him like that. Did you sleep last night?" His voice was warm, full of genuine concern, and for the umpteenth time that day, tears prickled Jess's eyes and she dabbed at her nose with the back of her hand.

"Oops," she said. "There I go again. I don't know what's wrong with me today, I guess you're right—must be delayed shock ..." She tailed off and Shay stepped closer.

"Come here," he said, taking the mug he'd just put into her hands and placing it down amongst the cyclamens. "Come here." He engulfed her in a bear hug, holding her firmly until her body relaxed into his.

Eyes closed, held firm, she felt safe and warm and had an urge to stand there forever, everything else locked out of her mind.

Eventually, minutes or hours later, he gently pushed her away, and passed her the mug of tea once more: "Drink up, before it's cold."

She laughed weakly. "No chance of that in here, it's like a sauna today. Thanks, Shay, that was exactly what I needed. Really, thank you."

They spent the next couple of hours sowing winter vegetables in comfortable silence punctuated only by occasional "Pass me those trays," or "What's next?" and the quiet squeak of marker pen on plastic labels. *Spinach, beetroot, late cauliflowers, winter cabbages, leeks.*

When the last tray was filled with almost-black sowing compost, and the seed packets all but empty, Jess took up the hose and showered the entire laden table. The water, cool after the first warm spurt from where the hose had lain in the afternoon sun, was refreshing, misting the air, and Jess sprayed a trickle across her wrists, then held it up to her face to slurp noisily from the spray.

"Want some?" she asked, swinging it in sudden playfulness towards Shay, sprinkling first his jeans and then up over his mud-smeared T-shirt.

He took it from her, taking his turn to catch the cool flow in glugging mouthfuls. "A good few hours work there, partner. Come on, let's go get another cuppa, and that'll do you for work today, I reckon?" He held out a hand to pull her to the doorway, letting go only as they stepped outside into a fresh breeze and a darkening sky. "It's going to rain. Long overdue. Hope it's a good heavy downpour." The last few weeks had been unusually warm and dry, much to the delight of Jess's farming neighbours, who had enjoyed a late second batch of haymaking.

"Not until after I get home, I hope," Jess countered, squinting at the steely clouds. "If it's as heavy as those clouds predict, there'll be flash floods all over the roads and I'll be driving home in a river—" The image of a face-down body rising in an angry swell, tumbling in a torrent of swirling black water, flashed into her mind. She blinked the vision away, forcing brightness. "Make me that tea? Come on." She walked away from Shay, towards the portacabin where the kettle waited for them

Only once she was back in the car and about to set off for home, the first fat raindrops bouncing off her windscreen, did

she check her phone and find Marcus's reply to her earlier message.

Sure, let's bring the dogs out for a run Sat morn? Love to.

Chapter Eight

Eric had never been the promptest at responding to messages, and Jess had forgotten all about the "I found a fisherman" text she'd sent her brother on Tuesday by the time he answered on Thursday evening. The message flashed across the top of her screen as she idly flicked through television channels: *Sorry sis, what's up? A dead what? What mystery?*

"Eric!" She glared at the phone as if he would somehow hear her irritation, before opening the message fully and bashing out a reply: *Dead fisherman. I told you.*

His reply was instant. *Oh yeah. Chippy, prob. Irate chip shop owner, doesn't want people catching their own? With no fish to batter, he's going round battering fishermen instead?*

Jess groaned. *Don't be stupid. Real dead guy, Eric, not joking.*

How do you do it? Miss Marple, on the scene again! Haven't you had enough after last time? Stop looking for trouble.

I wasn't! Even in a text, she knew she sounded like the petulant little sister. *I was just walking Fletch, honest. This bloke was just there, floating face down in the water. I didn't plan it! But ... you know ... good mystery!!*

Eric shared Jess's passion for mystery, and her earlier reference to the Lollipop Club was a flashback to their childhood and their secret club based on mystery-solving, clue-hunting, and sleuthing around the neighbourhood they'd lived in, spying on friends and strangers alike. Their club had been dubbed 'The Lollipop Club' by their older sister, Alice, in mockery of Jess's depiction of a magnifying glass on the badges she had drawn in her childish hand.

Annoyed now, Jess hit the call button, rather than sending another text. "It's not funny, Eric. I found a body!" she snapped into the phone, before he had the chance to even speak. For what seemed like the umpteenth time that day, her voice wavered and her eyes filled with tears. "Dammit Eric!" She broke off, sobbing loudly into the phone.

"Oh shit, Jess ... Come on, it's okay ... Tell me what happened?"

Between sniffs and gulps, she relayed the events of the last two days: the finding of the fisherman, the discovery that he was someone she knew, albeit only vaguely, and the recurring images of the floating body.

Eric offered little in the way of interruption, bar the odd "Go on," when Jess paused to blow her nose or catch her breath.

Finally cried out, her burst of emotion gave way to their more typical problem-solving, and after twenty minutes or so, curiosity about the dead man had overshadowed her distress. "But what I really want to know," she said, "is why someone would have killed him? And who? I mean, the last thing we need round here is another murderer on the loose. What if he's someone local, Eric?"

"Or she."

"Guess so ... but they'd have to have been quite strong, I'd think, to get him into the river. He wasn't exactly small. I met him once, did I tell you? He was quite bulky—muscly, I think. I doubt *I'd* have been able to push him into the river, you know?"

"What if someone gave him a clonk over the head, first, and he fell in because he got hit? You know, a hefty whack and he'd overbalance, and ... Splash!"

"Hmm, s'pose ..." Jess paused, thinking. "Why though? Give me some reasons? Sensible ones, not chip shop owners."

For another forty minutes, the two fell easily into their childhood games of speculation and theories, batting ideas back and forth, until Jess heard Eric's wife muttering in the background about him saying goodnight to his daughters.

Belinda came nearer to Eric's phone so Jess could hear her clearly. "Hi Jess! Do you want to say hi to them before they go to bed?"

She did, and another ten minutes passed in chatter about going back to school, ballet, and soccer practice with her nieces, before blowing loud kisses into the phone and promising them they could come and stay soon. "Actually, put your mum back on for a minute; let's see if you can come before the holiday ends. How much longer have you got? Only a week ... hmm ... put her on, goodnight."

Jess had an easy relationship with her sister-in-law, and it took only a little wheedling to persuade Belinda to promise a flying visit the weekend after the coming one—the last weekend of the holidays. After a few more minutes of chat, the two women hung up, having agreed that they'd all come up to Ballyfortnum the following Friday, and head home again on the Sunday morning.

"Something to look forward to, eh Fletch?" Jess tousled Fletcher's ears and turned the volume back up on the television, choosing an old comedy film over her usual choice of mystery. She hadn't got far into it before she was interrupted by another text.

Kate. Hey, what's this about you finding Vik in the river? followed by a string of sad-faced emojis and another few question marks.

How the heck did she always know everything so fast? And how did she know the fisherman well enough to know him as 'Vik'? Was he another of her Get Slim clients? Surely this wasn't to be a repeat of the Get Slim murders? Kate was the local slimming group consultant, and for a while, Jess had even suspected her of being responsible for the deaths of three members of her group, earlier in the year. As it had turned out, although Kate was innocent of their demise, she was guilty of having been involved with one of the victims and was currently heavily pregnant with his child.

How're you? But more to the point, how the heck did you know that, and how do you know Viktor?

I know his brother more—they used to drink with Dec now and then, and their sister goes to my other group—the one in Ballymaglen—hear he was bashed around the head and knocked into the river? How come you were there?

Bloody hell Kate! Is there anyone you don't know?

She didn't come to weigh in last night, and someone said. Big shock!! There'd be a few from their estate in that group, it's much busier than the Tuesday one. Terrible thing.

After a few seconds, Kate sent another message, countering Jess's questions and echoing Marcus: *Also: Bloody hell, Jess. Is there any murder you aren't involved in?*

Jess snorted. "Touché," she said to her empty room, and fired off another text to her friend: *Come over tomorrow eve? Fill me in? I've work in the afternoon, come later? See what you can find out?*

Kate sent a row of laughing emojis in answer, followed immediately by a second text: *You detecting already, you mad cow? Knew it!! See you tomorrow x*

Jess sent only a smiling face in response, and turned her attention back to the film for approximately five minutes before her phone buzzed again.

Just checking how you are? Shay

I'm okay. Thanks for earlier, see you tomorrow x

And then another, only seconds after, saying much the same thing, but with Marcus's name on the screen. Jess felt suddenly loved, reassured, and happier than she had all day.

Yeah, I'm ok, thanks. How was your day? Tell me the updates on Sat? I'm trying not to think about it anymore today now! Good night, and thanks again xx

Chapter Nine

In Ballymaglen post office, Jess sifted through the limited range of condolence cards, discarding the overly religious or twee for a simple, elegant design. After her stint at the garden centre, she would pop round to Mila's to offer sympathy and a tin of Linda's shortbread.

Sheelagh Flannery, the postmistress, knew Jess by sight, and was chatty in the absence of the usual queue of people awaiting her attention. The Flannerys lived at the opposite end of Ballyfortnum to Jess, in almost the last house in the parish before the main Dublin road.

"Mike okay?" Jess said, making conversation.

Sheelagh's husband, Mike, attended the gardening course with Jess. The postmistress raised her eyebrows. "Shouldn't he be?"

"He didn't stay on Wednesday—most of them left after the news about Viktor." Jess nodded at the card she held. "Everyone was a bit shocked, I think … I didn't really notice—I was too gobsmacked myself." She gave a small laugh, devoid of humour.

Sheelagh frowned. "He didn't mention it," she said, rubbing her shoulder with one hand and taking Jess's money with the other. "Didn't realize he knew Viktor." She handed Jess her change, tucked the sympathy card into a small brown paper bag, and passed it across the counter.

"He might not've," Jess clarified. "I didn't—well, except for finding him, you know—but his sister is on the course with us. I'm surprised Mike kept up the course after it officially finished—it never quite seemed to be his thing, really..." Jess tailed off, remembering Mike's constant moaning about the course back in the spring.

He hadn't wanted to come. He'd said so right back in the beginning: "Who's got time for this fancy flower growing? Sure, isn't land for grazing and crops? And sure, can't herself get me a nice bunch of carrots in the supermarket anytime she needs to?" he'd grumbled, seemingly oblivious to the fact that someone had to grow those carrots somewhere. He'd also told them his wife had urged him out of the house to try something new while he was out of work, to see if it kindled some new direction for him.

"True, that," Sheelagh said, serious-faced, and without obvious emotion. "He didn't have much interest in it. He doesn't seem to know *what* he wants half the time. And him now, moping about, complaining no one will employ him ... Don't they only want the young ones so they don't have to pay a fair wage, eh Jess?" Sheelagh did a fair job of mocking her husband's grumbling tone, causing Jess to flash her a conspiratorial smile.

"He did say that ... once or twice." She gave a sympathetic half-laugh. "He isn't happy about it, is he? Gardening might not be his thing, but then he never really said what exactly was his thing. What was it he did before? He doesn't chat as much as the rest of us; keeps to himself mostly."

Mike, Sheelagh explained, had been let go just before Christmas in a redundancy merger shake-up and hadn't stopped bellyaching about it since. "He got a fair handout, for the redundancy," she said, "but it doesn't go far now his wage has stopped coming in. I've been arranging to sell off some of the land." She folded her arms across her body, her fingers kneading at her collarbone, then ducked her head. She busied herself with a stack of envelopes, letting her dark blonde fringe fall across her face, but not quickly enough to hide her sudden blush.

Jess made her excuses, conscious of Sheelagh's embarrassment at having divulged more about her finances than she'd intended with their idle chatting. "You take care now." She waved a hand as she turned to leave. "I'll be late if I don't get a move on. Bye." She stood aside for a new customer to enter, before stepping out onto the damp pavement and letting the door swing shut behind her.

As she strolled back towards the garden centre, she wondered vaguely which land Sheelagh Flannery had meant. The Flannerys owned a fair few fields, mostly around their bungalow, but some of it stretched away from the village and alongside the busy Dublin road. Most of the land would have been transferred to Mike with the house, when his elderly parents had finally given up their lifelong farming endeavours to move into a small retirement cottage on the outskirts of Ballymaglen.

There'd been some talk a few years back of the compulsory purchase of some of the land around that end of the village, with plans for a new road skirting around the built-up area along the main road. A few farmers had willingly sold up, but then the recession put a halt to the development, and everyone who had refused to sell hadn't been forced to hand over their land after all, much to their relief. Perhaps the Flannerys were wishing they had let the land go when they had the chance, rather than joining the protest committee and digging in their heels. Those who had sold had not only got a lump sum in their bank accounts, but still farmed the land they'd previously owned, for only a nominal rent to the Roads Authority. The road plans had been long-scrapped, and the farmers who had sold were still laughing about their good fortune in the local pubs and shops.

Mrs Dunne, proprietor of Ballyfortnum's tiny village shop, was one such villager who had benefitted from the buyout, selling up her family's derelict farm—a good seventy acres of scraggy land and a poky tumbledown bungalow. For the past seven years, she had lived instead above the little shop in the centre of the village while—as she was fond of saying—her retirement fund continued to grow healthily and undisturbed in her bank account, thanks to those generous folks of the Roads Authority.

Jess hadn't lived in the village back then, but her parents were not long resident when the plans had been announced, and her father had been active on the Ballyfortnum 'No Road' committee. "I didn't move out here to retire just to have a motorway zipping past," he was fond of saying, and he'd been nominated easily into the Treasurer position on the committee by his new community.

"Dreamin' again, Jess?"

She looked up to realise she was already at the entrance to the garden centre building.

Jack, an older man with a white beard worthy of any garden gnome, and a permanent twinkle in his eyes, gave her a nudge as he opened the door, ducked into a bow, and ushered her inside ahead of him. "Good ter have ye 'ere today," he added. "There's a funeral an' we're short. Can ye mind the till fer a bit?"

Of course. She wouldn't be calling in on Mila today after all—today was Viktor's funeral—she had, if not exactly forgotten, blanked it from her mind in her efforts to stop the image of his body haunting her thoughts. Now, as Jack reminded her, since the dead man was local, there were a few from the garden centre staff who would attend. The shop would probably be quiet enough, but you never knew; much of their trade was from further afield, and those zipping up and down the Dublin road between Lambskillen and the next big town. Ballymaglen Garden Centre and Plant Nursery had a reputation for quality, service, and unusual plants that stretched well beyond the limits of the little town.

Jess stashed her things behind the counter and headed for the portacabin to make a mug of tea before starting work, not entirely sure if the tea-making was an excuse to venture into the plant area to look for Shay, or not.

Chapter Ten

Instead of finding Shay, she found a note on the biscuit tin. *Jess. Sorry, missed you, gone to pay my respects to Mila, see you later p'rhaps. Shay.* She smiled at the realisation that he had known she would head straight to the biscuit tin, helped herself to two, and took them and her tea back into the shop.

Jess didn't often spend time behind the till, preferring the hands-on gardening outside or in the polytunnels, but today, with the day greying under increasing drizzle, and Shay not there for company, she was content to potter around the shop, tidying, checking stock, making small talk with the handful of customers who came in. The mixed scent of treated wood products, open compost bags, and trays of autumn flowers placed invitingly in strategic locations reminded her of her dad. She hummed along to the old songs on the radio, swept the floor, and rearranged a display of bird seed, and then it was five-thirty and the day was gone.

Jack locked the main doors, and Jess retreated out the back to the portacabin to rinse her mug and grab another biscuit.

The tinny murmur of a radio from the smaller portacabin that served as the office told her someone else was still around, and she stuck her head through the open doorway on the pretence of checking for mugs to wash.

Shay, behind the desk, hung up the phone, ran a hand across the front of his head and stifled a yawn. "Hey, how're you?" He threw her a tired smile. "I just got back in time to phone that order through. I was about to come in to check on everything and close up. How was your afternoon?"

"It's all done; Jack has locked up. All's well. How was it?" She looked him up and down, encompassing his uncustomary smart shoes and dark tie, and nodded in the general direction of the church. "Many there?"

"Decent turnout, considering ... Do you fancy a drink? A cuppa, or something stronger? In the pub, if you like? No, maybe not, it'll be busy, what with the funeral crowd, I guess ..." He yawned again, and the weather-beaten lines around his eyes deepened into dark creases.

"Looks like you need coffee more than anything? Will I make you a cup? Or there's a couple of cold cans in the fridge?"

Shay stood up behind the desk, shuffled some seed catalogues into a loose stack, tossed a crumpled piece of paper towards the wastepaper bin, not bothering to retrieve when it missed the bin and settled on the floor with a soft *phwft*. "C'mon, I need a beer. Keep me company? But not in the pub; I'm done with people and polite conversation today. Let's go sit in the tunnel, shall we?"

Jess didn't need persuading. They often dragged a couple of folding chairs across to the furthest tunnel, and enjoyed their breaks in the quiet warmth, surrounded by soft damp earth and tiny green shoots of new promise. Jess loved the peace of sitting there, silent and undisturbed. The far tunnel was mostly Shay's domain and even when all the staff were present at the busiest times of the day, they rarely intruded. Jess, learning the ropes, had quickly discovered that it was her favourite place at the garden centre too. Being among the rows of soft, brown earth, dotted by fresh sprouting green, that far tunnel was the calmest place she could imagine, and felt like the magic behind the scenes. It was here in this tunnel that she had felt the first stirrings of realisation and excitement that she had found something she wanted to do.

"Sure," she said. "You get chairs, I'll get the beers?"

Entering the tunnel, Jess laughed properly for the first time all day.

Shay had set out three chairs. Two faced each other, only about two feet apart, and the third stood a little further away. Shay wasn't sitting on any of them, but standing at a bench picking out a sprinkling of tiny weeds from a cluster of seed trays. "One for you, one for your feet." He nodded at the chairs.

"I would expect no less, if I'm to give up my sofa to sit out here on a folding garden chair." She threw him one of the cans.

He caught it deftly, one-handed, and popped in open. "I'm ready for this." He raised his can to her. "*Sláinte.*"

"*Sláinte.*" Jess held her own can aloft in reciprocal salute, before opening it, taking a large gulp, and collapsing onto one of the chairs. She obligingly swung her legs onto the other, as he had predicted.

"I know you'd have only put them on mine, if I hadn't."

Jess acknowledged the truth of this with a smile, and gestured for him to sit on the empty third chair. "C'mon, sit, you look knackered. Was it that bad? I didn't think you knew him anyway?"

"Ah, no, it was all right really—just, you know, busy week, could have done without it." Shay swigged from his own can and wiped his mouth on his shirt sleeve. "I know, I know ... they didn't exactly want it either. I'm an insensitive eejit ... It was awful. For the family, I mean, not for me. I'm just behind with work this week. Sorry, that's terrible to say when a young lad has been killed, but I didn't know him at all. I'd only met him once or twice when he came to collect Mila or pick up something for his mother. She—their mother—pops in for plants now and then. Nice woman. Not much English, but she's a sweet old dear. I wouldn't say I really knew them though." He sat heavily and stretched his long legs, digging the heels of his smart funeral shoes into the dusty ground until the chair tipped backwards, balancing precariously for a moment, before it thudded back to earth and stability. Shay let his head fall back, eyes closed, and took several large gulps of the beer.

"Jess?" He leaned forward suddenly, elbows on knees, and looked straight at her.

"What's up?"

Shay's tired face wrinkled into frown lines reminiscent of the ripples the breeze had blown across the puddles in the yard, and he looked down at his can. "Jess..."

She swung her legs off the chair but as she leaned towards him, ready to listen, her phone rang in her pocket.

Shay raised his can and his eyebrows—*Are you going to answer?*

Jess pulled her phone free from her jeans and hit the answer button. "Sorry," she mouthed at Shay as he drained the drink. "Kate? What's up? Is everything okay?" She paused while Kate answered. "Huh? You what? Who? ... What? ... When?" There was a longer pause. Jess, on her feet now and pacing away from Shay, walked around the end of the bench, and back along the far side, brushing her outstretched palm gently over the seedlings as she passed them. "Kate! How? And seriously ... how the heck do you always know what's going on around here before anyone else?" She stopped pacing.

Shay, also now on his feet and walking around the bench in the opposite direction, was coming towards her.

"Okay ... call me if you hear any more? Take care, call you later." She looked at the phone for a long moment.

Shay, an arm's length away now, stopped in front of her. "What is it?"

Jess met his quizzical gaze, phone still in her hand. "Ah, nothing important. She says gossip at the funeral was that Viktor was definitely killed deliberately. A hefty thump to the head with a blunt something or other. And it's definitely a murder investigation now. I knew that part—about it being murder—but how she heard about him being bashed on the head, I do not know. She knows everything, does Kate."

The lines on Shay's forehead deepened as he took another step towards her. "Wow. Murder. What is it with you and murder? Maybe I should back off?" He raised an eyebrow, held up his hands, and took a theatrical backwards step.

She shoved the phone back into her pocket and moved to close the gap between them, but he turned and left the polytunnel, leaving her standing alone amongst the seedlings.

Chapter Eleven

"I'm sorry, I shouldn't have answered it," Jess said, "but she's close to her due date, and I promised to be there if she goes into labour. To get her to hospital, or whatever, but I didn't expect that news—not from her at least. Seems Viktor was a small-time drug dealer. Mila hinted at that before, too, come to think of it."

Shay, having returned only minutes after he'd left, carrying two more cold beer cans in each hand, held one out to her. His eyes were gentle, and as she met his gaze, she felt a sudden thump in her chest.

"What was it you were saying? Before Kate called?" She took the fresh can gratefully from him and rubbed the cold metal across her forehead.

"Come here, Jess?" He stood his own unopened can on the nearby bench and held out his arms to her.

This time, she allowed herself to look up at his face as he put his arms around her, and when their mouths met, it was with a gentle intensity she hadn't known in the last few years. Kate's news; the image of Viktor Dąbrowski floating in the river; the overwhelming sadness she had felt on her way to work yesterday, all of it slipped away as she focused only on the man who was kissing her amongst the plants and seed trays and damp earth.

After hours, or minutes, Jess drew away. "So," she asked, deadpan, "what was it you wanted to say?" She turned away and prised open the ring pull on the can she still held.

"I've wanted to do that for months," he said. "Did you mind?"

She shrugged, a small smile tugging at her mouth. "It was quite nice, I suppose." She flickered her eyes up at him, her head lowered in sudden shyness. "It's been a while; was it okay?"

"I think you need more practice, since you ask. I can help with that." He put a hand on each of her upper arms, drawing her close again, and she flinched.

"Ouch! Sorry, carry on." She moved his right arm down a little, away from the tender spot on her left arm, and slipped her hands around his waist, raising her face to him once more.

"What hurt?" he asked, between kisses.

"Just a bruise. When Mike grabbed me the other day to stop me falling. It's nothing." It wasn't anything much—just a row of fingerprints where Mike had gripped her as she'd reacted to hearing the dead fisherman she'd found was someone she'd actually known. "I'd have fallen flat on my face if he hadn't caught me." The bruising was at the tender purple stage, but he'd saved her an embarrassing faint.

Breaking away from another kiss, Jess pulled the back of Shay's shirt free from his waistband as he groaned softly. She stroked his bare skin with her fingertips, and then held the cold can against his back, laughing as he leapt away from her, squealing like an angry piglet.

He swatted at her with a gardening glove he snatched up from the bench, and they giggled together like school kids, the heavy mood of the earlier part of the day forgotten.

"Let's take it slow, yeah?" she asked him, hoping he'd understand the plea in her eyes as she met his. "I'm not sure what I want, to be honest. I like you, I do, but I ... I don't know if I want a relationship right now. I ... I'm ... finding myself." Jess chuckled at herself. "Listen to me! But you know—you definitely know—the course I'm signed up for ... This—" She gestured around her at the plants, the soil, the polytunnel. "And all the stuff that's happened recently. It's a lot, all at once ..."

He traced the line of her T-shirt sleeve, running soft fingers across her arm. "I know. And it looks like there's more on your plate again now too; finding another dead body in your neighbourhood and all that. You attract trouble, you know." He smiled at her, a lop-sided grin that made him look young and boyish, and the now familiar lump rose again in her chest.

"Oh, Shay ..." This time, it was she who pulled him to her, reaching her arms up around his neck and guiding his mouth to meet hers. "I should get home ... I've left Fletch for too long."

He kissed her softly, briefly. "Oh, yes, Fletcher—the other man in your life. When do I get to meet him? Can I see you at the weekend?"

Driving home, she replayed the moments over and over, aware that she was grinning like a fool as she sang the wrong lyrics to the cheesy '80s tracks on the radio.

Fletcher greeted her at the door as if he had been abandoned for weeks, jumping up and licking her face.

"Okay, okay, I'll walk you first, eat after ... Stand still a minute while I get your lead on." She shoved him down so she could grab the leash from the hook beside the door, and snapped it to his collar. "Let's go."

At the entrance to Orchard Close, Fletcher pulled left, towards the village and their more usual choice of direction, but Jess, remembering Kate's call, tugged him to the right instead. "Let's walk round this way, boyo."

Turning right again at the next junction, they headed towards the river but didn't get that far. Tired and lazy after an emotionally-charged day, Jess nudged Fletcher back towards home after only ten minutes of walking, and still a good ten minutes away from the gate to the river path. She stopped to tie a bootlace, resting her foot on the bars of a gate. A cluster of curious cows ambled over, gathering to investigate. "Hello cows," Jess murmured, hastily tying the lace and stepping away from the fence. As she moved away, a car engine diverted the cows' attention, and as one, they turned their heads to seek out the cause of this new distraction.

The yellow and blue checked paintwork of a Garda car swept into view, crawling steadily over the rise of Tractor O'Sullivan's pot-holed driveway, and slowing further to pass her, before turning into the road and accelerating away to the junction.

A prickle of worry inched up Jess's back, immediately followed by the recollection that Tractor's land reached down towards the river. *Of course, they'll be talking to him about that.* She hadn't really considered it before, but he probably owned the riverbank she loved to walk along, and therefore the land that Viktor had died on.

"I s'pose they'll be questioning him, huh, Fletch? I wonder what *did* happen." Concern abated, hunger edged into its place and she turned her back on Tractor's drive to continue homewards. "Marcus'll know." As she remembered her plans to meet him tomorrow, her thoughts segued to the recollection of kissing Shay in the polytunnel only an hour or so ago. She gave herself a mental shake to dislodge the niggle that popped into her mind: Of course, thinking about her meeting with Marcus didn't have *any* connection to her kissing Shay, that would be ridiculous. Marcus was her friend. And Shay was ... well ... *we'll see*. She replayed the events in the polytunnel, humming one of the cheesy pop songs that'd been playing on the radio earlier. When they turned the final corner into Orchard Close, her face was warm from the sun and her mouth ached from smiling.

Chapter Twelve

Marcus, as arranged, called for Jess a little before eleven on Saturday morning—not too early, as they'd agreed. Snowflake and Fletcher jumped over each other like long-lost brothers, while Marcus greeted Jess with a more restrained peck on the cheek.

"How are you? Sorry I've been so busy I haven't checked up on you properly. Are you ok?"

She turned away so he wouldn't see her flush. After last night, it seemed as if weeks had passed since she had walked to the river on Thursday morning, and she felt silly for calling Marcus to walk with her. "I just got a bit spooked," she admitted to him now. "I love walking up there, and so do the dogs, and suddenly I felt a bit ... I don't know, scared, I suppose, and I don't want to be too scared to go up there anymore. It was your men, I think; they said something that unnerved me and I freaked out—"

"Jess." Marcus reached out and clamped a firm hand over her mouth. "You are rambling. I get it. Shut up. Are you going to invite me in for a coffee or are we going straight out?"

"Walk first, coffee after?" They agreed to walk the twenty-minute stretch to the river, rather than waste the pleasant late-August sun and lazy Saturday morning with driving. With Fletcher pulling to get ahead, and Snowflake trotting primly at Marcus's side, they retraced the steps Jess had taken the previous evening; right out of Orchard Close, right again, and past the corner where Tractor's fields met the road.

Jess gestured to Tractor's land with a sweep of her hand that encompassed his house, the farm buildings, and the wedge of dark green forestry that bordered the Tunny. "I guess it was his land? Where Viktor was found? I saw a Garda car there last night." She pointed along Tractor's drive, emphasising the gesticulation with a jerk of her head as they passed his gateway.

Marcus stopped, following her gaze. "Yes. He owns right up to the water, all along his north boundary. A couple of miles, almost, in total. They'd need to talk to him about who has access and suchlike."

"But surely anyone does? Any old dog walker, fishermen ... ramblers ... anyone who knows they can hop over the gate at the bridge and follow the path, anyway?"

"True, but aside from locals, I'd say not many know they can." He walked on, Snowflake still trotting sensibly beside him, even though Marcus had unclipped the lead as soon as they'd rounded the corner onto this quieter lane.

After yesterday's rain, the grass along the roadside was refreshed and greener than it had looked all summer. In the shady patches below trees, dampness still lingered, giving a soft sheen to the mossy shadows.

Fletcher bounded this way and that, sniffing at every tree and gatepost along the way, until they reached the gateway to the riverbank walk.

Snowflake, small enough, scrambled beneath the gate, while Fletcher bounded up and over the same low piece of fencing that his mistress scrambled across, almost knocking her flying in his eagerness.

Marcus caught her with a chivalrous hand, and as she jumped down, he gave her fingers a soft squeeze.

Remembering Shay—and the events of yesterday—she pulled away, stooping to tie a bootlace that wasn't loose, ducking her head away from Marcus's gaze.

The dogs had already crossed the stony access track beyond the gate, and were sniffing their way, tree by odorous tree, further into the woodland.

Although they'd often walked the dogs together, enjoying each other's company, over the summer, now Jess felt suddenly shy in Marcus's company. It had seemed like a good idea to ask him to walk here with her, the day she had aborted her walk after talking to his colleague, but now, as the sunlight bounced shimmering shards off the water, she didn't know what to say. The walk along the road to get here had been uncharacteristically silent, her drifting thoughts quieting her tongue. She remained silent as her thoughts meandered, swirling and bubbling like the river beside her. Whichever way she looked, trees were thinking of turning their colours for autumn. The swans bobbing silently on the water had paired off into old married couples now their cygnets were grown. A lone heron stood frozen, balletic, on one outstretched leg. A splash so fleeting it was only the lingering ripples that gave evidence of the fish darting below the glassy surface ... A hover of trout gathered in the shadow cast by the rushes ... Viktor's body ...

She shuddered at the unbidden image, rising again to bob in the forefront of her mind, and Marcus reached out to touch her arm as they came level with the first thin strip of forestry that divided the fields from the river. Marcus, perhaps presuming her to be nervous of revisiting the place where she had found a dead man only a few days ago, hadn't questioned her silence, but the longer she said nothing, the more awkward she felt.

"Worried?" He broke her reverie as they rounded the first bend.

She shrugged, looking out across the water. "Not really ... I don't know; everything's a bit weird ..." Let him think she meant the location and the memory.

"Come on." He held out a hand she pretended not to see. "It's okay. You're with a top-level Garda now, you know."

She smiled, gave a small half-laugh, and called to the dogs. As they came bounding towards her, tongues lolling, Fletcher making running at speed look easy and the little Westie struggling after him on shorter legs, she laughed again, more easily this time.

Beside her, Marcus smiled his warm, uncomplicated smile, but it was fleeting and his face was concerned and kind as he glanced towards her.

"Your tail isn't so waggy today, Jess. You'll still be a bit shocked, you know. It's not easy seeing a body, especially an unexpected one. You never get used to it. At least, I hope I never do."

"Kate says it's definitely a full-on murder investigation now?" She stopped abruptly and looked directly at her friend at last, matching his worried look with one of her own. "Is that true?"

"That friend of yours." He sounded exasperated. "How does she always know everything?"

"Beats me." Jess would ask her again; she thought she may have asked her yesterday when she'd delivered the news, but she couldn't remember waiting for the answer. She couldn't remember much of the conversation actually, what with what happened after. Heat prickled her neck and she knew she was blushing again as she recalled the afternoon in the polytunnel.

Marcus gave her a strange look. "You hiding something again? Have you not learned that you can't solve every mystery alone?"

Relieved to change the direction of her thoughts, Jess rose to his bait. "Can't I?" She grinned at him—the usual natural ease flooding back as she teased him. "I pretty much solved the last one for you, didn't I?" She batted him with Fletcher's lead, which she had been swinging around as they walked.

"So," he pressed, "what do you know this time?" He stopped walking and caught her arm, bringing her to a halt too, so they faced each other on the grassy path.

She met his eyes, holding firm. "Nothing. Really. I only heard what Kate said: he was hit over the head with something. I don't even know if it's true, although I guess from your reaction that it is? You kind of said as much the other day anyway—yesterday morning? Was it only yesterday ... oh, no, Thursday then? I've lost days this week. So, she's not wrong, is she?"

"She's not wrong," he agreed, "but no details—not for you anyway." He dodged another swing of Fletch's lead. "It's being investigated. I can't tell you what happened. Don't look at me like that—I don't know myself. I should be working today, only for having already put in so much extra time already this week. I told them I was off today and that it was non-negotiable. Said I had arrangements I wasn't cancelling."

"And do you? What are you up to for the rest of the day?"

"I'm doing it now, Jess. I told you I'd come out here with you, and here I am. Silly girl." He flashed his crinkle-eyed smile and she turned away, walking onwards along the dry path.

"Look, a fish! Oh, it's gone ... they always jump so fast. But he was bashed over the head, right? What with? Did they find it?"

"I don't know Jess, really I don't, so don't look at me with those puppy-dog eyes. It could've been a plank of wood; a heavy branch, a dead fish..." He glanced sideways at her, his lips clamped together to stop a smile as he checked to see if she was listening.

"Blimey. Imagine if he'd caught the biggest fish he'd ever landed, and someone whacked him round the head with it! Poor man." As she laughed with Marcus, a familiar surge of warmth swelled in her chest and stretched across her face as he smiled his gentle smile and his dark eyes sparkled with humour.

They had walked as far as the spot where Viktor's fishing things had been abandoned, although it was largely indistinguishable from any other stretch of the riverbank. Jess recognized it only by the worn patch of earth that dipped towards the river that she'd noticed the other day, and the large cluster of gorse bushes just beyond.

Fletcher leapt down onto the grassless patch and lapped eagerly from the river. Snowflake, ever his mimic, scrabbled down to join him, and the large black dog and his small white companion stood together, heads bent, drinking noisily, with the sun on their backs and the river burbling around their legs. Another heron—or maybe the same one, flown to a new lookout—turned its elegant neck in their direction, then spread its wings and made a graceful retreat, swooping low as it followed the path of the river for a few yards before settling on a central sandbank. It stood, statuesque, steel in both colour and composure, watching to see if the intruders would follow and cause it further alarm.

"Did his things get returned to the family? Were you at the funeral yesterday?"

"Yes, and no. An officer went along—not me though, not this time. They'd have dropped his things to his family already, as far as I know. It's usually done as quickly as is practical."

"So," Jess continued, persistent as a dog with a bone, "did they find whatever it was he'd been hit with?"

Marcus shook his head and sighed, pretending exasperation. "No, Jess. No weapon was found, but any tree branch, fence post, suchlike; toss it in the river and it's gone."

"Hmm." Jess stared out across the water, as if the murder weapon might float past at any moment. "But why?"

"Er ... because it would float away ..." He swung around to face her, with his hands planted on his hips and staring at Jess with what she thought of as his Serious Policeman face. "So, Jess... wooden things, they tend to float on water—"

She slapped at his arm. "Not that! I mean why was he killed?"

"Jess." Now Marcus's firm-policeman gaze morphed into his stern you-know-I-can't-tell-you-that gaze, designed to silence that particular train of questions, but Jess was undeterred.

"Was it a drugs thing? Rumour has it that he was a small-time dealer?" She walked on again, and he fell into step beside her on the sun-browned grass.

"Where'd you hear that?"

"Mila. She was uncomfortable about it, but mentioned it once or twice. Said he'd had some trouble. Kate had heard it too."

"It's one line of investigation," he said, putting on his firm voice again. "But, Jess ..." He stared at her for a moment, then switched to his lighter I'm-your-friend tone. "How far are we walking? All the way to the bridge?"

It was a good forty minutes to the next road bridge, but she wanted to go on. "Yes," she agreed. "It's a lovely day, and if I'm to banish the threat of tree-trunk-wielding murderers, we should cover the whole stretch. Let's go on?"

They had already passed the spot where she had found Viktor; the area identified by the fence post she had tried to dislodge, the trampled grass, and the hacked-back area of reed. Now, they continued away from it, following the bald dirt-path onwards, the worn dry earth bordered on one side by the dark green forestry and on the other by the bright ribbon of reflected sunshine bouncing off the water.

Chapter Thirteen

Here and there, beams of daylight shot through the dim bank of trees, wherever drainage ditches or narrow tracks left a wider space between the neat rows of pines that grew beyond the outer edging of birch.

"It's weird that it's planted with trees," Jess spoke her thoughts aloud as they walked. "You'd think he'd use the river for the animals to drink, wouldn't you?"

Marcus laughed his easy laugh. "An hour ago, you didn't know it was farmland, and now you're planning better land management for it."

"I did know! I just hadn't thought about it. I like the trees better. If it were grazed right to the water, I couldn't walk along it."

"That's kind of the point." The narrow strip of land they were walking along was a public footpath—a right of way—albeit little-used, Marcus explained, but nonetheless a fact which would prevent any conscientious farmer from grazing right to the edge, for public safety.

"Or insurance claims, more like." Jess remained sceptical, knowing many local farmers preferred to graze or grow crops on every possible inch of their land, much to the detriment of trees, hedgerows, wildflowers and wildlife.

"Plus—" Marcus threw her a disparaging look. "—the trees are farmed forestry, so they need an access path for the machinery. I've been looking over the land maps in the station, trying to piece together what might have happened and where else there are access points to the river path. "I can't tell you what happened to your man, but I can give you a lesson on the lie of the land, if you like."

Jess smirked, giving Fletcher's lead another swing in his direction. "Nah, you're all right, thanks. I know what I need to know without the geography lecture."

In front of them, the sound of a car rushing by alerted Jess that they'd reached the next bridge. Sure enough, as they rounded the curve of the path, they were barred by a padlocked gate, and beyond it, the road. "Will we turn around, or climb over and walk back along the road?"

Marcus, chivalrous as always, batted the decision back at her. "You choose."

"We'll turn? Go back the way we came?" That way, the dogs could stay off-lead, enjoying the freedom of the river path.

Some thirty minutes or so later, they had once again passed the fence post marking the spot of Viktor's demise. As they approached the bend where his fishing gear had been found, a small patch of red amongst the trees to their right caught Jess's attention. She ducked between a couple of straggly birch trees, and into the pines beyond. As she neared, she could see the flash of red was a piece of fabric, and not rubbish as she'd first assumed. She jumped across a narrow ditch to discover a dark red cap lying on the loamy forest floor.

Where the hat lay, the trees were shorn of their lower branches to make a track wide enough for pedestrian traffic, but not wide enough for a vehicle. She picked up the cap, turning it in her hands as she stood, looking down the line of trees where the rough-hewn path led away from the river and on into the forestry. Another drain ran parallel, giving further width to the cleared strip. The sun painted a bright streak of earthy brown, flanked on either side by the dense gloom of the tightly-packed trees. Underfoot, a thick layer of pine needles created a soft brown carpet. There was a faint smell of decay mixed with damp earth and the strong scent of pine that reminded Jess of childhood Christmases. To each side of her, the trees closed in, branches entwined to form a thick barrier, as if to deter anyone from straying off course.

"I guess this leads back up to the fields ..." she muttered to herself before turning towards the riverbank and calling out to Marcus. "I found a cap, look."

Marcus had walked on a little further along the river path, but at her words, he turned and came to meet her, ducking around the branches that reached out to snag him as he entered the little forest.

Jess held out the dusty red cap. "Looks like it hasn't been here for very long—it's dry, and quite clean; not all covered with moss or muck or pine needles, just a bit of dry dust."

Marcus reached out to take it from her. He looked it over, then twiddled it in his hands while silently looking up and down the path, just as she had done minutes before.

Jess watched him. She'd seen that look on him before. Weighing up information. *Was it important? Not? A clue...?* Of course he wasn't thinking anything as amateur and banal as "Is it a clue?" Jess couldn't help a small giggle, breaking Marcus's train of thought and causing him to throw her a questioning smile. But the thought was the same, regardless of the words he dressed it up in.

She made the most immediate decision for him: "Let's walk a little way in?" It felt like one of her and Eric's childhood adventures. They would spend hours off exploring, a packed lunch of sandwiches stashed in their backpacks ... cheese and pickle if they could persuade their mother, otherwise Marmite, or peanut butter, and a hunk of cucumber they would eat down to the stalk, fighting over whose turn it was to get the end bit. A bag of Monster Munch, or Hula Hoops, and an apple each, selected carefully from the fruit bowl. They would stay out for hours, returning home only as dusk fell, by which time their mother would inevitably be standing on the doorstep, waiting for them, arms crossed and an annoyed look on her face as she reprimanded them for staying out too long.

A ripple of excitement fluttered in Jess's abdomen, and she strode off ahead of Marcus, her steps large but cautious, always looking before she trod, in hope of further finds. "C'mon!" She turned to see if he was following. "Call yourself a policeman?"

He chuckled, called the dogs, who had gone on ahead of him and out of sight along the riverbank, and crashed through the trees to catch her. "Okay, okay, I'm coming, but really Jess, how old are you again? Seven?"

She spun around to face him, sticking her tongue out in feigned protest, both acknowledging his retort and playing into it by beckoning him forward with a theatrical flourish and a finger to her lips: "Shh!" she hissed, darting her eyes back and forth up the trail in an exaggerated fashion, as if they'd fallen headfirst into a Scooby Doo mystery.

Playing along, he attempted a cartoon-worthy exaggerated tiptoe, promptly caught his foot in a stray bramble, and tripped.

Jess doubled over with laughter and sank down against a tree trunk while she waited for him to untangle his leg and catch up.

Still giggling, she held out her hand for him to pull her up. Once on her feet again, she leaned back against a tree trunk, wincing as the prickly twigs dug into her back. "Look," she conceded, "it might be a child's game, sleuthing about in the woods, and I may have temporarily regressed twenty-five years or so, but really, aside from that ..." She became serious, her face stilled. "Whose hat is it?" And with that, thoughts of the dead man flooded back and she shivered despite the streak of golden sunlight.

Marcus said nothing but nodded and gestured her onwards.

With Jess in the lead, they progressed down the track, stepping over the odd loose bramble or strand of ivy that snaked into their path, ducking under the odd branch that stretched out to snag Jess's ponytail or to spill a sprinkling of pine needles onto their T-shirts like confetti.

"We'll just see where it comes out," she whispered over her shoulder, then jumped in fright as something moved fast and loud to her left, beyond the thick entanglement of pines and bramble. She stopped so abruptly that Marcus bumped into her, placing his hands on her sides to steady them both, and first Fletcher, then his small white shadow, appeared on the path ahead of them. Jess's new flurry of giggles was underpinned by nervousness this time, and now she shoved Marcus in front of her, to lead them forward into the widening stretch of daylight promising the end of the path.

"I can't believe we are stalking around in the forest like kids in one of your Nancy Drew books." He stepped out of the trees into a bright patch of sunny green and ducked to pull a twist of spiky bramble from his ankle.

Here, the grass was long, yellowing in the late summer, overgrown beyond the reach of the startled cows who jumped away and scattered on the far side of a post-and-wire fence a couple of yards ahead of Jess and Marcus. The herd of young heifers regrouped and edged closer, curious and jostling, their heads nodding as if amused to see Marcus and Jess emerging from the trees covered in various degrees of foliage.

Marcus pulled a large twig from Jess's hair, and in turn, she swatted away a flurry of pine needles from the back of his T-shirt. They called the dogs to heel and Jess hastily clipped on Fletcher's lead before he could get any ideas about running around in a field of livestock. Snowflake, trained by a policeman who, when necessary, exuded authority, came obediently to his master's heels and sat demurely in a perfect portrayal of 'trustworthy dog'.

Beyond the last few scattered birch trees that edged the evergreen plantation, the pasture stretched for acres. In the far distance was the white-painted, two-story, double-chimneyed farmhouse that belonged to Tractor O'Sullivan.

"Closer than you'd think," Jess said.

"Probably still a good half mile. Maybe not quite that far."

"Still, I liked the river best for not being able to see a single building from it," Jess complained.

"You still can't." Marcus poked her shoulder, laughing. "We can't see the river now, and you can't see the house from the river path. Come on, let's head back." He clicked his fingers for Snowflake to follow and they disappeared back under cover of the trees.

Jess shrugged, tugged at Fletcher's lead, and ducked into the trees after him.

Chapter Fourteen

They emerged from the trees, blinking in the bright sunshine that warmed the path along the water's edge. Just as they had done at the far end of the forest trail, Jess and Marcus stopped to brush forest debris from their clothes and hair—although this was more of a problem for Jess, with her tangle of pony-tailed curls, than for Marcus's closely-shaved head.

The dogs bounded ahead, running, chasing, bouncing over grassy hummocks, and darting in and out of the clumps of tall dark rushes that grew prolifically along this stretch of riverbank.

As usual, Jess swung Fletch's lead in loose circles as she walked, the sun warm on her face. Marcus, beside her where the path was wide enough to walk two abreast but dropping behind wherever it narrowed, was silent. She liked this about Marcus; this comfortable companionship without need to fill the silence with mindless chatter. She shifted her focus between the uneven path ahead and the sparkling sun-kissed ripples of the river.

"A fish! Look—oh dammit, it's gone. I don't know why I bother to say it—it's not like they'd ever just hover there, waiting for you to turn and look." They were always too quick; a flash of broken water, a gentle *splsh*, and the river calm and smooth once more with only the concentric circles rippling on the surface to show they'd been there at all. She loved these glimpses of wildlife, however fleeting. She'd seen an otter once. Only once. She longed to see another, although with Fletcher's boisterous presence it was unlikely. Even the swans stayed away from him, although she'd often watched them glide silently towards other, smaller, quieter dogs, swaying their elegant necks as they peered in beady-eyed curiosity.

"Jess?" Marcus touched her arm, guiding her back to the path she'd veered off. "You're in a complete daydream. I'd really rather not have to get wet pulling you out of the river today, if you don't mind." He gave her a quick half-smile, accentuating his laughter lines as usual, then frowning as a new thought occurred. "Have you actually seen James O'Sullivan recently? I suppose I should've asked you sooner, come to think of it—we need to ask him some questions, but no one seems to have any idea where he might be. Or if they do, they aren't saying."

Jess snickered. "Tractor? Well, if he's on form, he'll be somewhere he shouldn't be with someone he shouldn't be with, and will have all his tracks well covered. And anyone he is with won't tell, and anyone he's not with won't tell either—they won't want to let on that they know his habits that well!"

Marcus nodded. "Exactly. And then there's the added problem that at this time of year, they're all out getting silage cut from dawn to dusk and on through the night at times. Silage; women. He could be anywhere. Everyone thinks he might be somewhere else but no one knows where that somewhere actually is. Slippery as your vanishing fish, that one."

"Yeah, there's been a lot of farm noise at night this week. Starts Fletcher off barking when the tractors pass along the road or cut the fields behind us. Not to mention the light from it. I still don't really understand why they need to work through the night."

"Weather, apparently. And time."

"Wouldn't catch me working overnight. I don't know how you do it, either. But, to answer your question, no, I haven't seen him, but I don't often anyway. I'll look out for him if you like?"

Just before the river narrowed and burbled to flow under the road bridge, the bank sloped gently into the water, allowing access for small fishing boats or pleasure craft like canoes and kayaks. Here, Fletcher stood belly-deep in the river, lapping noisily, as if he hadn't slithered down a steeper incline just five minutes beforehand to drink just as thirstily. Snowflake stood on the very brink of the water, feet firmly on dry ground, neck stretched towards the water, delicately dabbing at the water with his tiny pink tongue.

"Do you think he'll enforce that sign; put a better fence up now?" Jess gestured towards the NO TRESPASSING sign that hung drunkenly from a tree in full view of the gate and the road. "I do hope not. Dead fishermen aside, it's a lovely place to walk."

Marcus looked at the sign, then back along the riverside path they'd walked along, and back to Jess. A flash of understanding passed between them. He loved being here too, alongside this peaceful river, where they could walk for miles without seeing anyone more than a fellow dogwalker or a scattering of fishermen, still and watchful as the herons that watched the fish with as much interest as any angler.

Tired, hungry, with a scratch across her arm from the foray into the trees, but feeling ridiculously happy, Jess waved Marcus off and made herself a sandwich. Cheese, but no pickle. She must buy some. She carried her plate to the patio and sat in the cooling afternoon sun to reminisce some more about the 'sleuthing' she and Eric had enjoyed as children. It would be fun to see him next weekend; they could take the girls down to the woods—not that riverside forest, with its regimented rows of unfriendly pines, but a kinder, softer, more magical woodland, with moss and mounds and fairy dens. They would do tracking ... she'd lay a trail for them to follow ... it was ages since they'd done anything like that. Maybe Marcus would like to come. Or Shay.

Oh yes; Shay. Her phone displayed a little envelope symbol, reminding her Shay had sent her a text she hadn't yet opened. She shoved her phone aside and took a large bite from her sandwich. She'd read it later when she'd had time to think about what she wanted from him. What he wanted from her. All the while she hadn't read his message, she wouldn't have to think about how to answer. Whatever the question might be. She closed her eyes, turned her face to the sun and let the kiss replay again. Mmm. It had been nice. And she liked Shay, really she did ... quite a lot ... She reached up to touch her face where he had touched it yesterday, and her fingers moved on upwards to where Marcus had pulled the twig from her hair. Dammit.

She shook her head, propped her chin on her hand, and called her sister. "Hey, how're you? Wanna come down on Saturday? Eric and his lot are coming. I thought we'd go tracking but it'd be better with another person—two teams of three?" Her voice took on a childish wheedling, but she knew Alice would come if she could.

For too many of Jess's childhood years, Alice had been unwell, moody, unreachable, as she'd battled for years with her eating disorder. Only now, in these last few months, did Jess feel that Alice was truly recovering and ready to make up the lost years when Jess had needed to be 'the responsible one', 'the mature one', and 'the one who takes care of everyone'.

"Say you'll come, Alice. It'll be fun."

Alice was already sold. Eric had mentioned he was coming, she said, and she'd planned to invite herself along anyway. Since the spring, Alice had been spending more time in Ballyfortnum, coming down to stay a night or two every few weeks. She'd even admitted to "quite liking it here now" in a rare lapse of what Jess referred to as her 'Aliceness'.

Half an hour later, still ignoring the text from Shay, Jess hung up on Alice and promptly dialled a different number.

"Hey Kate, how're you? Listen, did Tractor O'Sullivan join up in the end? Your group, I mean. Do you remember, way back in the spring when you were flirting shamelessly with him that day we delivered your leaflets ..." she tailed off, leaving Kate to fill the gaps as her memory was jogged.

They'd been out in Kate's car—sometime around St Patrick's Day, or thereabouts, Jess thought—delivering leaflets for the Get Slim group. Of course, Kate had flirted with Tractor O'Sullivan; of course she had. Even though she was secretly struggling with the death of her secret lover, Kate's innate ability to flirt with anyone had switched onto autopilot, and she'd left with a promise from Tractor that he'd give her group a try. Trust Kate. Trust Tractor too ... as well as his reputation for being the most eligible bachelor in the village, and rich with it, he was also well-known for having tried it on with almost every woman within a good ten-mile radius of Ballyfortnum. Jess never knew whether to feel relieved or offended that he hadn't come knocking on her door in the few years she'd lived in Ballyfortnum.

Kate conceded that he had indeed been to a handful of meetings, but, she suspected, more to check out the talent than any serious notions of dieting. "He's already pretty fit," Kate said with a snigger, "so I didn't expect anything else from him. He asked me out, of course."

"Of course." Jess didn't even try to hide the smile in her voice, but Kate carried on, unhindered by Jess's interruption.

"I was tempted, what with him being loaded and me being ... well ... you know ..." Kate tailed off, and Jess knew she was remembering the awfulness of her clandestine affair with Dave, a local farm labourer who'd died suddenly back in January.

As if that hadn't been bad enough, it turned out he'd been knocked off his bike by a local woman, who'd also poisoned another of Kate's group members and attempted to poison one more, in a fit of jealousy over their achievements in Kate's slimming group. A few months after Dave died, Kate realised she was pregnant. Declan, Kate's husband, knew it couldn't be his and left her, and her secret had finally come out. Kate, with no more income than the group brought in, and now no husband to supplement her bills, admitted to Jess now how she'd briefly, but seriously, considered 'taking up' with Tractor O'Sullivan as a way out of her misery.

"Thank God you saw sense there—talk about out of the frying pan and all that ... you'd have been mad," Jess said.

Kate laughed. "Mad, but loaded. Could've worked out okay, you know."

"So do you know him better than I do, would you think? Sounds like it—you didn't sleep with him, too, did you?" Jess's voice rose in horror. "I mean, everyone else around here has, if you believe Mrs Dunne." She paused for a second, twisting a strand of hair in her finger. "Hmm ... probably everyone except Mrs Dunne, to be honest. And me. He's never even asked me."

Kate was definitely in better form these days, having accepted her situation and made a tentative peace with her husband. She laughed again. "No, Jess, I did not. I do have some morals, you know." She was silent for a moment. "Jess, guess what? Dec is moving back in, at least at weekends. We've been talking a lot. He thinks us not being able to get pregnant was the main reason for our problems. He says he will support us—me and this one."

Jess could imagine Kate rubbing her enormous belly with a tenderness that suited her far more than the harsh angles and bitterness of the earlier part of the year.

"We're going to see if we can make it work," Kate said.

Jess said nothing, glad Kate couldn't see her mouth opening and closing like the clichéd goldfish, as she grasped for the right words. Eventually, she offered an unsubstantial, "Wow!" And then, after another pause while she tried unsuccessfully to come up with something better: "Wow."

"I know, right?" Kate agreed. "But, yeah, to answer your question, I would say I know Tractor well-ish. Why do you ask?"

"I was on his land earlier. You know? Where I found Viktor? Well turns out that it's O'Sullivan land. He owns right down to the river, Marcus said, and we followed a kind of track—a rabbit path, really—through the trees, and it came out on the edge of his fields. We could see his house, and well, I was wondering about asking him about how he knew Viktor—*if* he knew Viktor, I suppose—or who else might be on his land who would know that there's a way through to the river from his fields—"

Kate snorted into the phone. "And you want to turn detective again and find out did Tractor sneak up on Viktor with a short plank and thwack him on the head and kill him?"

Jess grinned. Her friend knew her well. She shook her head, then nodded it slowly, although Kate couldn't see her. "No ... well, yeah ... I guess so. I mean, I want to know what happened. I mean, I found the poor man, didn't I?"

Chapter Fifteen

Sunday passed quietly, with too many of Linda's latest batch of cookies in Jess's belly for her to summon any desire to leave the house, aside from a quick walk around the park to placate Fletcher. It was a dull, rainy day, suiting—or perhaps fuelling—Jess's lethargy, and she'd spent most of the day cosied up on the sofa with some old favourites on the television: *Death on the Nile* first, followed by *A Pocketful of Rye*. She didn't usually mix her Marples with her Poirots, but was feeling a pang of nostalgia for the familiarity and comfort of long Sunday afternoons spent watching the old Christie films with her dad, and these two films had always been her favourites.

Fletcher, sympathetic to Jess's inertia, lay curled beside her, snoring softly, but the long riverside walk yesterday alleviated any real guilt that Jess may have let creep in for today's laziness. She hit the PAUSE button and pulled herself to her feet to refill the kettle.

As she waited for it to boil, she scanned her phone for social media updates and messages. The usual Sunday scrawl of cats, dinners, and children offered little of interest but the envelope icon showing unopened texts reminded her she'd not read Shay's message, nor yet replied. Without bothering to open the message, she typed an apology for her silence: *Sorry, think the shock finally caught up with me a bit—have been ignoring the world. See you in the week xx*

She stared at the screen for a moment after she pressed SEND, recalling the security she had felt as she'd stood wrapped in his arms, and added a second text: *Thanks for the hug. It was exactly what I needed x*

And then, worried that still seemed inadequate, she typed a third one: *And the rest was nice too.* Smiley face; SEND.

The kettle rumbled to a boil and clicked itself off. Jess poured water over a fresh teabag and opened the door to let Fletcher into the garden for a pee. Despite the rain, the air was warm, so, tea in hand, she stood in the doorway to inhale that special smell of wet earth after a long dry spell. These past few days of heavy showers had done wonders for the parched garden after the unusually hot August. The ground had needed the rain, for sure, although there was a sorry-looking montage of soggy, browning flower petals under the rose bush where the downpours had stripped the last of the blooms. Autumn was on the way; she could feel it in the air.

"Fletch," she called, "that'll do. In you come."

He gave a wet clump of herbs a final sniff and ambled back inside.

Jess grabbed the kitchen towel from the back of a chair but by the time she had it in her hand, the rain-drenched Labrador had already given a vigorous shake, spraying water across her jeans and the kitchen wall. Pyjama-time had just arrived early, Jess decided, sliding down her dog-splattered jeans and hopping out of them by standing on first one leg and then the other, while Fletcher tried to help by tugging at the flapping material. She shoved him off as the jeans fell into a crumpled blue heap at her feet.

Fletcher abruptly lost interest in the game and scuttled through the living room and into the hallway, barking madly, his paws scrabbling on the hall floor.

A moment later, there was a knock on the front door.

Dammit. Jess froze; a rabbit in headlights. Would she pull the wet jeans back on, or leg it upstairs to find something dry to put on? The glass panel on the front door would give her caller a frosted-glass glimpse of her knickered-arse as she made for the stairs, so the wet jeans won the mental toss.

Shay stood on the doorstep, a bottle of red in one hand and a slightly embarrassed look on his face. "Sorry, I hadn't heard back from you, and I knew you might be feeling a bit ... well ... you know?" He shrugged. "And then I was only about two minutes away when your message did come, only I was driving, so I didn't look at it till I pulled up, and ... well ..."

Jess waved his words away and ushered him in. "It's fine. Sorry I didn't answer before." She pushed him into the living room, taking in the evidence of her slobby afternoon as she did so: the blanket draped half-on, half-off the sofa; the two plates bearing tell-tale biscuit crumbs; the half-drunk mug of tea, and the paused movie. "Lazing," she explained, gesturing towards the sofa. "Look, I need to get out of these wet jeans. Go through and put the kettle back on. Or open that." She nodded at the bottle he was still holding. "You'll find a glass in the cupboard over the kettle. Or tea stuff is on the counter. I'll just be a minute." And with that, she scarpered upstairs and wriggled out of the wet jeans for the second time in five minutes.

Back downstairs, Shay paused mid-dunk of a tea bag as Jess walked into the kitchen, and raised his eyebrows. "You saw my message then?"

Jess ducked her head, not wanting to admit she hadn't opened it. "Er..."

"The one I sent first? Or the second one? Or the one I sent about thirty minutes ago to say I was pretty much passing and would pop by to see how you are since you weren't answering your messages?" He grinned at her, self-confident and unabashed.

"Er ..." He'd sent more than one? She couldn't confess that the text she'd sent to him a few minutes before he'd knocked on her door was a guilty excuse that really meant "sorry I was too emotionally challenged this weekend to think about what to do about us". Nor could she admit she'd only sent that text to buy herself more time before having to think about him properly. "I didn't know you'd sent me more than one. Sorry." She shrugged guiltily and held her hands out towards him, in a gesture she hoped asked for understanding and forgiveness. "You found the teabags."

"Jess." He dropped the teabag into the sink and took a step towards her. "I know you've had a rough time lately. The reason I called by is not to hassle you or push you into decisions, but to check that you're okay." He flashed his boyish smile, belying the seriousness of his words. "Although ..." He held out his arms, inviting her into his embrace.

Once again, as Shay encircled her in a warm, solid hug, Jess felt herself relax and melt into him, a feeling of calm washing over her.

They stood in comfortable silence, arms wrapped around each other, and as she pressed her head against his chest, she let herself be lulled by the steady thudding of his heart through his soft flannel shirt.

"I'm sorry I didn't answer you," she finally said, pulling away and looking into his eyes. "I've been a bit crap this weekend." As she held his gaze, he inclined his face very slightly towards her, a questioning look in his eyes. She answered with the tiniest of nods and tilted her own face upwards to kiss him gently.

"So—" He pointed at the still-paused television, once they were settled on the sofa, the tea cold and undrunk. "What did I interrupt? And why were you wet?" He pulled away and looked at her in bewilderment. "I mean, how did you manage to get so wet if you were just sitting here watching TV?"

Fletcher, having eventually stopped bouncing around Shay as if he were a long-lost friend rather than a stranger he had only just met, looked up briefly from where he lay on the other side of Jess.

Jess patted her dog's head absently and explained. "... and I was just about to put my PJs on when you arrived," she admitted. "So, how come you were in the area, and do you want a glass of this wine you brought?"

As it turned out, they hadn't opened the wine. Shay, needing to get home to finish some paperwork before morning, had only stayed for another half hour or so, and several more kisses on the sofa, before gathering himself up and telling Jess he would call her the next day.

Jess stood on the doorstep to wave him off, filling the space created by the open door with her body, to block Fletcher's attempts to follow Shay out. As she watched his garden-centre logo'd van pull away, a pang of longing fluttered under her rib cage, and she wished she had persuaded him to stay after all. Maybe, just maybe, she told herself, this could work out as a good thing. Even after the van disappeared out of sight around the bend, she remained on the doorstep for several more minutes, willing him to turn around and come back to her.

When it became apparent that this wouldn't happen, and the evening chill brought goose pimples to her bare arms, she closed the front door with a soft click and padded back to the kitchen to grab a wine glass and the unopened bottle. She poured a generous glassful and returned to the sofa. With Fletcher's head on her lap, she finally read the trio of messages Shay had sent over the weekend. Warm happiness enveloped her like a blanket; the texts were friendly and caring, without any hint of 'pushy'. She fired out a text—a proper one this time.

Hi again! Sorry I didn't read your messages. Thank you for caring. Thank you for being exactly you. Thank you for coming by, I'm glad you did. When you left, I realised I wanted you to stay. How about one eve in the week? Let's do things properly, shall we? We could go out. Or I can make dinner—nothing special, just time together that isn't at work? Would that be ok? Xx

She hit SEND, rubbed Fletch's ears, and restarted the film, trying to concentrate as Miss Marple solved the crime and avenged Gladys's murder. Luckily, Jess was familiar enough with the film's storyline to not need to give her full attention to the unfolding plot as she glanced down at her phone and typed out a postscript: *wine's good too, btw, but maybe better if you were here to share it xx*

That sent, she pulled the blanket around herself and sank back against the cushions, still smiling to herself, and let Miss Marple lull her to sleep.

Chapter Sixteen

Monday morning brought a return to the hot, sunny weather Ireland had enjoyed and moaned about in equal measures for most of the summer. Jess woke early, feeling refreshed and well-slept. She lay in bed, drifting for a while, in and out of the remnants of a dream in which she—a small white dog—played in a sparkling river with Fletch, who turned into a policeman, morphed into a gardener, then back to a policeman, while glistening fish jumped in and out of the rippling water in graceful arcs.

The sound of a siren nearby jolted her awake again. A glance at her phone told her it was a little after eight, so she threw back the covers and swung herself out of bed. The siren's wailing loudened as she padded to the bathroom. Police? Ambulance? Fire? Her heart fluttered with a moment of worry but the siren faded away, passing Orchard Close and continuing on its way to bring bad news to somewhere else.

Fletcher, already downstairs, scratched at the French doors, eager to get outside.

Jess shoved open the door, switched on the kettle, and tipped a measure of dog biscuits into Fletch's bowl. Barefoot, still in pyjama bottoms and the old T-shirt she'd slept in, she took a bowl of cereal out to the garden table. The air was quiet again, the siren all but forgotten now it had receded into the distance. Aside from a handful of her neighbours leaving for work at various times between about seven-thirty and eight-thirty each day, and the odd rumble of a passing tractor, little other traffic disturbed the peace this early in the morning this far into the countryside. A solitary wood pigeon cooed mournfully somewhere towards the bog lane, but other than that, all was calm. Jess glanced at her phone again. Marcus would be here soon to drop Snowflake off for the day, but Jess's only plans for the morning were to think about what to do with Alice, Eric, and his family at the weekend, and what to cook for Shay on Wednesday evening.

Breakfast only half-eaten, she went back to the kitchen to get paper and pen to write a shopping list for the week ahead. She'd make the list, walk the dogs, and then head off into town. She'd pick up something nice for dinner tonight too; Marcus could eat with her, he'd be back to collect Snowflake at sevenish, and he'd be hungry and grateful for food after his long day at work. As she scribbled her list—*pasta, veg, fish*—her thoughts drifted back to Viktor. She drew a line through *fish* and wrote *halloumi* instead, followed by ingredients to make a sponge cake. On Wednesday after the gardening course, she could call and see Mila, since she'd be in the area, and take her a cake. A week was a respectable amount of time to pass, wasn't it? Not too soon, not too late ... Late! Marcus would be here any second! She shoved aside her empty cereal bowl and ran upstairs to get dressed.

When Fletcher's excited whining announced Marcus's arrival, Jess, hair still dripping after her shower, spat the last rinse of toothpaste into the sink and yelled out of the open bathroom window to the doorstep below. "Come in, I'll be right down." She pulled on jeans and a vest top, swung a towel around her hair, and thudded down the stairs, where Snowflake and Fletcher greeted her like a long-lost friend: jumping, barking, slobbering until Marcus heaved them off and dragged them into the kitchen by their collars and thrust them outside.

He slammed the door shut and leaned his back onto it, arms stretched out to the sides, palms turned flat against the glass as if to stop a barrage or stampede.

Laughing, Jess switched her gaze from Marcus's antics to look beyond him at the capering dogs, still charging around like children in a playground. "I don't know why they're so excited; I hadn't even told Fletcher his friend was coming, and I haven't any bones or treats waiting for them. Mad dogs." She took a couple of steps forward, to stand beside Marcus, and side by side, they watched the two dogs racing around the garden in ecstatic circles.

Marcus slung an arm around Jess's shoulders and pulled her into a side-hug. "How're you doing? Better today?"

She leaned into him for a moment, before ducking out from under his arm. "Much better, thanks. Have you time for tea? Or coffee to set you up for the day?"

He checked his watch and nodded. "Go on then, but it'll have to be quick. I suppose you heard the sirens earlier?" He nodded his head in the direction of the closed end of Jess's cul-de-sac, away from Ballyfortnum village and towards the river and the next village over. "Not like you to not be interrogating me. Are you sure you're okay?"

Jess swiped at him with a hastily-grabbed tea towel. "Haven't had a chance, with all that barking." She spooned instant coffee into a pair of stripey mugs, then stopped, mid-task, and faced him again. "I guess it's something interesting, since you mentioned it?" A trail of coffee granules fell from the spoon, leaving a grainy path across the countertop.

Marcus muttered something Jess didn't catch, and Jess guessed he was kicking himself for having let something important slip.

"Come on, out with it. What's happened?"

Marcus took one of the coffee mugs from the worktop, and took a few large gulps. "Ouch! That's hot. I have to get moving. I'll know more later. Be patient, and I promise I'll tell you what I can when I see you later?" His dark eyes met hers, imploring her to wait for news.

Jess picked up her own steaming mug and wrapped her hands around it, inhaling the rich coffee aroma but not drinking. She stared at him, unblinking, about to protest and demand he tell her more, but he intercepted her curiosity with a gentle hand on her arm.

"I don't know the details. I will find out more when I get to the station. I will tell you what I can later. Please Jess, trust me."

She nodded, biting back the stream of unsaid questions that bubbled in her mind. Who? What? Where? It had to be something newsworthy or he'd have not said anything.

Marcus gave her arm a gentle squeeze, called a goodbye to the dogs, who had stopped chasing each other and lay panting on the other side of the French doors, and didn't get up or respond to Marcus's wave. He downed the last mouthful of coffee, gave Jess a peck on the cheek, and saw himself out.

His car was barely out of Orchard Close—she could still hear the faint purr of his engine—by the time she had her boots on and the dogs' leads in her hand. She let herself out through the French doors, clipped on the leads, and ushered the excited-again dogs out of the garden gate.

"Come on boys; we've some investigating to do!"

At the open end of Orchard Close, she stood for a moment, wondering which way to go. She recalled how Marcus had looked away from the village centre as he'd mentioned the sirens, so she turned right, tracking the implied direction of the source of the trouble.

"We're just having a walk, right, boys?" she said to Fletcher and Snowflake as Fletch tugged on his lead and the little Westie trotted at her heels in his usual display of perfect manners. "Just an ordinary walk, just like we normally do."

Chapter Seventeen

Having found no answers on their walk, Jess conceded temporary defeat and returned home, shut the dogs in, and drove into town.

She'd already texted Marcus, to ask if he wanted to eat with her that evening; Linda, to see if she needed any shopping, and Shay, to check on his preferences for Wednesday's dinner. The needs for all those, combined with ingredients to bake something to bring to Mila's family, led Jess to the big out-of-town supermarket and almost two hours of traipsing up and down the aisles. The reward was a large slice of fruitcake at Linda's kitchen table on her return.

To Jess's surprise, Kate was already there, an empty mug and plate on the table in front of her suggesting she'd been there a while.

"I was waiting for you, really," Kate admitted, accepting another slice of cake with an apologetic gesture towards her enormous belly. "This little one is always hungry; I can't wait to get him out."

Linda tapped Kate's shoulder. "And we can't wait to meet him." She topped up Kate's mug, refilled the teapot, wiped some crumbs off the counter, and offered yet more cake to her younger friends, clucking and flitting, until, in unison, Jess and Kate urged her to stop fussing and sit with them.

"Don't you answer your phone these days? Am I not important now you're juggling so many admirers?" Kate folded her arms across her chest and glared in feigned annoyance as Jess rooted in her pockets for her phone.

"Must be in the car," she said, through a large mouthful of fruitcake. "What's up?"

Linda glanced anxiously at Kate and reached across the table to cover Jess's fingers with her own wrinkled hand. "More bad news, love."

Jess froze in her seat, the mug of tea partway to her mouth. A gentle whooshing filled her ears, and she felt the room begin to sway.

"Put your head down, quick—" Linda was on her feet, moving around the kitchen table as fast as her slippers would allow, simultaneously moving Jess's mug to safety and putting her other arm across Jess's back. "Steady now; deep breaths. That's it, love."

"What's happened? Who ...? Kate?" Jess turned to look at her friend, who was unmoved, and still munching her way through her second slice of Linda's fruitcake. With Kate nonplussed, Jess forced her breathing to slow to normal and her hands to stop shaking.

Linda was immediately apologetic. "Oh, love, I'm sorry. That was tactless of me. It's no one close to you." She pressed the mug of tea back into Jess's hands. "Drink." The older woman looked at Kate again, and gave a small nod, which Kate interpreted as an invitation to fill Jess in.

"Tractor O'Sullivan has been shot."

Jess put her mug down again with a loud thump. "You what?"

"Shot. Tractor. He's dead."

"Bloody hell. Sorry, Linda." She glanced up at her neighbour. "But ... Bloody hell!"

Linda smiled weakly. "I said some strong words myself, love, so don't be apologising for it. What a shock."

Jess picked up her tea and gulped it down.

Linda refilled the mug wordlessly, watching in concerned silence while Jess absorbed the news.

After a few false starts, opening and closing her mouth without forming a coherent question, she finally managed a full sentence: "How the heck did you know, Kate?" Without waiting for an answer, she voiced the other thought that had bubbled over the tangle of mixed emotions and questions. "I guess that's what Marcus wasn't able to tell me this morning then. So, Kate, go on. How ...? What ...? I mean, how ...?"

Kate, apparently, had not only turned down an "offer I could refuse" from Tractor back in the spring, but also knew a couple of his brothers and three of his cousins. Declan, Kate's husband, was a drinking buddy to some of them, and two of the men and an assortment of their wives and daughters had attended Kate's Get Slim classes over the past year.

"Do you know *everyone*?" Jess glared accusingly at her friend, pointing at her with her half-empty mug.

Kate shrugged. "Gotta network. Ouch!" Her smirk turned into a wince as she rubbed her belly.

Jess shook her head. "Don't think you can fob us off with baby kicks. Let's hear it. And you—" She jabbed a finger towards Kate's pregnant belly. "—can keep still and be patient until this story is out."

Kate ran her hands protectively over the baby and laughed. Tractor's brother's wife was, it transpired, also heavily pregnant. Kate had been to an ante-natal class early that morning, as had Tractor's sister-in-law, Jane. Jane, apparently, had been mid-pant, concentrating hard on practising breathing techniques, when her husband had answered his phone, turned ashen, and sat down so hard on a yoga ball that he'd slid off it and landed in an ungainly heap on the floor, while a room full of third-trimester woman looked on. Kate, she relayed to a speechless Jess, had helped Danny up off the floor, comforted an angry Jane, and managed to learn the entire contents of the offending phone call, almost before the midwife could collect the bouncing ball from the far side of the room. Then Kate had driven the pair of them to the home of the oldest of the O'Sullivan brothers, Charles, who also lived in Ballyfortnum, and left them there on the doorstep of Charles's farm. "I'll run Danny back into Lambskillen later, to collect his car, if he needs me." Kate sat back in the chair and plucked a crumb from her plate with a manicured finger.

Jess, still speechless, stared at her friend in disbelief, her mouth hanging open like some gormless village idiot.

"What?" Kate's voice was shrill with indignation. "I had to help! He was in no state to drive, and she hasn't been driving since she had Braxton Hicks a couple of weeks ago."

Jess didn't know where to begin, so went with the most obscure of all the many questions that jostled for precedence. "What the heck are Braxton Hicks?"

Kate didn't answer immediately. Her face was taut with strain, and she clutched her belly again. She took a long, deep breath in, closed her eyes, and slowly breathed out; her face drained of colour. After a moment, she opened her eyes and looked at Jess. "That," she said, "is a Braxton Hicks. Basically, they are practice contractions. Preparing for the real thing."

Linda pushed back her chair and stood up, wiping cake crumbs from her hands on the tea towel hanging over the back of the empty seat. "Kate, love, that is the fourth time since you arrived. I'm not so sure these are Braxton Hicks." She checked the kitchen clock and made a note of the time on a magnetic shopping list notepad hanging from her fridge. "Is Declan home? Have you a bag packed for hospital?"

Chapter Eighteen

Despite the three of them spending the next thirty minutes staring at Kate's belly as if it might explode, she didn't have another contraction, proving Linda's predictions wrong. Nonetheless, having determined that labour was not immediately forthcoming, Kate took herself off home, to ready her bag and come to terms with the inevitable nearness of her baby's arrival.

Jess tried to push her questions about Tractor O'Sullivan's demise to the back of her mind by focusing on an afternoon of baking. First, she mixed the promised cake for Mila. While that baked in the oven, she assembled a quiche to have that evening with salad and potatoes from the garden, and then she made up a double batch of scones—half cheese and onion, half cherry and apricot—to last her through the next few lunches, mid-morning snacks, or to munch with countless afternoon cups of tea.

As she mixed and kneaded and whisked, her thoughts kept tumbling back to Kate's news. Who would shoot Tractor? Why? Was this connected to Viktor being found dead on Tractor's land? She glanced at the clock. Almost five-thirty; not long till Marcus would be here and she could get some answers. She lifted the scones out of the oven and decided she still had just about enough time to rustle up something sweet to tempt Marcus into sharing more information. Chocolate brownies should do the job. In the cupboard, she found a bar of chocolate to break into chunks and a bag of hazelnuts. Marcus had a distinct weakness for the chewiest, crunchiest, nuttiest, gooiest brownies. She'd get him to spill the beans on Tractor, if it took all her cooking and bribery skills to do so.

"Mm, smells delicious," Marcus was not even in the door before the scent of fresh-from-the-oven cooling brownies caught his attention.

"Good!" Jess flashed him a smile and ushered him through to the kitchen. "Shall we eat outside? It's still warm."

In easy agreement, Marcus rummaged in Jess's cupboards and kitchen drawers, gathering plates, cutlery, and glasses.

The ease of their relationship gave Jess a warm flutter in her chest and she wondered, not for the first time, whether she'd been on her own for too long now. Much as she liked her independence—and her last boyfriend, had, quite frankly, been an absolute tosser—she relished these companionable dinners with Marcus, who was easy company and comfortable in her kitchen. Maybe things would work out with Shay... Feeling her cheeks flush as her thoughts once again segued from Marcus to Shay or vice versa, she turned away from Marcus so he wouldn't see her blushes, and busied herself with arranging the salad.

Once seated at the little garden table, plates laden with fresh green leaves, tiny new potatoes, and the quiche Jess had made earlier, she could hold her curiosity no longer. "Tractor O'Sullivan, then?" She looked up at Marcus, biting the inside of her cheek to hold back her smile; trying to maintain an innocent expression while she waited to see how long it would take him to realise that, once again, she knew something she shouldn't know, and knew it before he had told her.

Fork halfway to his mouth, luckily not already mid-mouthful, Marcus spluttered and dropped the still-loaded fork back on his plate. "Jessica O'Malley!" He stared across the table at her, open-mouthed.

Aiming for nonchalance, she took another large mouthful of her own slice of quiche. "Don't you like it?" She inclined her head towards his uneaten food, then looked at him again, raising her eyebrows. "I grew that myself, and spent all afternoon cooking that." She pointed with her fork to the respective items, enjoying his bewilderment as to how she could possibly know about Tractor already.

Not rising to her pretence of innocence, Marcus shovelled quiche into his mouth, chewed slowly, carefully, infuriatingly, and swallowed before speaking. "You know what I mean. How in the world did you know about James O'Sullivan?"

It always sounded strange to Jess when anyone called Tractor by his real name. Only a very select portion of the village ever called him anything but Tractor—his elderly mother, for one, and a few of the other older villagers. She took a moment to process Marcus's question, then smiled sweetly up at him. "Kate."

"Kate?" If Marcus had seemed surprised moments before, he was now a picture of wide-eyed, open-mouthed amazement. "Kate?"

"Kate," Jess affirmed.

"Oh, come on Jess! How did Kate know? And more to the point, *what* does she know? What do *you* know?"

Jess was suddenly serious. A man was dead, after all. And not just any man, but another of her neighbours. Not a laughing matter, she told herself firmly, and then explained to Marcus that Kate had not said much, because of the contractions that weren't really contractions but had been enough to distract the three women from worrying too much about Tractor. "She only really knew he'd been shot. And is dead. Presumably that's what the sirens were about this morning?" She looked up at Marcus for confirmation, and he nodded.

"Yes, I knew this morning there had been an incident at his farm, but not all the details. I didn't actually know he was dead when I saw you earlier, only that someone had been found injured up at his farm."

"So, what happened?"

"We're not sure yet, but it is being treated as suspicious. I don't mind telling you this, as it will be in the papers by morning—it's already made the television and radio news. I'm surprised you didn't know that."

Jess had been too engrossed in her latest audiobook as she was cooking, and, swept up in *The Mangle Street Murders*, had not thought to check the news all afternoon. As she said this to Marcus, he laughed at her again.

"Not much of a detective. Not hearing the latest updates on a real crime because you are too busy in a fictional one." He leaned back in his chair and smiled broadly; eyes creased into rippling laughter lines in that endearing way they always did when he was amused.

She waved her fork at him again. "But I have you to tell me everything, and you will be far more accurate than the news." She stabbed her fork down into a buttery new potato to emphasise her point. "So, go on. Spill."

Tractor O'Sullivan—James in Marcus's officially-voiced version of events—had been discovered in his old stone farmhouse by one of his labourers, when he'd arrived to help with the milking at about five-thirty that morning. At first, the man who'd stumbled across the body had assumed Tractor was drunk.

"That's fair. It wouldn't be the first time." Jess, along with most of Ballyfortnum, had heard the rumours about Tractor's laddish lifestyle. His reputation for being a fun-loving, woman-seducing, Jack-the-lad was a favourite subject of village gossip, and one of the most colourful rumours involved a cowshed, a girl from the next village, and a stack of empty bottles. That time, if the rumours were to be believed, one of his farmworkers had arrived for early-morning milking and met the girl stumbling out of the shed, straw in her hair but otherwise naked and nonchalant. According to the legend, she'd merely asked the labourer to direct her to the bathroom, and made no attempt to cover herself or spare his blushes.

"And then he noticed the blood," Marcus continued as if Jess had not interrupted him. "Still thought he was drunk, maybe had knocked himself out. Simon—that's the lad who found him—tried to rouse him, and that's when he realised his boss was dead. Turned on the light, saw the mess, called us, then went to milk the cows by himself. Said they couldn't wait, dead farmer or no."

"True, that." Jess had lived in the village long enough to know that you don't keep a herd of cows waiting to be milked, not for anything.

Marcus raised an eyebrow and expressed disbelief both of her farming knowledge and of the likelihood that anyone would discover the body of their dead boss and then calmly continue with their work as if nothing was amiss. "But, then," he amended, "shock can do funny things to a person. He probably just went into autopilot. By the time he'd finished the milking and the yard was full of Gardaí, he was a bit pale all right."

"So where was he—Tractor? Out in the yard?"

"No, in the kitchen. Dead on the floor. The labourer had let himself in, after he realised no one was around to help him with the milking. There'd been another bloke around the last few mornings, as James had been busy in the week with silage 'or summat', and usually didn't milk on weekend mornings, on accounts of his, 'um, lifestyle, yer know what I mean, sure yer do. Don' like ter speak ill of t' dead, but he were a player a'right,'" Marcus did a fair impression of a midlands country accent, and Jess nodded.

"Ah sure," she agreed, mimicking the accent. "They all say that, an' cross theirselves, a'right, but then they go on an' tell everything they ever heard. They'd sell their grannies for a bit of gossip, people round here. Bit of gossip beats speaking ill of the dead every time." She laughed and scraped up the last of her quiche.

Marcus stretched his legs out under the table, rubbing Fletcher's belly with his foot. He nodded at Jess, eyes sparkling with agreement, amusement, or both.

"And," Jess continued, "I suppose that by 'lifestyle,' he means Tractor was usually either out on the lash all weekend, or shacked up in someone's bed ... or hiding out upstairs with someone in his?"

"I'd say that's exactly what he meant. O'Sullivan certainly had a reputation. It seems everyone we've asked today has begun their comments with that. Well, except his mother. But even she mentioned his 'liking for the ladies'. He wasn't killed this morning though. Looks like he'd been there a while." He grimaced, shook his head with a jerk, and gave the tomato he'd speared on his fork a disgusted look before letting it drop back onto his plate. "We haven't the results yet, so don't ask, but it certainly wasn't pretty." He shook his head sharply again, as if to dislodge the image. "There's no more to say just yet, but it's obviously suspicious. There was no gun at the scene so he didn't do it himself." Marcus frowned at his almost-empty plate, then pushed it away, with a slight shudder. "Lucky I was just about done eating." He got up and cleared their dishes, scraping the last scraps of his meal into the compost receptacle beside the sink. "Will I put the kettle on?"

As it rumbled to a boil, Jess realised that she hadn't even needed the brownies as a bribe. He'd told her what he knew quite willingly for a change. Nonetheless, she held the still-warm selection out towards him, wafting them gently to maximise the chocolatey smell. "I suppose I'll let you have one anyway, in promise of future information."

Marcus's smile was as warm and melting as the brownies. He helped himself to the largest. "Deal."

Chapter Nineteen

For once, Jess was ready early on Wednesday, and already sitting in her car fiddling with the radio when Linda opened the passenger door and slid in. The morning news had offered nothing she didn't already know in relation to Tractor O'Sullivan's death, so Jess was searching for music she could sing along to during the short journey to the garden centre for their class.

Linda settled herself into the passenger seat and balanced a cake tin carefully on her lap while she fastened her seat belt. As Jess gestured to the tin, shooting her neighbour a questioning look, Linda prised off the lid to reveal a tempting stack of shortbread biscuits. "I wasn't sure if you'd remembered, but we said we'd call on Mila today, so I made goodies in case you had forgotten."

Jess pointed over her shoulder with her thumb, gesticulating towards her own offering, lying on the back seat in a large Tupperware container. "Fruit cake. I decided to make something that would keep well if they're overwhelmed with food." She gave up with the radio and hit 'play' on the CD instead, put the car into gear, and pulled smoothly away from the kerb.

Mila wasn't at the garden centre, but all the other course participants were present. As Jess looked around the stuffy portacabin—airless despite the open windows—she realised with a flash of guilt that she hadn't spoken to Shay since Sunday evening. She felt her face flush as she caught his eye, and a flutter of butterflies rose in her chest. Looking quickly away, she turned to Linda, saying, "Tea? You sit down, I'll make it."

In the corner of the room, Jess busied herself at the kettle. "Anyone else?" she called into the portacabin, still avoiding looking at Shay, and willing her face to cool before she had to sit at the table with the others. She wasn't ready for everyone to know that she and Shay were ... well, whatever it was they were. Still, the heat of the portacabin under yet another day of blazing August sun would give anyone a convincing excuse for a red face.

She carried a pair of steaming mugs of tea to the table, trying to tune in to the chatter of the room. As she picked up on snippets of conversation, she realised that for the second Wednesday in a row, the talk was predominantly of a dead man. While not all the members of the course knew Tractor in person, most knew him by reputation, at least. With a jolt of amusement, Jess realised she wasn't the only one blushing: Lucy, a part-time artist and full-time mother of three from just outside Ballyfortnum, was squirming in her seat and fiddling with her hair, doodling into her notepad and studiously avoiding eye contact with anyone. Jess scribbled on her own notepad, *Bet she slept with him!* She added a curling arrow pointing across the table towards Lucy, and angled the page towards Linda.

Linda raised an eyebrow and shot Jess an unconvincing glare of disapproval, definitely trying to suppress a chuckle. Linda may be eighty-something, but she still had a wicked sense of humour that Jess was relieved to see gradually reappearing. Since Bert's death in February, Linda had been understandably sombre, but over the past month or so, her old sparkle was emerging again. Kate had done her good, bringing out all of Linda's maternal instincts with the revelation about her pregnancy; the drama of the baby's father and Kate's affair, and that Declan had subsequently left her. Linda had vowed to help Kate as best she could, and had diligently stuck to her mission. As Kate blossomed and bloomed, so, it seemed, did Linda. That; the gardening course, and the stray cat Linda had tamed and taken in were doing wonders for giving Linda a happier focus while she mourned her beloved husband.

Tea drunk, notes taken, chat subsided, the gardening group moved out of the portacabin and into an equally airless polytunnel, where they spread themselves around a workbench laden with seed trays for sowing with spring cabbage, red cabbage, and winter spinach.

Jess jostled for a space nearest to the open doorway, but there was no breeze to give relief from the humidity. As she lifted the hem of her T-shirt to wipe sweat from her forehead, one of the older women leant in conspiratorially.

"Well, Jess. What do you think? He was your neighbour, wasn't he? What happened? My daughter knew him, you know? He was bit of a ladies' man, by all accounts."

Jess was saved from answering by Shay, who'd nudged his way in between the two women.

"You can firm that compost down a little," he said, "and fill it to the brim."

Although his words were aimed at Jess's companion, it was Jess's back on which he rested his hand; a light, tickling touch that sent a shiver coursing through her and caused her to tip an excess of compost all over her seed tray. She pushed her shoulder against his hand for a moment, savouring the brief moment of intimacy in the crowded polytunnel, but careful not to look at him or openly react to his presence.

"I'll go and grab some more bags of compost; looks like we're running low in here. Give me a hand, Jess?" He nodded towards the doorway.

She brushed the loose soil from her hands and followed him out.

Like a pair of errant teenagers, they ducked quickly out of sight inside the cool darkness of the large storage shed.

"How are you?" Shay reached out and brushed something from Jess's face, stroking gentle fingers down her cheek.

She leant into him, suddenly craving the warm solidity of his body.

He wrapped his arms around her and pulled her close. "You doin' okay? You knew that farmer, right?" His voice was muffled by her hair, and she closed her eyes and sighed, allowing herself to take comfort in being held.

"He lives—lived—around the corner. I didn't really know him to be honest. Kate knows—shite! Knew. Kate knew him better than me. He had quite a reputation. Any number of jilted lovers or their irate husbands could have had it in for him." She gave a small chuckle and Shay took a step back, relaxing his hold to place one hand under her chin and tilt her face up to meet his.

As he bent down to kiss her, a thud behind them caused Jess to jump backwards, putting a couple of feet of distance between them.

"Sorry." Mike stepped into the gloom of the shed. "Just came to see if you needed a hand with shifting that compost. I'll grab a couple of bags and leave you to it." He gave a half-smile, stepped around them, and pulled two bags of potting compost off a large stack. He left as silently as he'd appeared, carrying the heavy sacks easily, as if they were no heavier than a plate of biscuits.

Jess, cheeks flaming once again, covered her face with her hands. She peeked through her fingers at Shay, who was pretending to straighten a stack of already straight pots. As their eyes met, she giggled like a schoolgirl, leaned in to give him a quick peck on the cheek, then spun away from him to pull another bag of compost from the pile and follow Mike back to the polytunnel.

For the rest of the morning, she kept her head down, acutely aware of Shay's eyes on her, but certain that if she looked at him, she would either dissolve into uncontrollable giggles or die of embarrassment. Bloody Mike. She jammed the dibber hard into the trays of compost, making holes far too large for the tiny seeds she would drop into them.

Linda, working at the bench beside her, looked at her quizzically. "What's got into you love? Has someone upset you? You'll have holes put in the bottom of those trays if you carry on. Why don't you go and make us all tea? It's almost time for a break."

Jess ignored her friend for a moment, continuing to jab at the soil.

"Jess?" Linda persisted, and Jess threw down the dibber and strode out of the tunnel.

Back in the portacabin, the kettle bubbled loudly in the quiet of the room. Jess prised the lid off the biscuit tin and helped herself to a couple of broken pieces. With her free hand, she set out a row of assorted tea-stained mugs, threw a teabag into each one, and rummaged in the tiny fridge for milk, enjoying the cool air on her face as she opened the fridge door. As she splashed milk into the mugs, she found herself thinking of Tractor O'Sullivan again. The image of his cows grazing peacefully in the fields flanking his driveway merged with the memory of the startled heifers she and Marcus had disturbed.

Who would be minding the cows now he was gone? Would they get milked? She laughed aloud as she realised that Tractor not only had an army of labourers, but also several farming brothers and cousins, all living locally and probably only too happy to take on extra animals without having to pay to get them. She splashed water into six of the mugs and refilled the kettle to do the next batch, stirring the six filled mugs along with her thoughts. Who might have killed him, and why? Could one of his brothers or cousins have a grudge? Or found a quick way to get hold of cattle or land acreage?

Surely not. From what little she knew of the O'Sullivans, they were a close-knit family who helped each other out and worked together when the going got tough.

Who else, then? She absently stirred each cup, then emptied two of the mugs out into the little sink, remembering that Moira took her tea black and Mike would prefer coffee.

As she boiled the kettle for the third time, to start the last two drinks again, she remembered that she and Linda were to call round to Mila after the course today, and she made a mental note to ask Mila whether Viktor and Tractor had known each other. Two deaths on the same land, in the space of a week, could surely not be coincidence. Surely there must be *some* connection between their deaths? She put the milk in the fridge and pushed the door shut just as the door to the portacabin swung open and the chatter of her classmates snapped her out of her reverie.

As the little group filed into the stifling portacabin, Jess's phone vibrated in the back pocket of her jeans. She eased it free and squinted at the screen. Shay.

Looks like we won't get a moment. Still on for tonight? Miss you x

Smothering a laugh, she looked around for him, finding him watching her from the doorway. She flashed a smile in his direction and nodded. "Seven?" she mouthed across the room, waiting for his nod of acknowledgement before turning to talk to another of the course attendees about whether the humid air was warning of another imminent thunderstorm.

Chapter Twenty

A young man inched open the door to the neat semi-detached house in the large housing estate to the south of Ballymaglen and greeted Jess and Linda warily. "Yes?" he said, not impolitely, but as if he had answered the door many times already to people he didn't really want to talk to.

Linda stepped forward, holding out the tin of shortbread. "Hello, love." Her voice was soft; kind and grandmotherly. "We just wanted to call in and pay our respects. This is shortbread. It will keep for a while in its tin. I'm Linda. We know Mila from the gardening course." She smiled her gentle smile, and the man's face softened into a more welcoming expression.

"Jess." Jess stepped forward now, holding out the hand that wasn't clutching her own tin of consolation. "And fruitcake. You're probably overwhelmed. We don't want to intrude; just to see how Mila is and let her know we are thinking of you all. And to tell her we are here for her if we can help with anything. To give her our love. And cake, of course." Jess chuckled nervously. She hated this; the grief that shrouded a newly bereaved family like a heavy curtain. She felt suddenly tired. So many deaths in the past few months. Far too many for any one community. Although, of course, Viktor wasn't from the Ballyfortnum community, but still ... his family was connected to it now by so many threads—his death in the locality; Mila's growing friendship with her colleagues on the gardening course, many of whom lived in Ballyfortnum, and by Jess having found Viktor's body. She opened her mouth again to explain to this young man that it had been she who had found Viktor, but he'd turned away from them, gesturing them to follow him down the narrow hallway and into the lounge at the rear of the house.

Like Jess's own house, this one had French windows opening onto a well-kept garden bursting with late summer blooms surrounding a sun-scorched lawn.

Mila was outside, on her knees, trowel in hand, scraping at the dry earth. An older woman sat in the shade of a large green patio umbrella that threw cool relief onto a worn and greying plastic patio set. As Jess and Linda approached, Mila stood, brushing the dirt from her hands and knees.

Jess engulfed her in a warm hug. "How are you doing? I am so sorry I didn't go to the funeral. I thought I couldn't face it, but I realised too late that if his family had to face it, then of course I could have. I'm sorry." She turned to encompass the older woman in her apology. It had been weighing on her since Friday, and she felt guilty for allowing her own emotional reluctance to face Viktor's funeral to overtake the family's grief.

"It is okay. I understand. This is my mother, Katarzyna. Mamo ..." Mila switched to her native Polish and spoke rapidly to her mother.

Jess recognised only her name and Linda's, and guessed that introductions and explanations were being made.

When Mila spoke Jess's name for a second time, her mother's face dropped and the greyness around her eyes seemed suddenly more evident. She smiled sadly at Jess, her mouth turned up but no light in her eyes.

Mila switched to English and spoke to her friends. "I told Mamo that you are my friends from the gardening course. I told her you found Viktor, also. She recognised your name, anyway."

Linda, while Mila was talking, had seated herself beside the older woman, and took Katarzyna's hands in her own, expressing sympathy and kindness through gestures more than words. Now, Mila's mother started to rise, but Jess waved her back into her seat.

"Don't get up, it's lovely to meet you. I'm sorry it's in such terrible circumstances." Jess had recognised instantly that Mila's mother had only fundamental English skills so she spoke slowly and clearly, gesticulating to urge the poor woman to remain seated.

Katarzyna released Linda's hands and reached out to take Jess's instead. She coughed softly, then spoke in hesitant English: "Dear, is sad thing for you also, yes? I thank you for—" She turned to her daughter and shrugged. "My English—I have forget. I thank you for help my son. Yes?" She held Jess's hands with a firm, soft pressure, and Jess's eyes filled with tears, reflected in the older woman's watery eyes.

Without thought, Jess leaned down to hug Mila's mother, and the two held each other for a long moment before the awkward position forced Jess to straighten. "I am so sorry," Jess murmured again, as she stood.

"Sit, sit." Katarzyna patted the plastic garden chair beside her and spoke to Mila in Polish again.

Mila nodded, and offered her visitors tea, coffee, or a cold drink.

Linda opened the cake tins that she and Jess had put on the table, and showed Mila's mother the contents. "This one is shortbread. Biscuits. And this, this one is fruitcake."

Jess rose from her seat. "Let me help you Mila?"

Mila nodded agreement and the two younger women stepped into the cool dimness of the living room and through the hall to a large open-plan kitchen-diner, where Mila began to gather refreshments.

The young man, who had disappeared once he had seen Jess and Linda through to the garden, now reappeared, ambling into the kitchen, talking rapidly into his phone. He cut off the call once he saw the women, and Mila introduced him as her younger brother, Bartosz.

"Bart," the man said, holding out his hand to shake, altogether more welcoming now he saw that Mila was comfortable in Jess's company and he wasn't expected to make small talk. "You found our brother I think?"

"Yes. That's me." Jess could almost feel the young man's grief oozing out of him as he stood before her with sagging shoulders and a haunted look in his eyes. "I'm so sorry."

"Not your fault," Bart said, gruff but not unkind. "I just wish to find the bastard who did this to my brother. This is all. You can help me?" He gestured with open palms, and Jess realised he was even younger than she had first thought—late teens, maybe. Very early twenties at the most.

"Bartosz." Mila's voice held a warning. "Jess doesn't know anything." She shrugged helplessly at Jess, but Jess was focused on the boy.

"It's okay, Mila, I'll help if I can." She turned back to Bartosz. "I can try, but I don't think I will be able to tell you anything you don't know. Perhaps you can tell me about your brother? What was he like? Who did he know?"

Bartosz pulled out a chair at the kitchen table and sat down heavily. He gestured at the chair opposite. "Sit down. I will ask you questions. You will ask me questions, yes? This is a good idea, yes?"

Mila sighed, gave Jess an apologetic look, took two mugs of tea from the tray, and set them on the table: one for Jess, one for Bartosz. She picked up the tray holding the remaining drinks and a plate of cookies. "I'll take this out to Mamo and Linda. I'll be back in a moment."

"It's okay, really, don't apologise. I have some questions too, actually. Maybe your brother will be able to answer them. Did you hear that another man was found dead, near to where I found Viktor?"

The police, perhaps not surprisingly, had already told Viktor's family of this latest development, quizzing them for possible connections. "We don't think Viktor knew this farmer," Bart said, "but of course, we don't know all of those my brother knows. Maybe he did, maybe he did not. I think no, but maybe yes." He shrugged, looking vulnerable and helpless, staring at something beyond Jess's shoulder.

Jess followed his gaze to a photo placed centre-stage on the dresser. Shoving her chair back with a noisy squeak of protest from the tiled floor, she got to her feet, reaching out for the photo as she stood. She picked it up, holding it carefully, and brought it closer to squint at the subject. "This is Viktor?"

"Yes, this is Viktor. He was handsome, yes?" Bart's voice was tinged with anger as much as sadness and Jess's heart ached at the despair emanating from him, but it was not Bart who had her main focus. In the photo, a beaming Viktor held a large fish up to the camera, happy and proud in a checked shirt and red cap. A red cap that looked remarkably similar to the one she'd found in the trees on Saturday morning.

Chapter Twenty-One

"May I take a photo of this?" Jess had pulled her phone from her pocket, already selecting the camera function as she asked.

"Sure."

"Thanks." She lined up the camera carefully to ensure the picture was clear and focused, taking a couple of shots to be sure of getting a good one. Should she tell Bartosz about the cap she'd found in the woods? Maybe it wasn't something she should share with him ... Instead, she gave another reason to justify her interest in the photo—one that even as she gave voice to it, she realised was true. "It will be nice to have a happier image of him." She tried, without success, to suppress a shudder as the unwanted vision of Viktor's bloated, floating body filled her mind. "I keep having flashes of how he—" She broke off. She most definitely did not need to share that image with Viktor's little brother. He didn't need to hear the details of her recurring, nightmarish flashes of his brother's dead body, that popped into her head with an unbidden regularity she couldn't yet shake off. "Sorry." She sat down again. "Bart?" She lowered her voice apologetically. "Was Viktor in any kind of trouble? I heard someone say something about drugs?"

Bart flashed another glance at the picture. "He was a good brother and a good man."

Jess, immediately contrite, began to speak but before she could garble an apology, he looked straight at her.

"There is always trouble on this estate." Bart shrugged again, and downed the rest of his tea before shoving back his chair and getting up from the table. "This trouble is not something new. Ah—" His body sagged and he sat down again, somehow appearing both very young and very old at the same time. "I don't think anyone would want him dead for it though. Even the worst ones have called with ... with ..." He faltered, searching for a suitable word and reminding Jess that English was not his first language. "How do you say it, when people tell you they are sorry for your loss and look sorrowful with you? Like you are calling today, yes?"

"Condolences? Sympathy?"

"So, even his enemies have condolenced to my mother, yes? And they have are sad in their eyes when they talk with her. I am certain of this. They are not his killer, I think."

"Yes." Jess raised her mug to her mouth—not to drink, but to hide her smile at his misuse of the unfamiliar word—and agreed that it seemed unlikely Viktor's drug rivals would kill him and then call round bearing flowers for his mother. She didn't know anything much about drug rivalry—she'd ask Kate, who was more familiar with the nuances and habits of the residents of Ballymaglen than Jess. Kate would either already know the gossip or would know how to get it. For now, though, she would take Bart's certainty at face value and trust his assurances that drug-dealing clashes were unlikely to be the motive.

"What about anyone he supplied?" she asked instead. "Might he have upset any buyer? Charged too much, cheated them, sold bad stuff or short-changed them?"

"My brother is no cheat." Bart's tone was adamant, his accent becoming more pronounced as his voice rose in defence of his brother; his English less fluent as he spoke faster and with increasing passion. "Beside, he only small timer. No big dealer-man. No bad dealing. He is most times just buying small-time good stuff for him to use only, yes?" Tears welled in Bart's eyes, unspilled, but full of raw pain and grief.

Jess was spared further discomfort by Mila's entrance, and gratefully stood to greet her friend. "We should leave you to it. I'll come and say my goodbyes to your mum, and if Linda is ready, we'll head on home."

"It is getting late. You will be hungry? I will make us some lunch? You are welcome to stay."

"Thank you, but I must get back for Fletcher. My dog. He's been left since before nine. He'll be desperate to get out by now." Jess smiled and waved away Mila's offer of lunch, not wanting to outstay the welcome, although it was also true that Fletcher would be waiting eagerly to be let out by now. "We really must go. I'll call in again next week."

Jess thanked Bart for the photo and assured him again that she'd let him know if she heard anything that might give them some answers. To her surprise, the young man took her shoulders in his hands and kissed her on each cheek, before thanking her and leaving the room.

"I'm sorry I didn't get to chat to you so much Mila," Jess said. "Your brother seemed like he needed to talk."

"It's okay," Mila agreed. "It is good for him to feel he can speak with you. He is trying to be strong for Mamo and he keeps his feeling inside. I am happy that he talked with you." A cloud of sadness darkened Mila's face and Jess pulled her into another hug. The two women stood quietly for a few moments until Jess pushed Mila gently away. "You must call if I can help with anything. I will come again after the class next Wednesday, if you don't get to come. But do call me if you need anything. Anything, Mila. You have my number?"

In the garden, Mila's mother and Linda were as Jess had left them—still sitting at the garden table drinking tea and, by the look of their gesturing hands, making good headway with communication. Linda was so good at mothering people, Jess thought, with a lurch of sadness. Linda had been so good to Jess when her father had died. Jess's own mother was quite hopeless; hadn't even come home until after the funeral, and then only stayed in Ireland for a couple of days in an upmarket hotel in Lambskillen before jetting back to her new life in Spain. Linda had been a far better mother to Jess during these last few years than Doreen had been in a very long time.

Jess shoved thoughts of her mother aside and turned her attention back to the two women in front of her. Linda was a true rock. Jess felt a surge of love for her elderly neighbour and reached out to touch her arm.

Linda correctly interpreted Jess's intentions and rose from her seat. She bent to kiss Katarzyna's crumpled cheek, clutching the grieving mother's hands in her own. "I will call again if you wish." Linda enunciated the words softly and clearly and Katarzyna nodded her understanding.

"You are kind. Thank you."

Mila walked with Jess and Linda to the door, to see them out. She stood framed in the doorway of the neat semi, reflected in Jess's rear-view mirror until Jess rounded the corner and could no longer see how long her friend stood there, alone on the doorstep of her grief-stricken home.

"That poor family," Linda said quietly and Jess stopped fumbling with the dial on the car radio for a moment to glance at her friend and nod in silent agreement.

Chapter Twenty-Two

With only a few hours before Shay was due to arrive for dinner, Jess made a hastily-scrawled plan of action on the back of an envelope—*walk Fletch, cook food, hoover, clean bathroom*—before disregarding it and making a sandwich while talking to Kate, phone on loud-speaker on the kitchen counter.

"No baby yet? ... Hurry up, I want to meet him." Not all the pleasantries were strictly true; Jess had little contact with small children and aside from her two nieces, whom she adored, she had no idea what to do with babies or children. "What do you know about drugs in Ballymaglen? Is it likely that Viktor was killed over a drug thing? ... Okay ... Try to find out? Be quick, in case the baby comes? You'll have no time for snooping for me after he arrives ... See you!" She shoved the phone into her pocket and carried her lunch out to the patio.

Lulled into inertia by the warm August afternoon, by the time Jess had moved from the patio, walked Fletch to the bog, and made another cup of tea, she hadn't left herself as much time as she'd intended to get ready for Shay.

After a hasty half-clean of the bathroom, and a quick change of plan for tonight's dinner, she was almost ready. She had tossed together a salad using ingredients plucked from the garden, and made a simple tomato and basil sauce to top a ready-made pizza base. It was a bit of a cheat, but she was determined to leave time for a shower and to shave her legs, just in case. A wave of heat rushed up her neck and across her face at the thought. "But," she argued aloud with herself, "I'll feel better for it wherever the evening goes." She might even ditch her usual attire of comfy jeans for a summery skirt. "Why not?" she said to her reflection, and stepped under the hot jet of the shower. "Why not?"

She gave her hair a final rinse and stepped, dripping, onto the bathmat just as her phone vibrated noisily on the bathroom windowsill.

Kate. That was quick. *Vik's big bro says Vik not into that level of dealing. Not likely drugs, unless it was a message to him, but that's not the usual style. Think dead end, prob. Have fun tonite. Do everything I would do xx*

Jess chuckled as she thought about the significance of Kate's last sentence and typed a quick reply: *Yeah, gonna focus on tonight now, will think about dead people again tomorrow. Don't have baby tonight unless I text you with orders to interrupt us!! Xx*

Noticing the time, Jess swore, grabbed a towel from the hook on the back of the door, and wrapped it around herself, snatching up a second towel to twist around her hair. Picking up the phone again, she sat on the edge of the bath to tell Marcus about the photos she'd found, before padding through to her bedroom to dry off properly.

She pulled on jeans and a clean blouse, then shrugged out of the jeans and switched them for a knee-skimming denim skirt instead. Hair still wrapped in its towel turban, she slid her feet into her slippers and ran down the stairs to tidy the kitchen and throw a colourful cloth over the table. As she rummaged in the drawer for cutlery and selected plates and glasses from the cupboards, she changed her mind. She gathered everything and carried it to the garden table instead. It was just about still warm enough. But would the midges be out by the time they sat down to eat? And it would get chilly soon enough, now August was almost over. Better inside, then. She collected up the tableware and brought it all back inside, where she dumped the pile of crockery and cutlery on the kitchen table in a disorganised clutter.

"Hair!" she said to Fletcher, who was watching her curiously as he tangled himself around her legs and generally got in her way. "I'll never be ready in time, Fletch! Help?" She unwrapped the towel from her head and used it to rub vigorously at her hair as she headed back upstairs to find the hairdryer.

Ten minutes later, still uncommitted to where they might eat, but at least with her hair dried and brushed, Jess ran back down the stairs to pull a barking Fletcher away from the front door, where the blurry figure of Shay stood beyond the frosted glass.

"Come in." She held Fletcher back by his collar until Shay had pushed the door shut behind himself. "Sit down and shut up! Not you, him." She stretched up to greet Shay with a kiss, shoving an excited Fletcher down as she did so. "Tell you what, just make a fuss of him first, then he'll settle down. Come through and find me when he's stopped jumping and slobbering." She gave Fletcher a gentle poke with her bare foot and gestured towards the kitchen. "Beer, wine? Tea? Something else?"

Shay squatted to give Fletcher the attention he demanded, including a thorough belly rub once the dog finally stopped leaping around and squirmed onto his back instead, waving his legs in the air like an upside-down beetle.

"What're you having?" Shay called after Jess, as she rolled her eyes at her dog and left them to it. "I'll have the same."

With Fletcher finally appeased, and shut outside in the garden, it was Jess's turn to snuggle up for Shay's attention. "He likes you," she murmured into his chest as they stood wrapped in each other's arms in the middle of the kitchen.

"I like him too, but I like you a lot more."

"Mmm ..." It was several more minutes before Jess stopped to top the pizza and slide it into the oven to cook. "You wanna eat inside or out? Why don't you go sit while I finish off here? I'll just sort the table and it'll only be about ten minutes 'til that's cooked." She nodded at the oven.

"Ten minutes, huh?" Shay pulled Jess to the sofa with him, and the table remained unset.

The smell of burning told Jess she'd forgotten to set the timer, and both the kitchen table and the garden table were eschewed in favour of eating slightly-blackened pizza on their laps as they flipped idly through Netflix, searching for a film they both agreed on.

"I can cook, you know. You clearly bring out the worst in me."

"I dunno, if this is you at your worst, I'm excited to see what you're like at your best." He pushed a strand of hair away from her face, holding her gaze until the pizza was forgotten. Without releasing Jess, he carefully manoeuvred the plates onto the floor, so he could pull her closer. The film played on, but when Shay glanced at the television screen and said, "What's this about then?" Jess couldn't answer.

"I guess we should start it again."

"Start the film again? Or start this again?" Shay stroked gentle fingers along her bare arm, and the film was ignored once more.

Later, having been interrupted by Fletcher's impatient and insistent scrabbling at the French doors— "Oops, I forgot about him! Sorry boyo."—they stood in the inky-blue darkness of the garden, Shay with his arms wrapped around Jess as she leaned her back against his chest, enjoying the quiet and the starlit sky and the cool slabs under her bare feet.

Shay nuzzled his lips against her neck and she wriggled in his arms until she was facing him again.

"Are you staying?" she asked.

Chapter Twenty-Three

Shortly after midnight, Jess stood on the doorstep waving as Shay drove slowly out of Orchard Close. For a change, as she drifted to sleep, her thoughts were filled with warm fluttery kisses instead of floating bodies or gunshot wounds.

So, on Thursday morning, she awoke refreshed and well-slept, a good twenty minutes before her alarm shrilled into life to usher in the day. By the time Marcus arrived with Snowflake a few minutes after eight, Jess was showered, dressed, and onto her second cup of tea. "You time for a cuppa?"

"Well, O'Malley, you're cheerful this morning. Good night's sleep?"

"Mm." She sloshed water into a mug, added a splash of milk, and pressed it into his hands. "Here."

In wordless agreement, they moved to stand side by side at the French doors, to watch the two dogs cavort around the garden.

"Oh, to be a dog," Marcus said, his face relaxed and wistful as he followed the canine antics.

"I think I'll take them to the river, since I'm up early," Jess said. "Give them a good long run before I go to work. We'll have to work out something for when my new course starts ..."

"Not long now, is there? We'll sort it out, as soon as you know the hours."

The single reservation Jess had about starting her new gardening course at the college in Kildare, was whether she would be out of the house too long for Fletcher. If she couldn't organise someone to mind him, then she wouldn't be able to commit to the course. "Linda would help, I know, but I can't ask her to do much—she's not able to walk him; he's too strong for her, too energetic. She'd cope with Snow, I'd think, but that only solves half the problem."

On Marcus's days off, he'd have the two dogs at his cottage, and even after a night shift, he'd manage them fine, so only on the days where his day shift clashed with Jess's college hours would they need an alternative dog-care arrangement.

"I'm sure we'll find someone who could either mind them or call in and let them out for a run and pee break for us. It'll only be once or twice a week—we'll cover the rest between us still." He rested his fingers lightly on her arm, taking his eyes from the dogs for a second to shoot her a sympathetic sidelong glance. "Don't worry just yet. Having got this far, I'm not going to give him up easily now." Marcus smiled affectionately at the Westie, who now sat on the patio gazing at his master with a matching expression of adoration. Since his ex-wife's decision to move to America with an old colleague of Marcus's, taking Marcus's young daughter with her, he was determined to hang onto this last remnant of his family: the little dog his daughter had adored so much.

"I spoke to Lily yesterday; it's so difficult—she hates talking on video chats and she doesn't sit still for long—but she's always happy to see Snow. She never knows what to say to me, but her face lights up when I lift him to the screen." He shot Jess another quick glance. "I'm planning to go over to see her before Christmas."

The sadness on his face tugged at her heart and she snaked an arm around his back to pull him to her side for a one-armed hug. "I'm sorry. It must be so tough."

Marcus leaned in towards her for a moment, the close warmth of their bodies softening the sad lines on his face. "I should go. I'll be late." He edged away from her, rinsed his mug in the sink, and stood it upside-down on the draining rack. "See you this evening. How about I go straight home and cook something for you for a change? I'll give you a buzz once I'm in; give you a half-hour warning? Would that suit?"

"Perfect. I'll get home from work around five-thirty myself so I'll give the boys a run in the park instead of cooking. That sounds wonderful. See you later."

Marcus pecked Jess on the cheek and let himself out.

Even on working days, it was unusual for Jess to be out walking the dogs quite as early as this, but at ten to nine, she clambered over the gate to the river path, having left Orchard Close just minutes after Marcus drove away. She set off along the riverbank after the dogs, who had already charged off into the trees, yapping and wagging in excitement. The single car parked in the lay-by opposite the gate suggested another early dog walker or a fisherman was also up early and taking advantage of the dry, bright late summer morning. Mindful of this, Jess called the dogs back to her. "Stay in sight, lads, just in case."

Sure enough, just around the next bend, a solitary angler stood poised on the bank, his fishing rod arcing across the glistening water.

Jess clipped on the dogs' leads and reined them in to her side before calling out a cheery "Hello."

The fisherman raised his hand in greeting but as Jess approached, his line jerked and dipped. He grabbed the rod with both hands, bracing against the sudden pull, all his focus on the straining fishing line. The rod bent; the line taut and glistening as the sun caught the water droplets that hung, then dropped to merge with the thrashing ripples below.

Jess froze, hissing to the dogs to sit down and be quiet.

The angler reeled in a writhing silver fish, deftly clasping it in one hand and releasing the hook from its mouth with the other.

"Nice one." Jess inched nearer, keeping her voice low and maintaining a tight hold on Fletcher to quell his quivering excitement. Snowflake, of course, stayed at her heels, unbothered and calm as ever.

The man held the fish for Jess to see better. "He is Trout. Not so big. I having a larger one already." He nodded to the long, green keepnet that snaked over the bank and into the water, anchored to the ground by a tent peg. "This one, I will let him swim free." He knelt at the water's edge and let the fish slip from his hands. With a small ripple and a last above-water flick of its silver tail, it vanished into the current.

"Will you eat the other one?"

He nodded, then shrugged. "Maybe. Or maybe I am catching a larger one next," he said in his stilted English. "Then this one too will be swimming." He gestured at the keepnet with an open hand.

"Where are you from?"

"I am Polish. My name is Seb. You are from here?" He gestured around himself as if they were surrounded by houses, and smiled.

"Jess. I live in the village." She pointed in the general direction of her home. "Nice to meet you." They exchanged pleasantries for a few minutes until Fletcher, bored with the confinement, pulled at the lead, whining to move on. "I'd better let these guys get moving again. See you on the way back."

She waited until they had rounded the next bend before letting the dogs loose once more, all three of them enjoying the increasing warmth of the still-rising sun and its promise of another hot day ahead.

Jess and her canine companions walked on, the dogs lolloping ahead, darting in and out of the tree,, running at full pelt along the path, or occasionally scrambling down the steep riverbank to slurp noisily at the water to cool off. Even when Jess couldn't see them, she could usually hear them, and confident she was unlikely to see anyone else now the single car was accounted for, she relaxed and allowed them their freedom.

Every now and then, she called them back to her, thus keeping loose tabs on their whereabouts, but was still frequently surprised by one or other of them appearing from a place she hadn't quite expected, usually from the thicket of trees to her right. Usually Snowflake, more obedient—better trained, if she was honest— would appear first, but Fletcher, not to be outdone by his smaller friend would always show up not far behind him, then overtake his small friend with a burst of speed, barging past if necessary, to ensure he get to his mistress first.

Jess laughed into the still air, causing a soft echo of laughter from the trees on the opposite side of the river, as the two dogs disappeared over the edge of the grassy bank with a loud splash. *That'll be Fletcher.*

Sure enough, seconds later, he bounced back into sight, dripping a trail of water across the path.

"No! Get down, you disgusting dog! Get off!" Jess pushed the wet dog away, as he shook vigorously, showering her with river water. "Yuk. Go away!"

Never one for heeding instructions, Fletcher licked her hand instead and tried to jump at her again.

She put her hands in front of her body to fend him off. "Get lost, you big brat." She laughed again, grateful for the heat in the still-rising sun, and flicked a lump of wet mud from her jeans. "Where's your friend got to? Snow? Snowflake! Come on, where are you?"

The Westie still didn't appear. He'd better not have fallen in; he wasn't as fond of water as Fletcher, and also, being smaller, not as strong a swimmer.

She covered the distance to the edge in a few long strides, calling his name until she found him, peering up at her with mournful eyes from where he sat at the bottom of the steep bank, perched on a flat, muddy ledge barely wide enough to hold him.

His tail wagged when he saw her, but he didn't rise from his haunches; a sorry picture of piteousness. He whimpered as if to ask, "What kept you? Can't you tell I can't get back up?"

"Ah you silly boy, come on!"

The Westie scrabbled half-heartedly at the vertical bank.

"Oh, you daft eejit!" Unable to reach him easily, and without enough ground below her at the water's edge to jump down to him, Jess dropped to her knees on the edge of the bank. The soft earth gave way slightly under her weight, dampness seeping into the knees of her jeans as she leaned over to try to grab Snowflake.

Fletcher, feeling left out, nosed against her, causing her to wobble precariously towards the water.

She grabbed at a clump of reeds, righted herself, and shoved him away with a firm, "Bugger off, Fletch."

He backed away, lay down, and inched forward on his belly as if she may not notice him creeping towards her.

"Sit down! Sit and stay there," she repeated firmly, waiting until he backed up and lay down a few feet away, head on paws and a sorrowful look of extreme rejection on his doggy face, before she leaned over the edge and grabbed Snowflake by his collar. She hoiked the muddy Westie back onto the path and let him go. "You eejit!"

He gave an indignant shake and scampered off to join the sulking Fletcher.

Still kneeling, Jess let her bottom rest onto her heels and sat there for a moment to recover her breath.

As she tipped forward onto her hands to push herself to her feet, a glint of sunlight bounced off a shiny object half-buried in the muddy earth where the river lapped against the shore below her. She leaned towards the water again, stretching down to scrabble in the soft mud, trying to loosen the object. Leaning quite precariously now, she worked at the object for a few moments, digging her fingers under its smooth surface until, slurping and squelching, it finally came free from the mud. Clutching it in her hand, she sat back to examine the thing she'd found: a slightly battered, very muddy Thermos flask. The cup was missing but the stopper still in place. The rattle of broken glass assured Jess the flask was far beyond salvage, and as she lifted it, she could feel the shifting weight of liquid inside. Strange thing to lose in the river. One of the fishermen must've left it behind.

One of the fishermen.

One of the fishermen who had been hit over the head with a hard object. She almost dropped the flask back into the water. A hard object. A hard object that could be picked up quietly, stealthily, when a branch could be too wieldy or too noisy to pick up without rustling the ground around it, or too weak to do the job without snapping.

A hard object like a metal Thermos flask, perhaps.

Again, she sat back onto her heels, frozen in thought. The dogs sniffed around her, curious as to why she wasn't getting up. "Okay lads, hang on a minute, I'm just coming." She shooed them away and lifted her weight off her heels, squirming to get her phone from her pocket.

She leaned over the edge once more, to snap a series of photos. She zoomed in on the spot she'd pulled the flask from, then straightened up to look around for landmarks to ensure she could remember the location, taking photos of every angle.

Photos taken, flask in hand, she slowly got to her feet, her legs numb and protesting about supporting her weight. She shook each leg in turn, stamping them to coax circulation, and limped to the path, with pins and needles prickling her ankles. She stumbled, glad she was going away from the water—*at least if I trip, I won't fall in; I'm wet enough already, thanks to those idiot dogs.* Back on the worn strip of the path, she tucked the flask under one arm and stooped to rub her calves and ankles, massaging vigorously until the pins and needles abated and proper feeling returned.

"Fletch! Snow! Come on lads, we're going home." The dogs bounded back to her, tails wagging and tongues lolling.

"Hello again!" Seb greeted her as she approached. "What happens to you? You are getting wet?" He pointed needlessly to her damp, mud-stained jeans.

"The little guy got stuck." She gestured to Snowflake. "He always thinks he can do what Fletcher can do, then realises too late that he can't. I had to pull him up from the water. Idiot dog."

The fisherman laughed, but with kindness and sympathy in his eyes. "I have dogs too. Here." He scrolled through his phone for a moment, then showed Jess a picture of two enormous Rottweilers. "They are no good for being fishing. I leave them in home with my wife." He pulled the phone back, scrolling again. "Here, she is my wife. Pretty, yes?"

"Very pretty," Jess agreed, peering at the tiny picture of the smiling brunette in the photo. "Oh, Seb, I found this." She showed him the flask. "Don't suppose it's yours?"

He pointed to a small blue tackle box next to his stool. "I having my drink in there. This one is not mine. It is not same." He peered at it more intently. "You know dead man? Viktor? He is having a flask same as this, I think. Maybe it belonged him."

A tingle crawled along Jess's spine and she shivered, as if the sun had gone behind a cloud instead of beating down on them from the cloudless blue sky.

At the road, Jess clipped on the dogs' leads, and, still deep in thought, they moseyed along the road towards home, dogs sniffing at passing smells, Jess oblivious to anything but her swirling thoughts.

Jess's reverie was broken by a passing car. She looked up, startled to realise they were almost at the junction already. In front of one of the houses, a familiar-looking man power-washing his car waved as Jess passed, calling out some greeting Jess couldn't catch over the noise of the hose.

A Dalmatian ran alongside the inside of the fence, barking loudly.

Jess waved to the man and pulled Fletcher and Snowflake away, not sure how friendly the large spotted dog might or might not be. Directly opposite lay the gates to Tractor's farm. From here, the old stone farmhouse was hidden by a slight bend in the drive and an unruly cluster of ugly conifers but there were no obvious signs of human activity.

Behind the fences on either side of the driveway, an assortment of cows in every shade of brown, and several black-and-white Friesians, lifted their heads, most of them still chewing mouthfuls of grass.

Jess paused by the open gates. "Hey, cows. What happened to Tractor? Do you know?" And to poor Viktor? Was this flask any kind of clue?

The herd ambled towards her.

Snowflake backed away; hackles raised.

Fletcher wagged his tail and strained to get nearer, eager to greet the young cows as they trotted towards their visitors.

The cattle jostled for space in the corners flanking the gateway, seemingly unperturbed by the loss of their master, watchful and curious. As curious as ... well, as curious as a herd of cows.

Chapter Twenty-Four

As soon as Jess was home, she stopped just inside her front door, not even bothering to take off her shoes, and texted Marcus: *Might V have been whacked with a Thermos flask? I found one at the river. Other f'man says maybe V's. x*

Jess hit SEND and hurried to the kitchen to grab something quick for lunch. She took a cheese scone from the tin, slathered it with butter and jam, and wrapped it in a sheet of kitchen paper. Before calling the dogs in from the garden, she ran to the bathroom, tidied her hair, and grabbed her keys, phone, and that scone, giving them every last second outside until she had to go to work.

Dogs shut in the house, Snowflake already dozing peacefully on one sofa, and Fletcher watching desolately from the back of the other, Jess drove out of Orchard Close, using one hand to manoeuvre the gear stick and steer. With the other hand, she raised the scone to her mouth and took a large bite, sprinkling crumbs into her lap as she ate. She was going to be late.

The scone lost the battle. She needed both hands for driving, so set it onto the passenger seat beside her phone, which vibrated, hopefully with a response from Marcus. "Later!" she told it, and it obediently fell silent. Curiosity about the contents of his answer battled with the need to get to work on time, and, conscious of her responsibilities to Shay—and her pay packet—she resisted the urge to pull over and check the message and put her foot down to pull out onto the main road. She'd have plenty of time to talk to Marcus after work. She shifted up through the gears and, now able to drive easily with just one hand, she flicked the radio on and retrieved the scone, catching the lunchtime news partway through.

"It has been confirmed that murdered farmer, James O'Sullivan, had lain dead in his home for some days," the reporter declared solemnly. "Investigations into his death are ongoing, but Gardaí are treating it as linked to the murder of Polish citizen Viktor Dąbrowski earlier this month. Anyone with information is requested to contact Lambskillen Gardaí station." The dispassionate voice of the newsreader read out the phone number for the station, then segued into the upcoming weather forecast.

Jess swallowed the last bite of scone, licked jam from her fingers, switched off the radio mid-promise of another dry week ahead, and rummaged in the glove box for a CD to play for the remainder of her journey. She pulled into the garden centre car park with a few minutes to spare; not late after all.

Shay, unusually, was behind the counter in the main shop. As Jess approached, his face broke into a relieved smile. "Thank God you're here! Ella had to go home, and we've been really busy. Can you take over?" He gestured to the till, but Jess was already behind the counter, stashing her bag on the shelf below the counter. Shay reached down, groping to find her hand without taking his eyes off the woman he was serving. "I'll make it up to you later," he said, handing a bemused-looking customer a handful of change. "Thank you, have a good day."

Once the sliding doors had slid shut behind the departing customer, Shay's shoulders relaxed. He sighed loudly. "It's been manic. Thank God you're here."

Jess laughed, "You said that already. Has it been that bad? I could've come earlier, you know." She glanced around furtively, and, seeing neither customers nor other staff, stretched up and gave him a quick kiss. "Go on, I've got this. Go make a cuppa. Looks like you need it."

Shay grinned at her. "You mean you want one."

"That too. Go on. Go put your feet up. Take a nap. After you bring me tea, obviously."

He ran a hand softly down her back, murmured, "Thanks," and left the shop, leaving Jess alone for approximately thirty seconds until the doors slid open again to admit a gaggle of elderly women, chattering like squabbling magpies.

Jess never enjoyed the busyness of the shop or dealing with the customers quite as much as she liked being out in the polytunnels, but this afternoon, she was grateful for the lack of time to dwell on the likelihood that she'd carried a murder weapon home from the river that morning. She still hadn't had a chance to check her phone, and the afternoon continued in a similar busy fashion with a steady stream of customers filling the next couple of hours.

Aside from Shay depositing the requested cup of tea beside her as she bagged up a packet of rat poison for someone, she'd not seen him since she'd arrived and she guessed he was deliberately keeping away from the shop floor. He also much preferred the plant care and growing over dealing with the public, and was probably hiding away in the far polytunnel—where Jess wished she was. To be fair, she conceded, he was more likely to be bogged down with paperwork in the stuffy office. Even Jack was kept busy, fetching and carrying garden supplies to and from shelves and out to cars for customers, rushing back and forth like a little clockwork gnome.

Finally, a little after four, things quietened down.

Jack fell into a plastic garden chair—part of a patio furniture display—with a heavy sigh. Jess stepped out from behind the counter and collapsed into a similar chair, and emitted a similar sigh. They looked at each other in mirrored expressions of relief.

"That was intense! Whatever brought them all out today? Is there something I've missed? Some promotion? A national campaign to get garden supplies before the end of August? What the heck was that about?" Jess slouched forwards, her elbows on her knees, and let her head rest on her upturned palms.

The older man shrugged. "Beats me. Back ter school rush? Late summer madness? It's bin the same all day. An' wee Ella tripped on a bag o' compost some fecker left in the aisle. Bumped 'er head, poor aul' flower. 'er man 'ad to come and fetch 'er; she'll 'ave a sore head on 'er for days, shouldn't wonder."

"Think you'll manage here while I go check in with Shay?"

Jack winked. "I'll be 'right, go on, 'e'll be 'appy to see ye. Don' be too long now; seein' the rest o' the day, I don't want to be alone in 'ere."

"I'll bring you tea." Jess gave his wrinkled cheek a peck and scampered out of the back doors into the yard before he could change his mind about letting her go.

Conscious of Jack waiting, Jess was quick. She found Shay in the office, busy with paperwork.

"We're not going to get anything productive done in the tunnels today now." His brow furrowed as he shoved papers out of the way to make space for the mug Jess plonked in front of him, then picked up the top sheet of paper and groaned. "It's never-ending today."

"I guessed it might be a coffee kind of day for you. Here." She stepped around his desk to give him a hug. "No, don't get up. I promised Jack I'd be quick. Just checking whether there's anything more urgent than fielding shop customers?"

He shook his head, so she dropped a kiss on his upturned mouth and left him to it.

To her surprise, Jack was now deep in conversation with Mila's brother, Bartosz. "Ah, 'ere she is now. Jess, this young un's lookin' to talk to ye. I'll find ye those peonies, while ye talk. Ta, flower." He took the tea from her and pottered off among the shelves to find Bart's requested peony tubers.

Jess took up her place behind the counter, gesturing to Bart to follow. "Hi, what's up? Is Mila okay?"

"She is well. Thank you. She tells me you are here today. I wanted to say to you about Viktor. I have two informations to give you. One—" He held up his forefinger. "His hat is not with us in his room. You asked me in the photo, is this hat he was wearing for fishing, yes? I have looked. The hat, he has gone. I think yes, Viktor wears this hat to go fishing. On day of dying, yes? This is important?"

"I'm not sure," Jess admitted. "I think I found his hat—did I tell you that? I can't remember. I found a red hat by the river. It was like that one in the photo. Did I tell you? But my friend is a policeman—Marcus Woo, have you met him?"

Bart shook his head.

"He's high-up. I guess someone else came out to your house. Anyway, Marcus is working on your brother's case. He has the hat now. I'll let him know it's probably Viktor's. What's the other thing?"

"Two—" He held up a second finger. "My brother Viktor is having no drug killing. I have friend in pub. He know this from hearing this news in pub. Everyone is saying it is no drug kill. This not happen here."

"And you think this is true?" Jess raised her eyebrows. She wasn't sure she'd be so quick to take dealers' gossip at face value.

"He is certain, yes. I trust this." Bart met Jess's eyes, holding steady with unwavering conviction. "This, I believe, is true fact. My brother is not killed for drug problem, yes? Also, his drug thing, just small-time, no threat. I am certain."

Jess nodded, watching the young man thoughtfully. "Hmm. It's strange, though, isn't it? There must be some connection between your brother and Tractor."

"Tractor? What is the tractor to mean?"

"Oh!" She laughed. "No, Tractor is the name of the farmer who was killed. His nickname, I mean. Not his real name. There must be some connection between Viktor and James O'Sullivan. Did you think of any connection?"

Bart shook his head slowly.

"Anything at all, even just a small thing?"

"No. No one I ask knows any connection. I think he not know this man. Just fishing on his land. Perhaps they said hellos at the river one day, this is all I think?"

Jess chewed her thumbnail. "It's weird, isn't it. So, if there was really no connection, maybe Viktor saw something. Or heard something ..." She fiddled with a stack of flyers on the counter, shuffling them into a straight pile. "I wonder if that was it ..."

Jack placed a netted package of peony tubers on the counter. "I'd say these are what ye are lookin' fer. Get 'em in now, in good drained soil. Give 'em lots o' space; don't be crowdin' 'em, so. Pretty, they'll be."

"Thank you." Bart nodded at Jack, who was already shuffling away, and turned back to Jess. "These are for Moma. I think this what she wants, yes?"

Jess looked at the packet. "They are good to plant now and have very beautiful flowers in the summer. Tell her to put them somewhere sunny, well-drained, and not crowded. They'll be happy in her garden, I should think. Mila will know, but I'll write it too. If they are the wrong thing, we can swap them." She scribbled bullet-pointed instructions onto a page of the notepad next to the till, tore off the sheet, and tucked it into a paper bag with the tubers. "I'll pass that onto Marcus—the policeman; what you said about Viktor."

At exactly five o'clock, Jack locked the main doors, having already dragged the display items in earlier to be sure that nothing would hold up closing time. "Might be good fer takin's but don' be givin' me too many o' those kinda days." He leaned theatrically against the closed door and wiped a sheen of sweat from his forehead.

"Go on, you head off," Jess said. "I'll just finish cashing up and then I'll lock the rest."

Jack smiled gratefully, not bothering to argue—a true measure of how busy the day had been—and left. Jess counted the coins and bound the notes with a rubber band, leaving just enough in the till for the next day's float. She wrote down the day's totals and pushed the cash register drawer shut with a satisfying ping.

"You okay?" Shay's arms sneaked around her, making her jump.

She passed him the bundle of money ready for the safe and allowed herself to be pulled into his hug. "Hey," she said. "Busy day, huh? How're you? I barely saw you. Hope it won't be like that tomorrow."

"Come here, I can't wait to do this any longer." He bent his face to hers and kissed her. "I've been stuck in that stifling office thinking of you all afternoon. Want a drink?"

"Definitely, but it'll have to be a quick one. I need to get back to the dogs. Come on, I'm finished here."

Chapter Twenty-Five

Jess unlocked her front door and tried to push it open, but an over-excited Fletcher leaped against the door, blocking her way. "Get down, you daft dog! Let me get in ..." She shoved at the door gently but firmly, forcing him back into the hall. As soon as she stepped over the threshold, he threw himself at her, whimpering in delight, licking and drooling as if she were the most exciting thing he'd ever seen. She put one hand each side of his head and rubbed his ears. "Oh, all right then, you big muppet, let's just go straight out. Come on Snow, you too." She threw her bag onto the hall table and grabbed the dogs' leads from the hook on the wall. "Round the park do you both?" Jess took their wagging tails as agreement, and they set off at a brisk trot, Fletcher tugging and puffing like a steam train, and Snowflake jogging sedately at her heels like the well-trained dog he was.

Once they were across the road and safely within the confines of the park fence, Jess unclipped the leads and let them run. Tired from her day, she decided against walking far and sank onto the second bench, barely a hundred yards along the path. She'd not been sat there for long when she was joined by Elizabeth, out walking her own spaniel, Stanley, and the whippet-mix she'd taken on in the spring after her neighbour had gone away.

Jess smiled warmly at her friend and bent to fuss over the two dogs. "Hello Stanley, hello Daisy. Hello Elizabeth, how're you? You know I still can't believe you took Daisy in, after ..."

Daisy's owner, Breda, had recently left the village under something of a cloud, somewhat distraught after an incident that had put Elizabeth in terrible danger and almost cost her life. Fortunately, Elizabeth's husband had found her just in time, and Elizabeth had recovered well. A couple of weeks ago, a FOR SALE sign had gone up outside Breda's home. In agreement that as they didn't want to live there, Breda's far-flung children had decided to sell the house. Breda wouldn't need a house for while—she wasn't likely to return to Ballyfortnum any time soon.

Before the unfortunate incidents of the spring, Elizabeth and Breda had been not only next-door neighbours but also close friends, enjoying daily walks together with their dogs. They even had a little pedestrian gate between their two gardens, and spent much time together.

"Ah, it wasn't Daisy's fault," Elizabeth said. "She's calmed down a lot already, haven't you?" She patted the whippet's head affectionately. "It's amazing what a bit of Henry's firm training has done for her."

Jess and Elizabeth passed the next ten minutes or so in companionable conversation; three out of the four dogs now sitting contentedly at their feet, while Fletcher, inexhaustible, charged around chasing birds or pieces of rubbish caught in the early evening breeze.

"I'm heading up your way in a bit actually; Marcus is going to cook dinner for us. I was going to drive up as it'll be dark once I leave, but I'll text him and see if he can run me home if I walk to the village with you. Hang on." Jess fished her phone out of her jeans and started to fire off a quick text. "Ah no, I won't actually." She deleted the half-written text and shoved her phone away. "He'll be knackered; I won't ask him to get me home. Besides, I'm still in work clothes and could do with a quick shower. I'll pop in and see you in the week instead; have a proper catch-up? I guess you heard about Tractor?"

Elizabeth sighed. "Yes. Who'd have thought it would happen again? This used to be such a safe little community." She frowned, squinting at Jess through half-closed eyes as her face crumpled in sadness. "But if I know you, Jess O'Malley, you'll have this solved before those Gardaí can even open the casebook. You did well there in the spring..." Elizabeth's words trailed off into a pensive silence.

Jess patted her friend's tissue-soft hand in sympathy; the fading scar from a cannula a stark reminder of her stint in hospital after her near-death in the spring. "I'll see what I can do." She smiled at Elizabeth, lightening the mood with a modest shrug. "Jess O'Malley, detective extraordinaire, at Ballyfortnum's service. I'd be failing my duties if I didn't ask you who you think did it. Let me get out my notebook." She patted imaginary pockets around her body, and Elizabeth let out a girlish giggle.

"Ah, sure, any one of a thousand jealous husbands or spurned lovers, don't you expect?"

"Funny how everyone says that. Any idea who he was seeing lately? Heard any rumours?"

"Mrs Dunne reckoned he'd someone up the far end of the village; didn't know who."

Jess smiled. "And if she had even half an idea, she'd not have kept it quiet."

The two women chuckled at the idea of gossipy Mrs Dunne keeping anything to herself. The shopkeeper's mantra seemed to be that rumours didn't need to be substantiated to be shared.

"Anyone else you could think of who might have it in for—oh get down you big eeijt!" Fletcher had come lolloping across the grass and leapt at Jess, heavy paws thumping down into her lap. "I guess I'd better head on back; get showered and changed, and get Snowflake home to Marcus in exchange for my dinner. I'll call in when I have more time."

The women said their farewells, and Elizabeth walked on around the park while Jess, Fletcher, and Snowflake turned homeward to Orchard Close.

It was only once she was clean, changed, and had the dogs bundled into the car that Jess suddenly remembered the flask she'd found. How long ago the morning's walk seemed after the long day. With a firm warning and glare directed at Fletcher, she jumped out of the car, slammed the door to keep the dogs contained, and ran back into the house to grab the flask from where she'd left it on the hall table.

Fletcher, predictably, had moved himself from the back seat onto the passenger seat and sat slobbering drool onto the dashboard.

"You disgusting dog." Jess glared at him again, but as usual, his deep, chocolatey, puppy-dog eyes melted her heart and she ruffled his ears with affection as she tried to sound cross. "At least one of you has manners." She flung a glance at Snowflake and blew him a kiss before turning back to Fletcher. "Sit down properly then, you big lump. Let's go see what Marcus makes of this flask."

The heady smell of spices greeted Jess as Marcus ushered her into his little cottage. She sniffed in appreciation. "Mmm. What are you cooking? It smells divine. I'm suddenly starving. It's ages since I had lunch."

"Thai green curry okay with you?"

"Would I ever say no?"

"It's too late anyway; it's almost ready. Go sit." He bent to make a fuss of his dog, waggy-tailed in delight to see his master after their day apart. "Has he been good?" Marcus always asked. It was never necessary.

One day Jess might say no, just for the fun of it, but he'd never believe her. Snowflake was *always* good. "I brought you this." Jess held out the battered flask. "I don't know if it's any use by now. It'll be covered in my prints, but it was stuck in the mud at the edge of the river, so it will've been beaten around a bit by the weather and the water anyway."

Marcus took the Thermos from her and placed it on his own hall table. "I'll bring it in tomorrow. See if it tells us anything."

Jess knew she looked disappointed when he laughed at her.

"I know," he said, unable to contain his smile. "You imagined I'd take one glimpse and tell you, 'yes, it was used to bash your fisherman over the head, knock him in the water, and we'll match the dent in the flask to the dent in his head, Miss O'Malley,' but it doesn't quite work like that. And no, before you ask, I can't tell you that it contains a brand of tea that only the killer drinks, either. Ask me again tomorrow, and maybe I'll be able to tell you that. Not tonight though. We need to take a proper look."

Jess swatted him lightly. "I do know that." But even to her own ears, she knew she didn't sound convincing. "Oh, damn you, Detective Woo, you know me too well. Of course that's what I wanted to hear! Never mind. You can feed me instead; that's a decent enough consolation, I suppose." She plonked herself at the kitchen table and reached for the open bottle of wine. "This all mine or will I pour you a glass too?"

"You're only allowed one; you're driving home. Bad luck, O'Malley, but nice try. Pour me a large one, it's been a busy day."

Chapter Twenty-Six

Jess didn't see much of her brother's family these days. As children, she and Eric had been very close, but since he'd settled down south in Waterford with his wife and children—a good three-hour drive away—and work and life had kept him busy, they saw each other far too infrequently. Jess had spent Friday morning flapping around her house, tidying, making up the spare beds, baking, and cleaning. She'd sat her battered childhood Teddy bear on the pillow of the small single bed in the box room, and pulled a few favourite old Enid Blyton books slightly out of place on the landing bookshelf, inching them forward to stand proud of the rest, hoping her eldest niece would be subtly drawn to one of those for bedtime reading.

After work that afternoon, she didn't linger, stopping only to give Shay a quick hug, a slightly longer kiss, and a rushed: "Sorry, got to go. I haven't seen them in ages, not since Easter, but come for lunch on Sunday; meet them all."

Not long after she arrived home, seven-year-old Bryony bounced into the house ahead of her parents and filled it instantly with noise and vitality, matched only by a bouncing Fletcher, who Jess hastily shooed into the garden before returning to her family in the hallway.

Eric dumped his armful of bags at the foot of the stairs and swung his little sister into a huge hug. "Good to see you Jessie," he said and kissed her loudly on the cheek.

"Put me down you brat! Good to see you too." She wriggled free, kissed him back, and turned to embrace her sister-in-law, who was holding shy five-year-old Clara. Wrapping the two of them in a warm hug, she dropped a soft kiss on her youngest niece's cloud of black curls. "Hello sweetheart, how are you?"

Bryony, hopping up and down on the bottom stair, held out her arms for her turn.

"Oh, come here, Kangaroo, before you bounce through the ceiling!" Jess held her own arms out in invitation and Bryony leaped from the stair, her plaits flying in all directions. Jess scooped her into a flurry of loud kisses and squished the child into a tight hug.

The clack clack clack of colourful beads in Bryony's hair lent a soothing beat to the lyrics of the adults' chatter as she bounced around the house with all the excitement of a new puppy.

Clara, calmer, quieter than her vivacious older sister all but welded her five-year-old self to Fletcher, following him around as closely as if she were a crazed fan stalking a pop idol.

"Read to me, Auntie Jess," Bryony pleaded, as she jumped step by step down the stairs, a pile of Jess and Eric's old mystery books teetering precariously in her arms as she made her descent. "Can we do these ones?"

Jess laughed as she rescued the unstable tower of battered paperbacks from Bryony. "All of them? I shouldn't think so, but we can start with this one." She plucked one of the ear-marked favourites from the pile and waved it at her niece.

"I have to finish dinner first though. Why don't you come and sit at the table and read this one to me while I cook?" Jess felt an unfamiliar flutter in her chest as she watched her niece sort through the rest of the books with the same reverence and interest that Jess herself had as a child.

Eric's daughters shared their father and their aunt's passion for mystery and it had become a well-established tradition that time spent in Ballyfortnum equalled time spent reading the old books Jess still kept on the landing bookcase, exactly where they had always been in every house the O'Malleys had lived in while they grew up. Even here, after her parents had retired to this house in Ballyfortnum where their children had never lived, the bookcase and its contents had moved too, settling comfortably onto the new landing as if they had always belonged there.

Jess loved revisiting her old favourites with Bryony and Clara, their dark heads bent together, warm bodies snuggling close, and the coconut scent of their hair oil reminding Jess of her childhood summers.

Bryony climbed onto one of the kitchen chairs, tucked her legs under her, and leaned across the table to rummage through the books. "Which one?" She'd muddled the one Jess had previously chosen back amongst the rest and now spread them out like playing cards across the kitchen table.

Jess sifted through the mysteries and plucked one of the Secret Sevens from the selection. "How about this? These are the shortest, so we can finish it fast and then have time for a longer one tomorrow?" This one would be easy for Bryony to read, and Jess was familiar enough with the old story to know what was happening without needing to give it her full attention. Listening to Bryony read would be a perfect accompaniment to juggling the dinner preparation of homemade burgers, fat potato wedges, and a salad mix fresh from the garden. She directed Bryony to tidy the rest of the books and take them through to the living room out of the way; called to Belinda in the garden to pick salad, and yelled at Eric to come and open wine. "Now best-mystery-solving girl," she said to Bryony, "climb up here and wash these potatoes first, because I won't be able to hear you read while water is running." She pulled a chair across to the sink and helped her niece climb up.

The next forty minutes or so were spent in peaceful harmony with Jess chopping, mixing, cooking; Eric keeping their wineglasses topped up; Belinda throwing the salad together; Clara still following Fletcher around like his shadow, all while Bryony read slowly, carefully, about the exploits of the Secret Seven.

A delicious smell of frying onions filled the air, wafting through the kitchen and into the garden, and the house hummed with activity and happiness.

"I wish you lived closer," Jess said to Eric as Bryony paused for breath and page-turning. "I wish we got together more often."

"We're here now," he retorted. "You'll be fed up with us by tomorrow and longing for peace and quiet."

Jess knew that this would be true by Sunday, at least, but for now, on this Friday evening, she relished having the whole weekend stretching out ahead of them.

"Tell me more about this mystery then?" Eric said, swiping a sliver of translucent onion from the pan.

"Later." Jess nodded towards Bryony. "I'll pick your brains once the girls are in bed. We'll have time enough then. Just don't pour me any more wine or I'll be slurring, or asleep." She flipped the burgers and sliced open a pile of bread rolls. "Butter these?" She shoved the plate at her brother and waved her knife in the direction of the fridge. "Butter in there. Top shelf."

Clara wandered in from the garden and clambered up beside her sister, thumb in mouth as she leaned in close to pick up the storyline. "I want a dog called Scamper," she said, without removing her thumb, appealing to each of her parents in turn with her wide brown eyes.

"That would be lovely. It's a great name. Scamper's a spaniel. Spaniels are lovely." Jess pretended to focus on the onions so that she couldn't see the glare she knew Eric was directing at her.

Every time they came to stay, Clara announced that she wanted a dog. Jess always did her best to encourage her, not least because she knew it wound up her brother.

He swiped at her with the knife he was buttering the rolls with.

Jess kept her face turned towards the oven, hiding her smile. "Spaniels can be golden like Scamper, or black like Buster. But Buster is a Scottie." She knew Clara would recognise the reference to another of Enid Blyton's storybook dogs from the stories they'd read last time they were here. "Did you know your grandad used to have a Scottie called Buster?" she added innocently to the pan of frying onions. "Is that you sizzling, Mr Onions, or the sound of someone's daddy getting mad at me?"

Belinda smothered a chuckle. "Or what about a poodle, with hair all fluffy like Clara's? Two poodles! We'd get you mixed up." She ruffled her younger daughter's afro. It was no secret that Belinda shared her daughters' wish for a dog, but her and Eric's working hours made it impractical for now.

The music of Jess's ringtone saved them from Eric's comeback. "Alice," she announced to the room, somewhat unnecessarily, since she hit the answer button and said, "Alice," into the phone a fraction of a second later.

"She'll be in at nine, as planned. One of us had better not drink anymore. And it can be you." She jabbed a finger at Eric, throwing Belinda a complicit smile. "We can't all go; we won't fit. Will I stay here and do bedtime, or you, Bel?"

Belinda groaned as the girls began a chorus of "We wanna see Auntie Alice. Wanna see Auntie Alice," only mildly placated by the setting of a plateful of burgers and chips in front of each of them.

"What salad do you want? Here." Jess passed the salad servers to Clara, knowing that trying to scoop up tomatoes without dropping them would distract the little girl from her thoughts of staying up late to see Alice, at least momentarily.

After dinner, Jess negotiated the job of bath and story, having agreed that Belinda would then settle the girls to sleep while Eric and Jess went to Ballymaglen station to meet Alice's train.

"They are tired enough; I imagine they'll drop off," Belinda whispered to Jess. "They can see her in the morning."

Sure enough, the girls were snuggled together and fast asleep, tangled like kittens in the narrow bed, before Eric and Jess were even ready to leave the house.

Belinda curled her long legs under herself on the sofa and flicked through TV channels while sipping from a freshly topped-up glass of wine. "Mmm," she sighed, closing her eyes and leaning her head against the cushions. "Peace and quiet. Bliss. Take your time. Go on, off you go."

Chapter Twenty-Seven

Saturday morning started early, with two small but boisterous bodies landing heavily on Jess's bed before the sun was up.

"Oy!" She feigned crossness. "You're in the wrong room. Go away and jump on your dad. Or Auntie Alice? Did you see Auntie Alice yet?" Even as she said it, she instantly felt guilty. Alice had offered with uncustomary graciousness to take the sofa for the night, despite Jess's insistence that she should have Jess's bed and Jess the sofa. "Actually, tiptoe to your room and get your book. Let's read another chapter first, before we wake everyone else." She forced herself into a sitting position, rubbed her eyes, and tugged the duvet up around her shoulders, dragging Fletch towards her along the bed as she did so. "Ten more minutes, boyo, then we'll go down and get the kettle on."

She managed to delay the getting up for another twenty-five minutes, before the lure of seeing Auntie Alice overruled the offer of "just one more chapter." Jess, confident she'd done her best, flung her hands in the air and whisper-shouted, "Oh all right then! You win!" To be perfectly honest, she was more than ready for a cup of tea and some breakfast, and six chapters was already five more than she'd promised.

The girls' attempts at tiptoeing downstairs were admirable but ineffective, as Fletcher bounded down noisily beside them causing Clara to squeal and clutch at the banister rail as he barrelled past her. Once they pushed open the living room door, however, they were met by empty sofas and a faint sound of running water.

"We didn't even need to be *quiet*." Bryony's voice rose in indignation as she stamped into the room. "She's not even *here*!"

Alice stood at the kitchen sink, tousle-haired and still in pyjamas, kettle in hand and the French doors flung open to the early-morning sun. "You're lucky I've decided I like being in the country and it's nice to see the sunrise," she mock-huffed as Jess and the girls entered the room.

Jess plucked the kettle out of her sister's hands, taking over the tea-making so the children could clamour for, and receive, Alice's attention.

"Sleep okay?" Jess asked, over the girls' chatter.

"Yeah, pretty good. The quiet is lovely." Alice's narrow Dublin street had far more residents than parking spaces and was non-stop jammed with traffic noise and all the sounds of city bustle.

"Tea? Coffee? I got a batch of croissants for breakfast; will they do you?" Jess was already pulling the buttery, flaky pastries from a bakery bag, but Alice shook her head.

"I'll make a slice of toast."

Jess glanced at her quizzically, hoping the sliver of worry didn't show on her face. "You sure? Have two pieces, yes?"

Alice obediently dropped a second slice of bread into the toaster and Jess's shoulders loosened. She hadn't even realised that she'd stiffened at the thought of Alice not eating. She had been so much better lately, and Jess had been quietly hopeful that the long history of Alice's eating problems was finally behind them.

Alice must have noticed Jess's unease. "I'm okay Jess, I promise. It's just early. I don't usually see this time of day on a weekend." Alice gestured out to the sun, low in the sky, but already climbing steadily.

"It's not that early, it's—" Jess looked at the oven clock. "Er ... you're right. It kind of still is. Sorry. Blame them." She pointed accusing fingers at their nieces, met Alice's eyes over the children's heads, and, as one, in unspoken telepathic agreement, Jess and Alice closed in on the children to launch into a tickle attack.

"Not quite seven, Jess! Not even seven o'clock, Trouble and Little Trouble." Alice jabbed a tickling hand at each niece in turn to identify which Trouble was which. "I don't know the last time I was up before seven on *any* day, never mind a weekend."

Releasing their giggling nieces, Alice grabbed her coffee from the worktop and Jess ushered the girls towards the television.

"Let's find some cartoons." She yawned and rubbed her eyes, but despite the sleepiness that still lingered, her overwhelming feeling was utter joy. Tickle attack was a rare childhood memory of a fun thing she shared with Alice. In childhood, the two had not been close. Alice, five years older, and aloof and suffering with an eating disorder by the age of twelve, had given little time to her baby sister, rarely joining in with Jess and Eric's games. Unexpected tears sprang to Jess's eyes and she felt a surge of love for her big sister. Only in the past few months, since Alice had come down to Ballyfortnum back in the spring, had Jess felt as if the age-old rift could be healed, allowing Jess to finally be the younger sister for a bit instead of shouldering the responsibilities of caring for them all for far too long.

She swirled a splash of milk into her own mug of tea and joined her sister in the living room. The adult sisters sank into opposite ends of the larger sofa, beckoning the little girls to cosy up between them. Jess pulled up the duvet Alice had slept under and tucked it around them all, cuddling them together snugly to watch old reruns of Scooby Doo on a nostalgia-filled children's television channel.

By tennish, Jess and Belinda had pulled a picnic together while Eric and Alice had pored over local maps, ignoring Jess's suggestions of where to go for some tracking adventure, only to eventually agree on the exact woodland area Jess had initially suggested.

The forest on the southern edge of the county, about fifteen miles from Ballyfortnum, was a popular spot for walkers and cyclists, and the largest accessible woodland within an easy drive. Jess took Fletcher there frequently enough to know the lie of its land, and it would lend itself well to laying trails for the girls to follow without needing to stay on marked pathways.

Marcus had dropped Snowflake off earlier—the event that finally persuaded Eric and Belinda to surface, well after an hour of Scooby Doo had already passed. The two little girls were delighted at now having a dog each to fawn over; Clara claiming temporary ownership of the smaller, easier Snowflake and relinquishing bouncy, exuberant Fletcher to bouncy, exuberant Bryony.

"Shame you're working," Alice had said as Marcus stepped inside long enough for introductions to Eric's family and an, "Oh, yes, we met before; nice to see you again," for Alice, whom he had met briefly back in the spring.

"We hear so much about you," Alice continued. "It would've been nice to get to know you better."

If Marcus had looked surprised by this statement, Jess didn't notice. She was too busy shooting glares at Alice and avoiding eye contact with Marcus. Once he had gone, she laid into Alice. "I don't talk about him!" Alice nodded obligingly but unconvincingly, and Jess continued to protest: "Besides, I told you; I'm seeing Shay. You know, from the garden centre."

"Oh yeah, course you are." Alice's carefree chuckle would have pleased Jess in any other circumstances—it was so lovely to see her happy—but for now, Jess was acutely aware of the heat in her face and the suspicion that her protests against Alice's teasing were only making things worse.

Chapter Twenty-Eight

Bryony's insistence to be on "both my aunties' team please" should have made the allocation of the teams easy, but Clara, smaller, younger, still clingy to her parents, was divided by the pull of being on the team with the dogs or staying with her parents. Nonetheless, by the time they'd arrived at the small car park in front of the entrance into the woods, parked the two cars, unloaded the two children, two dogs, and a plethora of backpacks with rations and supplies, the teams were settled, decidedly unbalanced, and arranged thus: Jess, Alice, Clara, Bryony, Snowflake and Fletcher versus Eric and Belinda.

Eric and Belinda, it was agreed, would lay the trail. Jess would have liked to be the trail-layer—it had always been her favourite part—but she had to concede that her young teammates would hinder the ability to simultaneously move fast and lay a coherent trail.

"I'm not actually confident we'll manage to follow one either," Alice whispered with a comical twist of her mouth.

Jess laughed. How lovely it was to see Alice wearing old jeans, trainers, her hair in a messy ponytail, and with not a care in the world beyond playing in the woods with her family.

She even had a glow in her cheeks and a glint in her eyes as she ruffled Clara's mop of springy curls. "Your hair is soft as moss,"

Alice told her youngest niece. "If we dyed it green, you could hide in the nooks under the trees and we'd win the game."

Clara giggled and tugged Snowflake's lead. "Come on!"

"Wait up." Jess called the excited girls back to her as they ran after their parents. "We have to give them a head start, remember! Let's wait by the river. We can play Pooh Sticks. That okay with you guys?" She directed the question at her brother, who nodded agreement.

"Give us a twenty-minute start? Is there anywhere we should avoid?"

Jess pointed them in the direction of the woodland's map, mounted on two wooden stakes beside the timeworn, moss-covered stone bridge. "You'll be fine. It's fenced anywhere it meets farmland, and the lake shore is a gentle slope. No sudden drops or deep falls. Up the hill takes you to the old house; down the hill gets you to the lake. It's all pretty safe. Off you go! Twenty minutes." Jess showed her nieces how to set the timer on her phone, and Eric and Belinda disappeared into the trees.

An hour or so later, Jess was bramble-scratched, dirt-stained, red-cheeked, but giggling, happy, and the most relaxed she'd felt since finding Viktor's body. Team Jess had successfully followed Eric and Belinda's trail of arrows to where the pair sat huddled behind a tumbledown wall, munching on chocolate bars and swigging tea from a Thermos.

Jess, Alice, and Clara flopped down on the mossy ground beside their quarry, leaning their backs on the cool stone of the old walls. These ruins marked both the centre of the woods, and its highest point, but the dense tree cover allowed no noteworthy view over the surrounding area.

Bryony, inexhaustible, clambered onto the wall, encouraging the dogs to jump up and balance with her.

Jess grabbed Eric's cup from his hand, and gulped down the dregs of his tea before he had a chance to protest.

Belinda wordlessly reached into the backpack, retrieved more chocolate, and threw a bar each to Jess and Alice. She then fished out two more cups, poured more tea for all the adults, and peeled wrappers off chocolate bars for each of her daughters, before anyone spoke again.

Jess blew a grateful kiss towards her sister-in-law. "I bloody love you, Bel. We are wrecked. Good trail though."

"We may as well eat the picnic here?" This was Alice's suggestion, and, not for the first time that weekend, Jess surveyed her sister in happy surprise. For Alice to be the first to suggest eating was a sure sign that she really was so much better.

Back in the spring, Jess had felt the first real stirrings of hopeful confidence that Alice had finally recovered from her long history of anorexia and almost thirty years of battling with food. And now: Alice, suggesting it was picnic time. Wow. Jess leaned against the wall and closed her eyes, allowing the dappled sunshine to trickle warmth, happiness, and an indescribable feeling of contentment across her face.

By four o'clock, even the children were ready to give up on the woods. Belongings gathered, Jess and Eric hoisted the girls up for piggybacks, Bryony bouncing on Jess's back and Clara clutching her dad's shoulders sleepily. With the dogs recharged and sniffing through the undergrowth, the happy party traipsed down the hill towards the cars.

"Fletcher!"

The Labrador had disappeared around a bend and out of sight.

Jess called again, without response.

Clara, sleepy on her dad's back, picked up the refrain, adding a tired "'cher, 'cher," to the call, echoed by Bryony, less subtly, shouting into Jess's ear as she bounced enthusiastically on her aunt's back.

"FLETCHER!"

Jess, without ceremony, dropped Bryony in a pile of moss, and tickled her under her arms. "That's for shouting in my ear, you brat!" She stuck her tongue out at her niece and turned her attention back to her absent dog: "FLETCHER!"

While Jess had stopped to dump Bryony onto the ground, the others had gone on ahead.

"It's okay," Eric called. "He's here. He's found a friend."

Jess held out her hand to Bryony and pulled her up. She kept hold of Bryony's hand, and allowed her niece to lead her, skipping, to join the others, where Fletcher ran in mad circles around an equally excitable springer spaniel. A second springer rubbed noses with Snowflake in comparable decorum.

As Jess approached, she realised she recognised the springers' owner. "Sheelagh! Hi! Sorry about him." She gestured at her dog. "He's usually a bit more obedient." She laughed, shrugging. "Ah, heck, no he's not. He's a brat. Come here Fletch." She grabbed at his collar and clipped on his lead. "At least Snowflake is trustworthy. But he's not mine."

Sheelagh fastened on her own dogs' leads. "He's fine. They're all friendly enough." Fletcher had met Sheelagh's dogs once or twice before, when they'd bumped into each other occasionally on random walks over the years since Jess had moved to the area. Really, though, the two women only knew each other in passing, and from exchanging general chat whenever Jess happened to be in Ballymaglen post office.

"How are you?" Now the dogs were under control, Jess saw the other woman looked tired and haggard, her face grey in the filtered sunlight under the trees. "Hey, what's up? Are you okay?"

Sheelagh looked away. "Yeah, I'm good."

Jess reached out and touched Sheelagh's arm. "You sure?"

"Hello, I'm Bryony. Are you Jess's friend? She's my auntie. Do you live near here? I don't. I live in Waterford. That's a long way. I have to go home tomorrow."

Jess and Sheelagh laughed; the moment of concern broken.

"She used to be such a quiet little thing! This is my brother's daughter. Bryony, this is Sheelagh. She lives in my village and works in the post office in the next town, too."

Sheelagh transferred both her dogs' leads into one hand, freeing her other to hold out formally to the little girl. "I'm pleased to meet you, Bryony."

"You do look a bit sad. I hope you feel better soon. You should eat an ice cream. That's what I like when I feel sad. Thank you for catching Fletcher. He is very bold sometimes but he is still my most favouritest dog."

Jess smiled at her niece's loyalty and squeezed her hand. "Go and catch up with the others; tell them I'll be there in a minute?"

Bryony skipped off along the path, not looking back, confident and sure-footed.

Jess watched her go, then turned to Sheelagh, "You sure you're okay, Sheelagh?"

Sheelagh let out a long sigh. "Actually, not really. You remember I told you I was selling some land?"

Jess nodded.

"I don't know if I told you, but I was selling to James. James O'Sullivan. You probably know him? He lives—lived—up your end of the village?"

Chapter Twenty-Nine

Once Sheelagh let the words come, they poured from her like tea from an over-filled teapot. Unlike everyone else around Ballyfortnum, Sheelagh offered a new angle on Tractor's demise: "I know everyone else is spreading rumours about jilted lovers or irate husbands," she told Jess, "but you know a lot of the local were dead set against us selling land to the O'Sullivans? It caused some problems; I can tell you."

Jess shook her head. "I—"

"I told you, didn't I? I had to sell some land; we've no choice, never mind what Mike says. With him out of work, and the farm not what it was ... well ..." Sheelagh flushed a deep scarlet.

Jess, sensing the woman's discomfort, nodded but said nothing—not that she could get a word in, as Sheelagh was talking again.

"And hadn't I got friendly enough with James O'Sullivan over the past few months? Known him for years, so I have, since we were kids, but we only got properly friendly again more recently." Tears welled, and she wiped them away with her sleeve, her face setting into a mix of anger and despair. "And now James ... James ..." She broke off into sniffly crying, pressing clenched knuckles against her mouth as if to try to push the sobs back in.

Funny how she called him James though, Jess thought, as she gave the woman a clumsy hug while the springers tangled themselves around her feet. Only strangers, a handful of the older people around the village, and his myriad of relations called him by his given name; to everyone else, the nickname had stuck. She supposed Sheelagh'd known him before that, if they'd been at school together? Couldn't think of him as James herself, but of course, she'd hardly known him.

Sheelagh spoke again, breaking into Jess's thoughts. "And now I just don't know what to do." Her voice rose in high-pitched desperation and she blew her nose loudly into a crumpled tissue. "Ah, I'm sorry Jess. You don't need to hear about my troubles. It's just—well, just that Mike is so feckin' pleased about it. I know he didn't want to sell, but a man is dead for Christ's sake! Dead!" And the tears came again.

"Oh Sheelagh, I'm sorry. Of course, it's a blow. He *is* dead, and of course that's terrible, but it doesn't mean that your own problems don't matter. I hope you sort it out. I really do. I'm sure someone else will buy you out?"

The two springers, impatient from being restrained at Sheelagh's side in the middle of such a lovely smell-filled wood, pulled at their leads, whining to move on.

Jess took a step back, also ready to move on and rejoin her family. "It's amazing what comes to you on a good long walk. I'll ask around a bit if you like? And I'll pop in to see you in the week when I'm in town, see how you are. We'd better get on now." She gestured at Sheelagh's agitated dogs, and then down the path in the direction her own family had taken a good ten minutes ago now. "I'd better catch them up. You take care now."

"Ah, it was good to share it with someone. Sorry. Thanks. You get on now. Sure, I'll be grand." Sheelagh untangled her dogs' leads and allowed them to pull her away along the forest path.

Jess jogged down the trail in the opposite direction, towards the car park, for about thirty seconds before reverting, panting, to a briskish walk. As she walked, thoughts of Tractor, Viktor, connections between them, and means and motives for killing them swirled in her mind. Good thing Eric was here; they could do some old-fashioned brain-storming this evening once the girls were in bed. Hadn't Sheelagh just said that loads of people didn't want Tractor to buy her land? She should've asked her who. Not to mention why. Why would anyone care if Tractor bought more land? Jealousy? The man owned half the land in the village already; what difference would a few more acres make? Greed? Did they want the land for themselves? Bit insensitive of Mike to be pleased—even if he didn't want to sell, he could have a bit of compassion, surely? She'd try to have a word with him on Wednesday.

The rest of the afternoon blurred seamlessly into the evening, with its combination of tired girls, mindless chatter, making dinner—which led to Eric's welcome suggestion of "Oh, let's not bother with all that cooking and washing up. I'll go and get a Chinese takeaway," and too much wine.

By the time Marcus arrived to collect Snowflake, the third bottle was already open and the half-empty foil takeaway dishes lay spread across the table. Noodles and rice were spilled around the girls' bowls from their determined attempts to manage chopsticks, and a large blob of sticky sauce glistened on the tablecloth, where it was slowly congealing.

Jess went the door to let him in, barefoot and with chopsticks still in hand. "Come on in." She pointed towards the kitchen with her chopsticks, aware that she was already slightly wobbly from the wine. "There's heaps. You'd better eat some."

Obediently, he followed her to the kitchen, kicking off his shoes in the hallway as he passed through.

Jess pulled out the chair she'd been sitting on and gestured to Marcus to sit. She cleared her own plate out of his way, replacing it with a clean one, a fresh pair of chopsticks, and a wine glass. "Help yourself. I can't remember what's what. Potluck, by now, I should think ... unless anyone else can remember ... chicken; lemongrass; hot ..." She waved a chopstick vaguely over a few different dishes, shrugged, and wobbled to the patio to drag a garden chair inside.

Marcus, instantly at home in the midst of the family he'd mostly only met that morning, scooped portions of the various dishes onto his plate, then, seeing Clara peering at him curiously from under her curls, feigned indifference with his chopsticks. "What do I do with these?" He directed the question straight at the five-year-old, and Jess smiled broadly as she noticed she wasn't too drunk to notice that Marcus was a natural with the child.

A natural with her family, come to think of it. A warmth that may have been pride—or may have been too much wine—rushed through her.

Bryony giggled. "Aren't you Chinese?"

Jess leaned slightly closer. She'd never liked to ask him this directly, what with political correctness and all that, but she wouldn't pretend that she hadn't wondered too, in the months since she'd met him.

"Only partly. My mother is from China, but I was born in England. I've lived here in Ireland since I was nine. My father's English. I've never even been to China, I'm sorry to say."

"You're part English?" Jess was more surprised by this revelation than anything—his accent was fairly non-descript and she'd never noticed even the tiniest hint of Britishness creeping in.

"Sorry." He shrugged, frowning in mock apology. "You never asked."

"True."

"My mammy is like you," Bryony added. "Only not Chinese. And my Daddy isn't English, of course."

"Of course," Jess, Marcus and Eric chorused as one, then tried without success to hide their laughter as Bryony looked affronted.

"Not exactly like you," Belinda explained. "My parents are British-Nigerian. My grandparents came over to England in the sixties—both sets. I was born in Bristol. Eric's Irish, though." They all laughed again at the superfluous addition of her last deadpan comment. Even without his accent, Eric's fading orange curls and freckled pale skin were a dead giveaway. Not for the first time, Jess was glad she'd escaped that full-on Irish stereotype and been blessed with a tumble of looser, browner, curls.

"Can you talk Chinese?" Clara was no longer pretending shyness and sat fully alert and straight on Eric's lap, looking with interest at their new dinner guest.

"Only about three words. Can you speak Nigerian?" he countered, deflecting his lack of linguistic skills.

The girls giggled.

"Yoruba. Bel is pretty much bi-lingual," Jess said. "But they know Alice and I are hopeless, so they speak English here. Anyway, how was your day?"

Alice nudged her sister's foot under the table.

Jess looked at her quizzically. "What?" she asked, indignant.

"You sound like an old married couple asking him that."

"I do not!"

"Do so," Eric said.

Jess took a large swig of her wine and glared at them both. "Shut up. I'm sorry about them, Marcus. I apologise for my family. How was your day?"

Before he could answer, Eric interrupted again. "What she really means—" He lifted his wine glass to Marcus. "—is have you solved these murders of hers yet?"

"Eric!" Now it was Jess's turn to kick out under the table. Never good with her aim, even when sober, she kicked the table leg instead. Drinks wobbled and sloshed, and an errant chopstick rolled to the floor. "Oh dammit! Right, you lot. Get up and get out of the kitchen. I'll quickly clear this up. Let's get these tired girls to bed, too, then we can have grown-up talk? Alice, help me clear this? Eric, get my darling nieces to bed. Bel, Marcus, you vaguely count as guests, so you can take wine to the other room or outside and get out of the way. Go on, all of you. Get out of the way." As she stood, the room swayed. She grabbed the edge of the table and the walls stilled once more. Balance recovered, she herded her household in the suggested directions.

"Why is Auntie Jess talking funny?" Bryony asked.

"She's had too much wine. She's so bold!" Alice wiggled her eyebrows at Jess, who tried to glare, but the room shifted again.

"Go on, girls, run upstairs. I'll come up and read once you're out of the bath but just a short story tonight, we've had such a busy day." Jess waved them away, poured herself a large glass of water, and began to scrape leftovers into the bin.

Alice grabbed a pile of foil dishes from Jess. "Stop. You put things away instead. I'll do this. You know where things go."

Fifteen minutes later, with the kitchen showing some semblance of clean and tidy again, Jess left Alice in the living room with Belinda and Marcus and went upstairs to take over from Eric and settle her nieces to bed.

In the bathroom, Eric had overdone the bubble bath, and the usually dark cloud of Clara's hair was an enormous cloud of fluffy white instead.

Bryony, meanwhile, sported a magnificent bubble-beard and an artistic bubble tower on top of her head, which she proudly claimed was a unicorn horn.

"Nice," agreed Jess, holding out a towel for Clara to step into, then lifting her soapy, bubble-covered niece up so she could admire her bubbly reflection in the over-the-sink mirror. "Come on then, let's dry you off and get you to bed."

Curtains drawn, Secret Seven chapter read, and kisses given, the girls surrendered to tiredness and arranged themselves top-to-tail in the single bed without complaint. Before Jess left the room, Clara's eyes were closed, and Jess was sure that Bryony wouldn't be far behind in letting sleep take over.

"Sweet dreams, sweeties." Jess gently closed the bedroom door and re-joined her guests downstairs, noting that the only empty seat was on the sofa that Marcus and Snowflake already occupied. Bel and Eric were cosied up on the other sofa, Belinda leaning comfortably against her husband, feet slung over the arm of the sofa and Fletch sprawled heavily across her lap. Alice was curled into the armchair, engaged in conversation with Marcus. Jess suspected Alice had deliberately taken the chair, ensuring that Jess had no choice but to sit with Marcus, given that last night, and again this morning, the two sisters had leaned comfortably into one another on the same sofa, eschewing the armchair or separate sofas for the new bond that was emerging between them. As she met her sister's eyes, she knew her suspicion was correct.

She stuck her tongue out, shoved Snowflake over a bit, and plonked down beside her friend.

"So, Marcus," she asked for the third time, "how was your day? And yes, I do mean have you got any news about Viktor or Tractor to share? Come on, I've fed you well, now you have to tell us everything you know."

Chapter Thirty

"You know I can't share confidential information Jess." Marcus waggled his wineglass towards her to emphasise his words. "And you can't get me drunk either. I have to drive home. Nice try."

"Here—" Jess leaned inelegantly towards the floor, stretching for the bottle that stood at the base of the other sofa. "Let me top you up." She smiled her most artificially sweet smile, fluttering her eyelashes to tell him that she knew he knew what she was up to but she wasn't giving up so easily. "Eric will drive you home."

Eric shook his head and echoed Marcus's words. "Nice try, baby sis, but you know I've already had far too much to drive, too. What can you tell us, Marcus?"

Marcus held out his hands in defeat. "Make me a coffee and I'll let you ask questions."

Jess swung her feet off the sofa, scooped up some of the empty glasses, went into the kitchen and filled the kettle. "Anyone else?"

She made herself a cup of tea, partly in a show of solidarity for her friend, but also because she was just about sober enough to realise that another glass of wine might tip her over the threshold of saying something she might regret, and sending Marcus running for home. She paused, mid-spooning of coffee granules as she realised what she'd just thought: She didn't want Marcus to leave yet. He was such easy company, and so comfortable in her home and amongst her family, and she relished feeling like half of a partnership for a change. But wasn't that where she was heading with Shay? She stirred the granules into the boiling water, watching the swirls. Round and round; round and round; swirling, mixing, swirling, mixing ... Could she imagine Shay sitting next to her on the sofa, surrounded by her family, scooping leftover Chinese takeaway out of foil dishes as if he belonged here?

Alice appeared beside her and ran herself a large glass of water, which she gulped down thirstily, before rooting in the fridge for a fresh bottle of white. "I'll have a mug of hot water and lemon, please. This is for Eric and Bel. He's nice, your Marcus." She lowered her voice only marginally for the last comment, and Jess glared, hushing her, before nodding in agreement.

"Yeah," she whispered, "I was just realising that too. He kind of is."

Back in the living room, she swung her feet up on the sofa again, tucking them under Snowflake's soft warm body, glad that he lay between her and Marcus, putting a physical barrier between them. Glad, because she was suddenly aware of a strong urge to push her feet up against Marcus's thigh. She gave her head a sharp shake, and took a sip of her scalding tea. *Come on, Jess, you're not that drunk. Sober up, girl. Don't do anything silly.*

"So, Marcus. We met Sheelagh Flannery in the woods earlier. She said a couple of things I thought were kind of interesting—" Jess relayed Sheelagh's musings about whether someone had killed Tractor to stop him buying her land. Was someone hoping that with Tractor out of the way, the Flannerys would be desperate enough to sell at a better price to another greedy landowner?

"Can you find out who else might have land bordering the Flannerys' land, or who else might have expressed interest in buying it?" Eric said, leaning into the conversation. "Might be a motive to consider."

"Sheelagh was a bit odd, actually," Jess went on. "She was really upset. I mean, I know the loss of the sale is a big deal, but she did seem excessively troubled. She said Mike was *pleased* about it, so I guess that hadn't helped. They're obviously having some problems."

"Pleased?"

"Well, pleased that the land sale has fallen through, I mean. He's a grumpy bugger at times, so I'd have thought she'd be pleased to have him happy for once, dead buyer notwithstanding." Jess eased her feet further under the little Westie, who shuffled over on the sofa to make room. She rubbed his belly with her toes. "I doubt she meant he's pleased he's dead. Mike, pleased Tractor's dead, that is."

Marcus scratched at his chin, rubbing his hand over the day's stubble.

Jess watched, noting how tired he looked and realising how long a day he'd had. "You must be wrecked. It's been a long fortnight, what with Viktor and then Tractor."

"Are you making any progress?" Alice looked at Marcus over the mug of cooling water she clutched in both hands.

"Can't say we are, if I'm honest," Marcus admitted.

"Any suspects?" Eric topped up Belinda's glass, then his own. "Any good leads?"

Marcus fractionally lifted one shoulder. "I couldn't tell you if we did, but that might be because we don't. But I didn't tell you that."

Everyone laughed, and again Jess felt a rush of something warm and comforting run through her. Marcus trusted them, she realised. He's saying far more than he should. He trusts them and feels at home here with us.

He must have felt the weight of her gaze, as he turned his face to her and caught her eye, raising an eyebrow in an unspoken question.

She looked away and slurped her tea, a familiar heat rising in her cheeks.

"What about the drugs connection? Did your farmer have any dealings with drugs?" Belinda had been following the conversation around the room as it bounced from one person to the next like an errant ping-pong ball. "Or, if he's the playboy you all imply he is, then there must be a string of irate ex-lovers you'd wonder about?"

"That's half the trouble," Marcus agreed. "There are so many of them, if what we've been told so far is even half true." He tried to suppress a yawn, pushed Snowflake's head from his lap, and rose. "I'd better head on home, or I'll be asleep on the sofa."

"That one's mine," Alice said, pointing to where he sat. "You'd have to move anyway, and the other one is shorter." She smiled and stretched out her legs, getting up to approach Marcus. "It's been lovely to see you again; get to know you a bit better. Jess talks about you so much. I'm glad she's got a friend like you; everyone else around here is a bit ... well ... old." She gestured with outstretched palms, and shrugged apologetically. "Nice, but old," she said to Jess.

Marcus gave Alice a brief hug and pecked her cheek. "Nice to see you again too. You too—" He encompassed Eric and Belinda with a wave. "No, don't get up. See you again, I hope."

Jess followed him into the hallway, where she sat on the second stair up, holding Snowflake on her lap while Marcus tied his shoes, only releasing the little dog once his master straightened up and held out his hand to her.

"Your family are lovely. Thank you for asking me to stay."

Jess recognised the flash of loneliness in his eyes and guessed he was thinking of his own family: the wife who had left him, taking their little daughter, about the same age as Clara, away from him.

He pulled Jess into a hug, which she returned with a fierce squeeze.

"They are, aren't they. Most of the time. I'm really glad you stayed. Thank you." She said it quietly, almost into his chest, before stepping back, reaching up to kiss his cheek, and stretching past him to pull open the door. "Drive carefully."

"I think I'll make it. It's only two minutes." He returned the peck and strode to his waiting car, Snowflake at his heels.

Jess stood at the door until he had pulled away from the kerb and rounded the bend out of the close. She pushed the door closed and leaned her head against its cool glass for a moment before rejoining the others in the living room.

Alice looked up with a knowing smirk, mouthing "Okay?" as her sister sank into the dent on the sofa that Marcus had just vacated.

Jess nodded slowly and raised her hand to her face, gently caressing the place on her cheek where Marcus had kissed her.

Chapter Thirty-One

"So, about this boyfriend," Alice said the next morning, nibbling at her toast and raising her eyebrows at her sister.

"Mm-hm?" Jess continued chewing, her eyes on the slice of toast in her hand, or on her cup of tea, or on the garden—anywhere but Alice. She knew where this conversation was going, and wasn't ready to hear it.

They'd been up since insane o'clock for the second day running, woken early by their nieces again, but this was first hour the sisters had managed to claim for themselves, just the two of them alone, all weekend. Eric and Belinda had taken the girls and Fletcher to the park. Jess tried to smother a yawn, feeling as if she'd already put in a full day shift even though it wasn't yet eleven. Belinda and Eric, in gratitude for their own lie-in, assuaged some of their guilt by leaving Jess to nurse the lingering dregs of her hangover and have a bit of peace with Alice.

"Well ..." Alice's voice was gentle and kind, but Jess could detect a certain firmness there too. "I think you need to have a word with yourself about what—and by what, I mean who—you really want to be with."

Jess swirled the tea in her cup, still not looking at her sister. There wasn't much point in denying it; Jess had seen how Alice had looked at her last night. Alice, it seemed, had seen it almost before Jess had. But what to do about it? "Mm. Alice ... mm." Yawning again, she rubbed her eyes. "Um ..." She couldn't decide on the words, and yawned again instead. She couldn't say anything; couldn't put voice to the feelings that, since last night, had churned inside her and kept her from sleeping. It wasn't just the hangover, or the children's early morning demands for stories, cartoons, and time with their aunts that had left Jess tired, bad-tempered, and red-eyed. She'd lain awake long into the night, thoughts of Marcus and Shay whirling in her thoughts until she'd eventually slid into an uneasy sleep and dreamed of the two of them running, running, while she floundered in the peaty, sticky bog, unable to move her feet. As she stood, helpless, sinking deeper into the black mud, she'd felt someone tugging on her arm, pulling her out. Bryony: tugging her arm, pulling her awake, what seemed like only minutes after sleep had finally come.

"Shay is lovely," she said at last. "I do really like him."

Alice wrapped her hands around her coffee cup and brought it to her mouth, peering over the brim at her sister. She sipped the drink, taking tiny, slow sips that reminded Jess of a kitten taking its first tentative laps of water from a dish, searching out her gaze until Jess had to return it. Alice raised her eyebrows, waiting.

"He's really nice, and he's been such a good friend. He's fun and I like spending time with him ..."

"But?"

Jess bowed her head, staring into her mug through almost-closed eyes, "That's the trouble; there isn't really any 'but'."

"Except Marcus?"

"Except Marcus." Jess's voice was barely audible as she whispered the words against her mug of tea. "Except Marcus."

"Oh Jess."

"I know. I didn't realise. Until last night."

"You always were a bit slow." Alice tried to raise a smile, but the one Jess mustered was weak and half-hearted.

"We only realised we fancied each other a couple of weeks ago—not even! Poor Shay. How can I tell him I was wrong?"

"Jess ..." Alice was tentative now. "You might not want to hear this, but have you considered that ... well ... maybe it's just about sex with Shay? It's been so long since you were seeing anyone. Might it be a physical thing, more than an emotional pull? Because ... well, because any idiot can see that you and Marcus have an emotional bond. He adores you."

At this, Jess did look up. "You what?" She was astounded. "He doesn't. We're just friends."

"Jessica O'Malley, I know I've not been the greatest sister to you, but count this as me rolling all the years I wasn't there for you into one big package of advice and observation. He flippin' adores you. Ask Bel, if you don't believe me." She waved a greeting to her sister-in-law, who had just pushed open the side gate and entered the garden; Clara, Bryony, and Fletcher tangling themselves around her feet.

"Ask me what?"

"Jess. Marcus." Alice said.

"Ah. Jess, he's lovely. What a lovely man he is. The girls love him. Clara asked will you marry him. Bryony has her bridesmaid dress planned."

Jess put her head in her hands and groaned.

"Trouble is," Alice addressed her sister-in-law, as if Jess wasn't sitting there between them at the garden table, "Jessica here is seeing someone else."

"Ah." Belinda pulled out a chair and sat with them. "Eric, make more tea. Stat. Snap to it."

He cast a bewildered look at the three women, but went uncomplainingly into the house, from where the sound of water running and cups clinking drifted to the garden.

"And," Jess whispered, "I've invited him to lunch." She pressed a button on her phone to light up the display. "He says he'll be here soon. He wanted to meet you all. Oh shite. What am I going to do?"

When Shay rang the doorbell at a quarter to one, Jess was saved from the worst of her awkwardness first by Fletcher leaping over Shay, licking and slobbering as if greeting his oldest friend, then by Bryony appearing, complete with a barrage of questions for Shay. Once he'd fended off Fletcher and fielded Bryony's inquisition, stopping only to give Jess a chaste peck on her cheek between questions, Jess felt more relaxed again.

I am pleased to see him. He is lovely and I like him a lot. Reassured, she followed him and her eldest niece through to the garden.

Bryony, never lacking in confidence, was already introducing him to everyone. "This is Jess's boyfriend. What's your name? This is my mam and Auntie Alice. That's my sister but she's only five, and there's my dad. He's called Eric. What's your name?"

Jess laughed, and slipped an arm around Shay's waist. "Everyone, this is Shay. I told you about him. He helped me get on the course I'm starting. He a gardening legend. Shay, this is my family, Bryony has it covered. Sit down. I'll get you a drink."

Shay didn't sit, but followed her into the kitchen, where he wrapped his arms around her and pulled her close for a hug. "Hungover?"

"Is it that obvious?" She craned her neck to cast him a weak smile, sank her head onto his chest, and relaxed into the hug. "Tired too. We had a late night. Marcus stayed for the evening, too." Was it her imagination or did Shay tense slightly? She really did need to get her feelings straight. It wasn't fair to play Shay along if that's what she was doing. Was she? She wished she knew. "I do have a slight headache; not going to lie." This, at least, was quite true.

Shay gave her a squeeze, then released her so she could get him a drink and check on preparations for dinner. "Can I help here?"

"It's under control. Eric did most of it already, to be fair. Come on, we're not eating till two-ish anyway, let's go sit in the garden with the others?" She took his hand, clutching it tightly, and led him back to the garden.

Despite their earlier conversation, and various degrees of hangover, Alice and Belinda hit it off with Shay, as did Eric. The afternoon passed easily, helped along by another glorious late-summer day of cloudless sky and bright sunshine. Bryony had artfully shifted Jess onto the periphery of the conversation by wriggling onto her lap, book in hand, and a petulant reminder that Jess had promised they'd finish another book before they had to go home. With an apologetic glance towards Shay, who was engrossed in conversation with Alice and didn't seem to mind, Jess sank gratefully back against the sofa cushions, held out an arm for Clara to join them, and lost herself in the adventures of Enid Blyton's Find Outers solving the mystery of a missing cat.

Alice seemed happy to keep Shay entertained, and Shay seemed comfortable in the midst of her family despite receiving little attention from Jess. When Alice got up to refresh everyone's drinks, Shay followed her to the kitchen to help, but when Jess stopped reading to try to hear what they might be talking about, Bryony nudged her with a sharp elbow. "Don't stop now Auntie Jess, we're nearly finished."

Chapter Thirty-Two

Much as Jess had enjoyed the weekend, the peaceful silence with which Monday morning arrived was most welcome. A glance at her phone told her she'd slept till almost nine, and even then, relishing the peace of her little home, she read for another twenty minutes, before realising that Marcus had been due to bring Snowflake early that morning and she must have slept through her alarm.

"Shite!" She shoved aside the duvet and ran downstairs, phone in hand and still in her scruffy pyjama bottoms and a baggy T-shirt. In the living room, she was greeted not by an impatient Fletcher, itching to get outside for a pee, but by Fletcher *and* Snowflake, curled up together on the sofa.

"How did you get in?" she asked the Westie, scanning the room in case Marcus was also there and she'd somehow missed seeing him. He wasn't. She glanced at her phone, hoping it might give her the answer. Nothing there either. The kitchen, then?

"Weird, huh?" she murmured to the kettle as she filled it. Outside, the garden was rain-soaked and green; vibrant against the dull, grey sky. Rain clattered onto the metal table, loud in the quiet of her kitchen. A cluster of wet pawprints darkened the doormat, but stopped not far into the kitchen, as if someone had wiped the floor, or the dog's feet, perhaps. She set the kettle in place and switched it on, and a scrap of paper fluttered to her feet. She stooped to retrieve it, then stretched up to select a mug from the wall cupboard, pausing mid-reach. "Huh?" On the worktop, beside the kettle, stood a clean mug. Inside the mug was a fresh teabag and a teaspoon. The beginnings of a smile pulled at her mouth, and she turned over the piece of scrap paper she still held, to discover the note it bore on the other side.

I did knock. About six times actually. Fletch was remarkably quiet. Your curtains were shut—guessed you were sleeping in. I came round the back and let Snow in + Fletch out—he seemed desperate! Also said he was ready for breakfast—I told him I don't know how he likes his cornflakes so he must wait for you. Was going to text, but didn't want to wake you.

And then, a scribbled: *PS Good morning—or afternoon, perhaps? See you later, M*

And under that: *PPS You should lock your back door. Have you learned nothing?*

Jess snatched her phone off the worktop and fired out a reply: *Morning. Yes, still morning. Sorry, I was dead to the world. You can't reprimand me for not locking my door when you are not only a policeman, but you also broke and entered and were so busy sneaking around that you didn't check that I really wasn't dead to the world. How'd you know the murderers hadn't got me?????* Ha! That'll dampen his smugness. She poured boiling water into the mug and stirred it, whilst typing a PS of her own: *PS Thanks for the teabag and Fletch's pee x*

She started towards the kitchen table, caught a glimpse of the grey downpour that persisted on the other side of the French doors, and went into the living room instead. Dropping inelegantly onto the sofa, she swung her legs up beneath her and flipped on the television, scanning channels for either local news or something even vaguely more interesting than *Cash in the Attic*.

Tea drunk, news half-listened to, her stomach growled, reminding her that she'd not eaten since the large late lunch of the previous afternoon. As Eric, Bel, and the girls had needed to begin their drive home no later than six-ish, they'd eschewed the notion of an evening dinner in favour of the two o'clock Sunday roast Eric had cooked, and now Jess was starving. "Get me some breakfast, Fletch?"

Fletcher cocked an ear, opened one eye, closed it again, and relaxed his ears back into a perfect picture of, "No. I'm asleep; get it yourself. Besides, I'm a dog," so Jess went to make some toast.

They'd finished the bread yesterday morning. "Dammit," she told the breadbin. Rooting in the cupboards instead, she pulled out a box of Crunchy Nut Cornflakes before remembering she'd all but finished the last dregs of the milk in her tea. She opened the fridge hopefully, taking the milk carton from the door shelf. Even after giving it a gentle shake, the few drops in the bottom remained steadfastly at the disappointingly low level of 'just enough for one more cup of tea'.

"Dammit. I guess we're going to the shop then." She glared angrily at the fridge as if it was to blame for her family's consumption of all her breakfast supplies, then glared just as bad-temperedly out at the rain. "In the car." She slammed the fridge door, causing jars of marmalade, pickled onions, and mayonnaise to protest loudly, and stomped upstairs to get dressed.

"You two, out. Pee." Jess held open the French door for the dogs to go outside. Neither showed any inclination to venture out into the rain, despite a gentle prod from Jess's foot. "Okay, fine, but you'll have to hold it till I get back. Don't say you didn't get the chance. Now, I'm going to the shop. Won't be long. Be good. Perhaps you'll clean the house while I'm gone?"

As an image of the two dogs on their hind legs in frilly aprons, one brandishing a feather duster and the other washing dishes popped into her mind, her bad temper dissipated and she dropped to her knees to give the pair of them a belly rub. "Okay, I'm off. See you in a bit."

As Jess entered the village shop, Mrs Dunne took up her familiar stance behind the counter; her bosom resting on her arms resting on top of the piles of newspapers on the counter.

"Hello, love. I've not seen you in a while, eh? How're you? Still keeping yourself busy down at that garden place, eh?"

Jess, no stranger to Mrs Dunne's insatiable desire for gossip, gave only a non-committal grunt in reply as she rummaged for the bread with the longest 'best before' date. She didn't remember having told Mrs Dunne about her new part-time job, but it was no surprise that the woman knew anyway. Between Mrs Dunne and Kate, the two women had a mutual instinct for knowing anything worth knowing, and plenty more besides.

Mrs Dunne, never one to expect an answer, continued talking. "It's a turn-up, so it is. James O'Sullivan shot; God rest his soul. And Father James still on his hols in Mallorca, too." She broke off to cross herself, as if in lieu of the usual parish priest being temporarily unavailable to oversee Tractor's demise. "I suppose you know all about it anyway, sure you do, eh? What with your knack of turning your nose into that sort of thing? Who do you reckon done it, eh love?"

Jess lay the bread on the counter and went to the fridge. "I've no idea. Who do you think, Mrs Dunne? Have you heard anything? Plenty of people round here wouldn't have much good to say about him, for sure, but I can't see they'd wish him dead, however much he'd broken their heart." She gave a half-chuckle and stood a bottle of milk beside the bread. "Actually, you might know the answer to something … Who might have an interest in the Flannerys' land? Now that Tractor—James, I mean, is dead? I saw Sheelagh the other day and she really needs to find another buyer." If she'd promised Sheelagh she'd ask around, it wasn't really gossiping, was it? And if she happened to find out anything useful while she was helping Sheelagh, so be it.

True to form, Mrs Dunne didn't disappoint. "There's a bigwig developer trying to get his hands on any bit of land that he can throw a few houses up on. Forget his name—ah no, Young, it could be, eh? He was in here not so long back, asking questions and nosying around."

"About what?"

"Ah, sure, he was just getting the lie of the land, I'd say. Seeing what's about the place. Wanting to know about the Flannerys, too, so he was, asking did I know them and did I see as they'd be willing to sell. Didn't think much of the man, so I didn't. Greedy fecker, if you ask me, eh? That'll be four euro twenty-seven please love."

Jess scooped the bread, milk, and a bar of chocolate off the counter.

"Henry would know your man, come to think of it, so he would," Mrs Dunne called after her as she opened the door. "You could ask him, if you're needing to know."

Jess paused in the doorway, turned slowly, and nodded to Mrs Dunne. "I might just do that. Thanks, Mrs Dunne."

The shopkeeper raised her hand without lifting her elbows from the counter. "Bye now, love."

On the pavement outside, Jess juggled her purchases in one hand while she rummaged in her coat pocket for her car keys.

She'd call in to see Elizabeth and Henry on her way home; she'd only told Elizabeth the other day that she'd pop in. No time like the present.

Chapter Thirty-Three

Marcus took the steaming mug from Jess's hands and sat down next to the French windows. Outside, the day was still dismal; heavy raindrops bouncing in ripples as they hit the patio slabs. "I'll bet you didn't walk far today." Marcus leaned down to ruffle Snowflake's ears.

Fletcher hadn't even bothered to get up to greet him—a sure sign of the lethargy the weather had brought to Jess's house today.

"Barely left the sofa, any of us, except to drive to the shop, and even then, these two wouldn't budge," Jess admitted, tipping a measure of rice into a saucepan. "But I did find out something ..."

"Me too, actually, but you go first." Marcus shifted in his seat to sit sideways on, back against the wall. He stretched out his legs, sighed, and sipped at his coffee.

Jess relayed the conversation she'd had with Mrs Dunne; Marcus interjecting only the occasional "mmhm" to show he was listening. "... so then I popped in to see Elizabeth and Henry—I hadn't seen Henry in ages, he's looking a bit worn out, poor man. I suppose you see them quite often?"

Marcus lived opposite Elizabeth and Henry, in the centre of the village, and yes, he agreed, he had made sure to check in on the couple at least once a week since Elizabeth had been poisoned back in the spring, causing the poor woman to almost drown in her own bathtub.

"And," Jess continued, "Henry does know the man who's offered to buy out the Flannerys. He said he—Nigel Young, he's called—has been shouting his mouth off about what a great price he would get on it now, and how the Flannerys will have no choice but to sell to him as they'll go under if they don't sell, and then the bank will take everything, including the house. He's a nasty piece of work, apparently."

"Nigel Young? I know the name. He's quite a player in the local property development market, by all accounts. I'll have someone speak to the Flannerys again; see if Young's been putting pressure on. He's been in a bit of trouble before, but low-key coercion and bribery is more his style. Nothing as serious as assault or murder."

"That you know of." Jess smirked. "Or yet."

Marcus rewarded her with a wry smile. "Maybe."

"Henry doesn't know him well; just a friend of a friend kind of thing, he said. He hadn't anything nice to say about him. You staying for dinner? I'm doing stir-fry?" She took a package of chicken breasts from the fridge and began to slice them into thin strips.

"Love to, if you're sure? I'll ask around, see what anyone knows. We got O'Sullivan's post-mortem results today. Give me something to chop?"

She passed him an onion, an inch of fresh ginger, and a couple of carrots, and gestured to a second chopping board on the countertop beside the sink. "Here you go. So? What's the verdict?"

"Don't know if I should tell you—" He backed away, hands up in pretend defence as Jess waved her knife at him. "It'll be in the papers in the morning, so I suppose it's all right ... How small?"

"Marcus! Come on. Out with it. You know you're going to tell me or you wouldn't have said it to start with. And you know full well how to chop an onion." She waggled her knife again. "Now, tell me, or I won't feed you."

"The way to a man's heart—" He broke off and glanced at her, but she ducked her head and concentrated on the chicken.

Damn this blushing habit. He must've noticed. She really needed to work out what was going on here and why his presence suddenly made her feel ... well, a bit weird. "I know, I know," she said to the chicken breast, her back to Marcus. "You have me sussed. I want to know something; I feed you. Guilty!" She glanced sideways at him, swinging her hands out in amused apology, still holding the knife.

"Works though."

Jess turned her back on the chicken and leaned against the counter, assessing her friend. "Come on then, you're dying to tell me. Spill."

"Well, the real surprise was just how long he'd been dead. You'd think with the heat, someone would've noticed much sooner, but those old stone farmhouses are like fridges inside, so that helped preserve things."

Jess shuddered. "Too much information. Cut to the chase. How long?"

"Probably the beginning of the week. It puts the time frame of the two deaths much closer that we initially thought. And gives us another clear link."

"Same time, same place." Jess toyed with the knife in her hands, looking into Marcus's eyes. They held each other's gaze for a moment while Jess let the news sink in. "Hmm." She swivelled round to finish shredding the chicken. "So, you're presuming the same person is responsible for both deaths?"

"We don't 'presume' in police work, thank you very much—"

"Marcus!" Jess said warningly.

"All right, all right! But yes, we are looking at that probability. We have enough to suggest that the deaths are likely to be linked in some way. If you want to be useful—"

She scraped the chicken into a sizzling frying pan on the stovetop, gave the pan a shake, and spun to face him once more. "Are you about to ask me to help? After telling me to butt out for all that time when Kate's Get Slim group were being bumped off? And now you want me to help? How exactly are you going to make it worth my while?"

"Well ..." Marcus stood and took a step towards her.

Heat immediately flooded her face yet again. *Oh shite, he thinks I was asking him to kiss me.* "I ... not ..."

"Your adorable nieces let on how ticklish you are," he said, and her discomfiture was replaced with—what? Relief? Disappointment?

"Don't you bloody dare," she rallied, grabbing the knife off the chopping board. "I've got a knife."

"Have you forgotten I'm a policeman? Trained in disarmament and deflection?" He plucked the knife from her and tipped his head on one side, flashing her a mocking smile. "Anyway, I don't really need to do anything to persuade you, do I? We both know you're itching to get involved and would be out asking questions regardless of whether I asked you to or not."

"Damn you, Marcus Woo." Jess pulled a tea towel from the counter and swatted his leg with it. "You know me too well. Now, give me that knife back, and those carrots, and tell me what you want me to do."

"Aside from getting that food cooked?"

"I don't have to feed you, you know. You're not as cute as a stray cat. You could go home to your little house and cook your own dinner."

Marcus looked at his feet. "Actually, I've been thinking about that ... it's long overdue for me to cook for you again. This staying and eating with you has become a very comfortable habit but I know I'm taking advantage of your kindness."

Jess instantly felt terrible. "God, no! You know I didn't mean I don't like you staying and eating with me. I know you've had a long day and you're wrecked, and we both like the company." She stared at him, eyes wide. "Don't we? Or is it just me who thinks it's nice to talk to someone at the end of a day instead of us both rattling around in empty houses? Like Alice said yesterday, everyone round here is so much older, and while I love my neighbours, it's so nice to talk to—well, you." She stopped abruptly, aware that her voice had risen, and she was sounding emotional. "I like you staying and eating with me, Marcus," she said, her voice even and collected again. "I like your company and I like having a friend who's a little younger than ninety-four."

"A little! I'm a long way off that yet. As are most of your neighbours. I like your company too, Jess. I like eating with you. I just don't want you to feel obliged, or to let this become a routine you feel obligated to adhere to. Especially now you're seeing that man from the garden centre." He backed away, but not before Jess noticed a strange expression cross his face, gone almost as she noticed it, as he smiled at her again. "You don't say much about him. How's it going?"

Jess spooned stir-fried vegetables and tender strips of meat onto the rice she'd heaped onto their plates, really not wanting to talk to Marcus about her stuttering relationship with Shay. "Chopsticks or a fork?" She pulled both from the kitchen drawer and held them out to him to choose. "Tell me what you want me to do?"

The mention of Shay successfully deflected, Marcus explained how they needed to find some links between Tractor and Viktor. "Someone who can place them together. Someone to confirm that they knew each other. A solid reason to connect them. With your nosiness, and your tenacity, you should be able to turn over a few stones, see what crawls out."

"And, if that gets me nowhere, I can always ask Kate."

"Just be careful. Don't be too obvious. There's a killer out there. Don't forget that, Jess."

The reminder hung in the air like the day's rainclouds. They chewed quietly, each lost in their own thoughts, as they finished their meal in relative silence until Jess stood to clear away the dinner plates.

"Sorry, no cake today; thought I should have something a bit healthier for a change. Help yourself to fruit?" She selected a crisp green apple for herself, and bit into it.

Marcus leaned back in his chair, peeling a satsuma and stacking the discarded skin in a neat pile in front of him, until he sat suddenly straight and clapped his hand to his head. "I can't believe I forgot to tell you! It wasn't just news of James we got today. Your flask?"

Jess stopped crunching, eyes on his, willing him to go on.

"Looks very much like it was what was used to conk Viktor over the head. I think you found our murder weapon, O'Malley."

She crunched up the mouthful of apple, swallowed, and said, "Well, Snowflake found it, really. I just pulled it out of the mud. Wow though. Really? He was killed by a Thermos flask? *Really?*"

He nodded and, speechless, she took another bite of the apple.

Chapter Thirty-Four

After Marcus had gone, Jess curled into her favourite spot on the larger sofa, a fleecy blanket over her lap and legs to stave off the threat of Autumn that had chilled the day. Although the TV was on, she was paying it no attention, pored instead over the open notebook on her lap. She chewed the end of her pen, staring at the doodles on the page, trying to join the dots and find a link between the dead men.

Fletcher, heavy on her feet, was of little help.

She scrawled three new headings—*Property Developer, possible greed? Other land-grabbers? Who?*—but quickly abandoned that train of thought, thinking of nothing useful to add to it.

At the top of a fresh page, she wrote FLASK in large capitals. Surely if Viktor had been bashed with his own flask, it had to have been someone he'd known? Someone he'd willingly let get close enough to pick it up and clunk him with it?

It didn't make sense.

If he'd been chatting to someone he knew, wouldn't he have been facing them, talking? Not standing with the back of his head presented for them to whack?

It was no good. Maybe she'd have to trust the Gardaí to work it out this time. Wriggling her feet out from under Fletcher's sleeping bulk, she turned off the TV and carried the notebook upstairs to her bedroom, no further on with her puzzle than before.

Ten minutes later, she closed the notebook, pen marking the page, and placed it on her bedside table. She shuffled into a cosy position against her pillows and opened her current novel instead, losing herself between the pages of a police procedural she'd borrowed from the library.

Awoken by a persistent vibrating sound, Jess groped in the dark until she found her phone. She squinted at the screen, one eye half-open, the other desperately clinging to sleep.

6.30 a.m.

What the—Kate!

Jess sat up properly, fumbling for the bedside lamp and pressing the switch.

"Kate?"

"Declan."

"Huh? What's up ... oh! The baby? Has she had it? When? Is she okay?"

"Jess, I'm trying to tell you!"

"Sorry. Go on?"

Kate's baby had arrived about four hours ago, Declan explained through stifled yawns. Kate had wanted him to call earlier, but he'd refused, not seeing the point of waking her when the news would still be there by morning.

"She wouldn't let me wait any longer though; she just woke up again herself and it was the first thing she said, almost. She wanted to know why I hadn't called you yet. She's insane."

Despite the words, Jess could hear a softness in his voice that she'd never heard before. She hadn't much time for Declan, but she certainly couldn't deny that he'd come through for Kate recently. Not every man would come back after his wife had got pregnant with someone else's child. That he had not only forgiven Kate's indiscretion but also been supportive for these last months of the pregnancy *and* been patient of his wife's mood swings and bouts of depression as she tried to come to terms with Dave's death and the unexpected pregnancy, was certainly commendable.

Jess also allowed another mental brownie point on Declan's file as she took in that he could have phoned her at three in the morning, instead of six-thirty, but had not.

Kate, Declan said, had gone into labour just before midnight, the baby making a quick arrival just a couple hours after they got checked into the Lambskillen hospital maternity ward. "A girl. No name yet. Healthy, crinkled, loud. Go and see her later," Declan urged. "She wants to show her off. Visiting times are between three and five or seven and nine. She'd love to see you. Take her biscuits."

"I will," Jess agreed, and hung up the phone. Wide awake now, she reached for her book and tried to read. Realising that she was reading the same paragraph over and over but not taking in any of the words, she picked up her notepad instead and turned to the page she'd been doodling on last night.

Under the heading *VIKTOR*, she added: *Flask. Hit on head. Hat. Why in woods?*

The red cap had belonged to Viktor, Marcus had told her, but they couldn't confirm how long it had been lying in the woods. No blood or anything useful on it, either, he'd said.

Under the heading *TRACTOR*, she added a list of bullet-pointed questions:

- *How did he know Viktor?*

- *Was he at the river?*

- *Was Viktor at the farm?*

- *Why?*

- *Who would know?*

None of the labourers had ever seen Viktor at the farm, Marcus had said, although a couple of them thought they vaguely recognised him from "roundabout; maybe in the pub, like," or some similarly undefined location.

She turned the page and added a new heading, SHEELAGH'S LAND, and below it, *Is there a connection?*

The letters danced and jumbled into an incoherent mess as Jess squinted at the page, hoping for inspiration. "Dammit."

Fletcher groaned and jumped off the bed.

No closer to reaching any sensible or logical conclusions, she closed the book and threw it roughly onto the bed, shoved the duvet off, and went downstairs to make a cup of tea.

Fletcher padded down the stairs behind her, nosed at the French doors until she pushed them open, and wandered into the garden to pee.

The kettle rumbled to the boil.

Jess made tea, rooted in the biscuit tin for a piece of Linda's latest offering of shortbread, and sat at the table staring out into the brightening morning, trying to make sense of what could have happened.

As she nibbled at the shortbread, she suddenly smacked a hand to her head, causing Fletcher to rush indoors, cock an ear and stare at her, whining softly. "It's okay boyo. Don't worry." Dropping her half-eaten biscuit on the table, she ran upstairs, grabbed her notebook, and leafed through to find the page where she'd written about the property developers. Perched on the edge of her bed, she drew an arrow from the heading and added *Nigel Young. And others. Find out more about. Estate agents in town, maybe? Pretend to be interested in land, perhaps?*

By the time Marcus arrived with Snowflake, a little after eight, she was halfway through her second cup of tea and her third piece of shortbread, with details of every estate agent in Lambskillen written on a neat list on a scrap of notepaper.

"Kate's had her baby," she announced to Marcus on the doorstep as Snowflake trotted over the threshold and disappeared into the living room. "I'll go and see her this afternoon. I've a few other things to do in town while I'm at it."

Chapter Thirty-Five

"Oh, my goodness, Kate she is just adorable!" Scrunched-up, wrinkled, tiny, but quite adorable. Jess, much to her own amazement, wasn't simply saying what she presumed any new mother wanted to hear about their brand-new offspring. The baby was indeed decidedly cute, with a little pouty mouth that made soft sucking noises as she slept in her mother's arms. Aside from Bryony and Clara, Jess knew very few people with babies or children. "I don't think I ever saw one as small and fresh as this." She couldn't take her eyes off the bundled-up infant.

"Fresh?"

"Erm, new then? Just out? You know I don't know anything about babies, Kate, but bloody well done!"

"There's nothing fresh about her nappies. Or the noise she makes when she's hungry. She's feckin' loud. Explosive at both ends."

Jess tore her gaze from the infant to stare at her friend. "Eugh. Anyway—" Her focus shifted back to the baby, although her words were directed to her friend. "How're you? You look bloomin' glamourous, for someone who just had a baby. Was it awful?"

"Mm, a bit. Apparently, I'm s'posed to forget it really fast, and pop out a few more, but tell that to my undercarriage when I pee."

"Eugh." Jess shuddered, flicking a quick sidelong glance at Kate. "Too much."

The baby shifted slightly in Kate's arms and let out a tiny mew.

"Aw! She's like a little kitten." Jess reached a tentative hand towards the baby's face, stopping an inch or so short of contact.

"Go on," said Kate, "she won't bite." Her face twisted into a grimace. "Not yet anyway. Here, why don't you hold her? Sit down."

A cheery-faced nurse checked the chart at the end of Kate's bed. "How's mammy this afternoon? Baby had a feed lately?"

Kate beckoned the nurse closer. "Can you help my friend hold her? Show her it's not that difficult? She's pathetic, really." Kate shot a dirty look at Jess, then grinned at her. "Only joking! But I can't lift her down to you without busting something, so …"

The nurse hooked the clipboard back onto the bed and obligingly plucked the sleeping bundle from Kate's arms and laid her gently into Jess's. "There now, like this. That's it now. Mammy can give me a buzz when you need to hand her back, if you need. That's it. You're a natural."

"What?" Jess was suddenly aware that Kate had been speaking to her. She wrenched her gaze from the baby's face. "What were you saying? Sorry. Say it again."

"Just that I was going to introduce you to Jane." Kate lowered her voice to a whisper. "That's her, over there. She had hers on Friday, but she's still here because she had a C-section, poor thing. Well, she can pee though, so there's that. Hey,

Jane!" Kate waved to the tired-looking woman in the opposite bed. "This is Jess. You know, she of the mystery-solving fame. Jess, this is Jane, Tractor's sister-in-law."

Jess, unable to move her hands for fear of dislodging Kate's tiny daughter, and unwilling to call out for fear of making the baby jump, wake, or scream, offered a smile and mouthed, "Hello."

"I'll come over," Jane said, slowly shuffling herself into a sitting position and swinging her legs off the bed. She put a hand to her stomach and winced.

"Oh God," whispered Jess. "Don't let her move!"

"It's okay, I have to move a bit, the nurses'll be round to nag me anyway. May as well do it while Jamie is asleep." Jane shoved her feet into a pair of fluffy slippers and shuffled slowly across the room, grimacing with every step.

Kate moved her feet sideways and nodded to the end of her bed. "You made it! Now, sit, quick, before anything falls out."

Jane gave a wry, rapidly-aborted laugh, shared by Kate.

Jess shivered, a rash of goosebumps suddenly breaking out across her arms. "I'm never having kids," she said. "Never. Although, this one is kind of cute. Hi Jane, nice to meet you. I live—lived—near Tractor ... Well ..." She faltered, "I mean, I still live there, of course ..."

"It's okay." Jane was reassuring as Jess floundered for the correct words to say to someone she'd never met before, whose brother-in-law had just been murdered. And who was sitting in a nightdress and fluffy slippers, had just acknowledged that "her bits might fall out", and was clearly currently living through a hazy mix of drugs, pain, grief, and happiness.

"No one knows what to say," Jane went on. "I wasn't that close to him anyway. I mean, he was a decent fella and all that, but I didn't see much of him. Danny would see him in the pub, or whatever, once a week or so, but aside from that, just family dos, that kind of thing. And to tell the truth, there's so many of them in that family it's hard to get a word in and talk to any of them anyhow. He was seeing some woman in the village, apparently, but secretive as ever about it. Married, of course. The woman, I mean. They usually were. No danger of him needing to make any long-term commitment if they were already married. He liked to play the field, in more ways than one." Jane laughed, her face relaxed and friendly, before the laughter was cut abruptly short as she winced and clutched her belly. "Oops. I keep forgetting. Laughing is totally off the menu for now."

Kate grinned. "Yeah, but so's vacuuming, so you're still winning."

The baby stirred in Jess's arms. "Oh help, I think she's waking up! What do I do now?"

"You should see your face." Kate giggled, causing Jane to let out another restrained snort and press her hands tightly against her belly with a grimace of pain.

"Stop it, Kate, don't start me off. It's your bed I'm sitting on if my stitches bust."

Kate got out of bed, moving slowly, cautiously, inch by inch, until her feet were on the floor and she could push herself upright. She took the baby from Jess and jiffled back onto her bed, wriggling until she and the baby were propped up against the bed head.

Relieved, Jess got up and held out her hand to Jane. "I can say hello properly now. Hi. Did I hear you call your baby Jamie? After Tractor—well, James, obviously? I guess you won't call him Tractor."

Jane snorted and winced. "Not likely! Funny thing was, Jamie was top of our list anyway, but we're not letting on to the rest of the family. They all think we did it for him—James, I mean, but he was always going to be Jamie. Don't tell."

"So, who'd you think he was seeing? James, not the baby. Come on little one, that's it, there you go." Kate had snuggled her daughter up under her silky baby-blue pyjama jacket, and loud guzzling sounds told Jess that Kate and her baby had already learned how to breastfeed.

"You make that look so easy." Jane nodded at the nuzzling newborn. "Jamie'll be on bottles in a week if he doesn't get the hang of it soon. There's only so many places on my body I'm prepared to suffer pain on his behalf. Some woman down near the Dublin road, I think—married to a 'useless wannabe-farmer who doesn't know a field from a flood', Danny said. He was buying some land from them; that's how they got it together. She was at school with them years ago. Somewhere between Dan and James, I think. Never met her. Well, not knowingly, anyway."

Jess knew she was gawping, but couldn't turn away. "You what? Do you mean ... no ... you couldn't. Surely not? You don't mean Sheelagh Flannery?"

Jane shrugged. "Dunno what her name was. Why?"

Across the room, a wail erupted from the plastic basin beside Jane's empty bed. "That's my boy. Don't s'pose you'd get him for me would ye?" Seeing Jess's face, she quickly added, "You can push the crib over; it's on wheels, you don't have to pick him up!"

Chapter Thirty-Six

Marcus might have given her the green light to seek connections between Viktor and Tractor, but he'd said nothing about permission to interrogate Sheelagh or Mike.

Jess deliberately hadn't asked, so he also hadn't said no. She fully intended to engineer a chat with Mike at the garden centre on Wednesday, so Wednesday morning saw Jess rapping lightly on Linda's door a full twenty minutes earlier than they usually left home for the short drive to Ballymaglen.

"Sorry Linda, I should've texted you. I want to talk to Shay before everyone arrives."

Linda looked knowingly at her friend, her pursed lips doing little to hide her smirk.

"Not like that! I want a good excuse to chat with Mike. I need Shay's help to make it happen."

Linda nodded her understanding, and beetled around her kitchen, grabbing keys, checking the whereabouts of her cat, and rinsing her teacup. Less than five minutes after Jess had knocked on the door, she shot one last look around her kitchen, slipped into her shoes, and said, "Okay. Come on. I'll drive." She ushered Jess out of the house and into her little Micra. "You can fill me in on the way."

A good fifteen minutes before the course was due to start, Jess sent Linda into the larger portacabin to arrange cups and biscuits, and went in search of Shay. As she looked in first the near polytunnel then the next, she tried to ignore the nagging voice of Alice telling her that she was stringing him along—she'd think about that later; this was about enlisting his help in trying to get Mike alone for a chat. Nothing to do with anything else that might or might not be going on between her and Shay. She found him coming out of the shop, calling instructions to Ella over his shoulder.

His face broke into a wide grin as she approached and she let him give her a swift welcome kiss on the cheek before leading him to the office.

"I need your help with something. I need to talk to Mike, alone. Can you initiate a reason?"

"Okay," Shay agreed, "I'll send you two off to do a job ... I'll think of something." He hugged her briefly, pulled away, and kissed her gently on the cheek. "And, Jess—" His voice became serious, almost sad, as he met her eyes. "I think we need to talk, don't we? Later? Go on, I'll be over in a minute. You go ahead."

True to his word, as the rest of the group settled themselves around the table with tea or coffee, Shay sent Jess and Mike off to the furthest polytunnel: "Would you mind? We need those veg plants out in the shop and no one's had a minute to do it. You can bring everything on the first two benches. Take a trolley. Thanks a million."

As soon as they left the portacabin, Jess seized her moment. "I bumped into Sheelagh on Saturday," she began. "Did she mention it? She was a bit upset when I saw her, actually."

As they lifted the plant trays from the benches and loaded a trolley, Jess deduced that yes, Sheelagh had mentioned meeting her in the woods, now he came to think of it, but no, she'd not in fact mentioned to Mike that she was upset.

"What was that about, then?" He didn't wait for an answer, moving away from Jess to lug a large pot out of the way of the trolley before wheeling it along to the next bench. "Nice walk, did you have?"

"It was fun. My nieces were with me." Jess could indulge in a little small talk if it made him chattier. "Bryony—she's seven—she loved meeting your dogs. She's very funny, would talk the ear off even a springer spaniel or two."

Mike chuckled and loaded another rack of plant trays onto the trolley.

"Is there any news on the land sale? I told Sheelagh I'd ask around; keep my ears open, but Mrs Dunne said she'd heard that a developer might buy you out?"

A cloud crossed Mike's face. "Been gossiping, have you?" His voice had taken on a harder edge and Jess cringed.

"I'm sorry, that's not what I meant, honest, I was just trying to be helpful." She decided not to mention that she'd made some inquiries at various estate agents on Monday afternoon, given his tone. It wasn't as if they'd been any help anyway. She'd learned nothing other than that the land was for sale, which she'd already known before wasting an hour or so traipsing around town after leaving the hospital. Waste of time altogether.

Mike stopped what he was doing and glared at her. "Yeah, well, we'd be better off without the likes of you nosing into our business. Ain't nowt to do with you really, is it now, Jess?" He looked straight at her, daring her to look away first.

Uncomfortable at having overstepped the bounds of their acquaintanceship, she turned away from him, pretending to search through the trays for the ones they were looking for. She ducked her head over the seed trays, letting her hair cover her blazing face. "I'm sorry, Mike. You're right. It's not my business."

He swung the trolley around in the widened-out space at the end of the tunnel and started towards the doorway. "Always people busy-bodying where they ain't needed. Suppose you've been gossiping about her carry-on too." He spat the words away from her, his back towards her as he shoved the trolley along the dusty earth.

"Mike." Jess strode to catch up with him and placed a conciliatory hand on his arm.

He shook it off. "You've said enough, Jess. Let's get on with what we're here for, right?"

"Sure." She muttered the word softly towards his departing back. "But Mike, let me just say just one more thing: I don't know any gossip about anyone 'carrying on' as you say. I've not heard anyone talking of any such thing." Lucky his back was to her, in case her lie was obvious. But Jane hardly counted, really. "I'm sorry. I overstepped the mark worrying about your land after I saw Sheelagh in the woods on Saturday, but that's the only interest I've taken in your affairs." As soon as the word was out, Jane's revelation reverberated in Jess's ears. Oh shite. "Shite. I'm ... I ...shite, Mike—"

He let out a snort and swung around to face her. "Some choice of words, Jessica. So you *have* heard about that too, clearly." The look he gave her could have cut through glass. "Stupid tosser got what he deserved. About time someone shot him; done the world a favour and I'm not sorry. Grab that last tray, and let's get on." With that, he pushed the laden trolley out into the damp air, and Jess stopped to pick up two extra trays of plants, taking a moment to recover her composure. These last two extra trays of late-season spinach weren't needed in the shop but she'd bring them to the portacabin instead, on the pretence of asking Shay if they needed potting on. Hopefully, her delay in leaving the polytunnel would give Mike time to stack the other trays outside the shop and settle his own thoughts before going back into the portacabin to join the others.

The spinach plants deposited on a shelf just outside the portacabin, Jess stood by the rack, unsure of what to do next. She was overwhelmed with a mix of embarrassment, anger, and annoyance. She'd upset Mike; Shay was being weird with her—heck, who was she kidding? He was only being weird because they both knew she was going to upset him too before the day was out—and she felt altogether out of sorts.

A low chatter spilled from the polytunnel nearest the portacabin. The rest of the group must have started work. Jess stepped out of sight behind the cabin and leaned her warm forehead against a metal post that supported the plastic rain shelter over the yard. Deciding she couldn't face the class just yet, she ducked into Shay's office and sank into his battered desk chair, closing her eyes and fighting back tears. *Dammit.* She'd really made a mess of things. She couldn't sit here all day though, and wallowing in self-pity would hardly help put things right. She blew her nose, tossed the tissue in the wastepaper basket under the desk, and got to her feet. She'd go and make tea before joining the others in the polytunnel.

The rest of the morning passed in notetaking and the banter of the others batting back and forth around her until break time.

"You okay hun? You're a bit peaky," one of the women whispered as she passed the plate of digestives along the table.

Jess nodded. "Thanks Moira, I've just a bit of a headache. I'm fine, honest." She forced herself to cheer up, making a valiant effort to join in with the chatter, avoiding eye contact with both Mike and Shay, but managing to pull herself together reasonably enough to fend off further concerns from anyone else.

After an interminable amount of time, the church bell sounded its one o'clock chime and the class stood as one, jostling to gather cups, notebooks and pens, and head for the door.

"I'll wash up," Jess said aloud to the dispersing group. "Go on, it will only take a couple of minutes and it's easier than us all doing our own." She flapped her hands to shoo them out, suddenly wanting to get it all over with. "I'll just be a few minutes," she told Linda. "I need to sort something with Shay for tomorrow too."

Linda must have sensed something was up, as she picked up her handbag without protest and said she needed to pop to the supermarket anyway, and did Jess need anything collected? "I'll meet you at the car in twenty minutes?"

Jess flung a grateful smile at her friend and nodded. "Thanks, see you in twenty."

Mugs washed and left upside down on the draining board to dry, she followed Shay to the office.

"Jess." He sat down behind his desk, shoved aside a pile of papers, and looked at her. "I like you a lot. I think you know that. But—"

"Shay—" She stood awkwardly in the doorway, feeling like a fifteen-year-old called to the principal's office for a telling-off.

"It's okay. Hear me out. It's easy to see that you aren't ready to commit to a relationship. Not with me, at least. Your adorably cute niece helped me to see that. I wanted to believe that you felt the same way as I do, I really did—"

"Shay—" Jess looked at her feet, unable to meet his eyes. "I ... I like you a lot. I thought it was more than that. I was sure it was for a while. I didn't—wait! What did Bryony say anyway?" She looked at him properly now, curiosity winning over awkwardness.

"She said was I really your boyfriend because nice Marcus is your boyfriend too, and I'm nice too but she didn't think someone should have two boyfriends, although she is friends with Jack and Patrick and Vithun, but they are only seven and not her real boyfriends, although Patrick might be when they are eight but she hasn't decided yet." He looked straight at her, biting his lip, but unable to disguise the amusement in his eyes.

Jess laughed. She couldn't help it.

And then Shay laughed too, and they were both laughing like a pair of pre-schoolers.

Tension broken, she took a large step forward and sank onto the wobbly plastic chair on her side of the desk. She reached across the table to take Shay's hands in hers. "I'm so sorry. I made a real mess of this, didn't I? I didn't mean to lead you on, I promise. I only realised at the weekend what Alice had guessed ages ago—I really had no idea that Marcus meant more to me than just a friend. He has no idea, and I don't know how he feels about me, but you're right. It's not fair on you and I should have realised sooner and not let us get this far. I am so sorry. You must think I'm a right cow. I like you so much Shay, but, yes, I ... I ..."

"Shh, Jess. I may understand and accept it, but I don't need the details." His eyes were momentarily sad, and he looked at her ruefully. "I'm sorry too. I should've made my move a lot quicker. But I'll get over it. Probably." He clutched the left side of his chest and grimaced but his familiar grin broke through, although it didn't quite reach his eyes this time. He dropped his hands back onto hers and squeezed gently. "Now, come round here and give me a hug, and then we will go back to being good friends? Yes? I will try not to drop weedkiller in your tea." He stood and held out his arms, which she fell into, grateful, relieved, and savouring the long embrace.

They stood in silence for several minutes, her head against his familiar chest, wishing that she could feel the same for him as he felt for her.

After a while, he pulled back. "Sorry about the weedkiller gag. I guess that wasn't the best joke, given your track record with poison and murder." He kissed her cheek and let her go.

Jess flashed him a weak smile. "I trust you. And I am sorry. I'd like to stay friends. You are so lovely. I really do hope we can? I'll see you tomorrow for work, unless you decide you'd rather I didn't come?"

"See you tomorrow. We'll be okay." He looked away from her, shuffling papers on his desk, but not before she caught the glimpse of sadness darkening his eyes.

"I'm so sorry, Shay, I really am." She gave him one last feeble smile and left the office to find Linda and go home.

Chapter Thirty-Seven

An entire flock of butterflies pounded their wings inside Jess's chest as she sat in her car outside the garden centre on Thursday. How could it be anything but awkward, seeing Shay, after yesterday? She wouldn't be late, but she wasn't going to be early enough for uncomfortable conversation either. With fifteen minutes to kill, she turned off the car engine and leaned back in the driver's seat, trying to shift the worry from her mind.

The song on the radio played out, and there were still thirteen minutes to go. Just enough time to run to the post office, and check in on Sheelagh. Feeling guilty about her tense exchange with Mike the day before, this was another conversation she felt a little nervous about. Nonetheless, she'd promised Sheelagh she'd call in, so she switched off the radio, locked the car, and strode quickly to the little row of shops just a couple of minutes' walk from the garden centre.

Catching the tail end of lunch-time closing, she arrived just as Sheelagh swung the sign on the door from 'Closed for lunch' to 'Open, come on in'.

Jess took a deep breath and did as the sign suggested. As she stepped forward to push the door, Sheelagh spotted her through the glass panel, pulled the door wide, and beckoned Jess into the cool, dim interior.

"I'm glad I caught you without customers." Jess closed the door and stood in front of it, blocking the entry. "I've only a few minutes before I have to start work, but I just wanted to check you're okay, after Saturday?"

Sheelagh smiled wanly. "Thanks. No real progress. We'll probably have to sell to the developer, unless a miracle happens, but Mike's coming round to the idea."

"Are there really no other options? Other developers? Someone less predatory than that Young bloke? He sounds like a vulture ... surely there must be someone else who'd be interested?"

Sheelagh sighed. "He's influential. Finger-in-every-pie kind of man. All he has to do is whisper in a few ears and no one else'll touch it."

"I'm sorry. Have you met him? In person, I mean. Is he really that bad?"

"Ah sure, he's probably no worse than anyone else, to be honest. All I really want is to get it all over with." Sheelagh picked a discarded crisp packet from the post office floor. "Anyone else would be as bad, I expect. And Mike would sooner deal with him than with James, so there's that, at least." A frown furrowed her brow and she turned away, straightening an already straight rack of greeting cards.

"I think I upset Mike yesterday." Jess tried to pitch her tone at the right mix of contrite and concerned. "I hope he was okay?"

Sheelagh didn't turn around. "Hm, well, he wasn't exactly delighted to find out people are gossiping." Her voice had a harsh edge to it now; not her usually friendliness.

"I'm so sorry." The apology came out as a hoarse croak. Jess coughed into her hand and tried again. "I wasn't gossiping, I promise, I just used a stupid word without thinking about what I was saying, and he must've realised that I realised what

I'd said, and it just went downhill from there." She swallowed and took a deep breath, steadying herself with a hand on the door handle. "I wasn't gossiping, I didn't even know anything was going on until Tuesday and I certainly wouldn't gossip about it." Even to her own ears, she sounded defensive and whiny. She took another breath and held her hands out in a placatory gesture.

"Look, Sheelagh, I am truly sorry, I didn't mean to upset him, and I certainly didn't mean him to think I knew all about your personal life. I don't anyway, I only heard a silly rumour and I haven't repeated it." Another wave of guilt washed over her. She had, in fact, told Marcus the little snippet of gossip Jane O'Sullivan had shared with her and Kate over the hospital beds. "I'm just trying to help find out who killed Tractor and Viktor. I found him, after all. Viktor, that is." The defensiveness had crept back; she was making things worse. "Ah shite, Sheelagh. It's just that all this—" She made a vague circling motion with her arms to encompass whatever 'all this' meant. "—has been playing on my mind. I can't sleep properly since finding Viktor, and then Tractor only lives across the field from me, and then when I saw how upset you were on Saturday too ... It's ... It's all just such a mess."

Sheelagh nodded and tapped in the code to open the little door that connected the public space of the post office to the secure area behind the counter. She disappeared momentarily, then reappeared behind the glass screen. "I know. It's a real mess."

"I have to go, but I had an idea about the land," Jess lied, improvising quickly for an excuse to talk to Sheelagh some more. "Are you around later? Why don't we meet up with the dogs? Give them a run and have a proper chat?"

Sheelagh didn't answer straight away, then visibly pulled herself together, straightened her back, looked Jess squarely in the eyes, and nodded. "Yes, that's a good idea. Let's do that."

They agreed to meet outside the pub in Ballyfortnum and walk up the farm track beside it; a midway point within walking distance for them both, bordered first by farmland and then opening into wide, open bog, and perfect for the dogs to run free.

"Seven-thirty?" Sheelagh suggested. "That'll give me time to get home, grab something to eat, and get back out again."

"Perfect. We'll have an hour or so before dark; that'll give us time for a chat, and time to walk home again. Seven-thirty." She nodded her agreement and glanced at her phone. Dammit; she'd have to walk fast to be at work on time after all. "See you later. Thanks, Sheelagh." She set off at a brisk walk, and arrived at the main entrance to the garden centre two minutes later, puffing and hot.

Jack looked up from where he was stacking piles of bagged compost, alerted by the noise of her trying to recover her breath and regain her composure. "Where's the fire?" he asked with a broad smile on his weather-beaten, gnomish face.

"I'm late, sorry." She stashed her bag under the counter and fumbled for the note Shay always left beside the till with the day's instructions. Today, it was wedged under the till, unusually folded in half to conceal the contents. Her stomach dropped at this deviation from the norm. Was he that angry with her? Was the note going to tell her he was sacking her? Or that she could carry on working, but must keep out of his way? With a tremor in her fingers, she unfolded the note.

Had to go meet a sales rep, won't be in. Not personal, or deliberate avoidance, I promise. Can you help Jack in the shop? See you tomorrow, S x

Not entirely sure she believed he hadn't purposely set up the meeting as an excuse to avoid her, she was overwhelmingly relieved at having twenty-four hours grace before seeing him. The tension drained from her shoulders and the uncomfortable flutter in her stomach subsided, as if all those butterflies had launched themselves from the depths and flown free. *Phew.*

She leaned onto the counter, resting heavily on her forearms, and took several deep breaths. Once her breathing was steady, and since the shop was momentarily devoid of customers, she stepped out from behind the counter and called out in the direction she'd seen Jack lugging the last few bags of compost: "Tea then, Jack? Since it's quiet for a minute?"

Chapter Thirty-Eight

Running late again, Jess drove to the village centre that evening, and left her car in the car park behind the pub. On the pavement in front of the pub, a scattering of tattered picnic tables congregated with the same kind of optimism as the wasps that crowded around a single beer glass with an inch of brown dregs in the bottom.

Sheelagh, as agreed, was waiting at one of the tables, her dogs at her feet.

Fletcher lurched forwards as he spotted the spaniels, tugging Jess off balance as she tried to restrain him whilst simultaneously shrugging into a light jacket, mindful of the chill that would creep in as the sun lowered on the horizon.

She staggered into a table, bumping her thigh on the solid wood. "Ouch! Stop pulling, you idiot! Sorry, I'm a bit late," she added as she regained her balance and came to a stop in front of the table where Sheelagh sat.

Sheelagh stood to greet her, brushing the apology aside with the cloud of midges plaguing the air. "It's fine, shall we walk first? Grab a drink after if we're back with time enough to still leave me enough daylight for the walk home?" She seemed keen to get moving, but that may have been more down to the springers, who'd got up as Fletcher had approached, and were now straining at their own leads, tails wagging as they rubbed noses with the Labrador.

The three excited dogs danced around each other, twisting their leads around the picnic table and Sheelagh's legs.

"Sure, good idea." Jess unhooked Fletcher from the tangle, and pulled him aside while Sheelagh sorted out her own two dogs.

They took the laneway that nestled beside the pub, leading past the beer garden and car park, then stretching onwards across farmland. There were a few scattered houses, including a couple of set-back farmhouses, reached by way of long hedge-lined driveways, but the road soon petered out into little more than a rough track with grass growing in a straggly line down the middle.

Once they'd passed the last of the cottages, Jess and Sheelagh unclipped the dogs and let them run free, bounding happily, tails wagging, as they darted from tree to tree. Now and then they stopped at a gateway, to nuzzle at nosy cows or bark at distant sheep. The late evening sun was losing its warmth, and Jess zipped her jacket.

"I'm sorry about earlier," she said. "I didn't mean to be tactless. I saw Henry the other day—you know Henry and Elizabeth?" She waved her arm back towards the village, loosely in the direction of Elizabeth and Henry's house. "He has some connections and may know someone better than that Nigel Young bloke. He said he'll make some inquiries; see if they might be able to make a better offer."

"Thank you," Sheelagh said it so quietly Jess wondered if she'd imagined the response, but then the other woman spoke again. "Jess? Mike said you know all about ... about ..."

Jess stopped walking and touched Sheelagh's arm gently.

Sheelagh halted beside her.

"Yes, and no," Jess said. "As I told you earlier, I just heard the tiniest snippet of a rumour, that's all. Please don't be angry—at least let me explain, anyway, first. I was visiting my friend in hospital; she just had a baby. Trac—I mean James's sister-in-law was in the opposite bed. We were talking about Tra—James, sorry. I only know him as Tractor. And she mentioned he'd been seeing someone. She didn't say who, but she said it was someone from your end of the village, a farmer's wife ... she gave enough clues that I guessed it must be you. I didn't know for sure, but then I stupidly used the word 'affair' when I was talking to Mike—"

"—you what?" Sheelagh's voice rose into a shrill squeal.

"Not like that!" Jess tried to defend herself. "It was in a completely different context, but—"

Sheelagh swung on her heel and marched onwards along the track again.

Jess lengthened her own stride to catch up. "Sheelagh, slow down! I can't walk this fast and talk." Jess gave tiny chuckle, trying to lighten the mood, but she was already panting a little with the exertion, and her attempt at a laugh came out more like a huff.

Sheelagh slowed slightly, allowing Jess to fall into step beside her again.

"It's just I ... well ... as soon as I said the word, I remembered what Jane had said, and at the same time, Mike gave me a funny look, and I probably went red—I have a horrible tendency to blush; it's awful—and I tried to fumble my way out and I just made everything far worse. Mike guessed I'd heard something—but I wasn't even talking about that! I said 'business affairs', for goodness sake!" Jess's voice had also risen, and she knew she was sounding angrier than was conducive to calming the other woman down.

Sheelagh, however, had slowed again, and now it was her turn to reach out to Jess. "It's okay. I understand. It was hardly your fault, anyway. I'm the only one who's to blame, really. It's my own stupid fault. And yes, it's true. I *was* seeing James."

"Do you want to talk about it?"

With that, the words spilled out of Sheelagh like milk from an upturned jug. She'd known Tractor since they were young, still at school. They'd been friendly, but not friends. They'd had mutual friends; siblings who got on, and always a vague idea of what each other was up to as their lives moved on. "When James heard on the local grapevine about Mike being made redundant—that we may lose the farm—he got in touch. I was so grateful to him. I knew his reputation—who didn't?" She broke off and gave a choked, humourless laugh. "And at first, we were just a pair of old acquaintances trying to solve a problem. Then, in the past few months ... Well you've heard that rural post offices are being closed all across the country?" Sheelagh looked at Jess for confirmation.

Jess nodded. "Yes, the one over in Glendanon is already gone, I know. It's shocking."

"So, first Mike, and now my own job under threat, too, and then things got even more difficult with Mike and he got a bit down about everything—moody, you know? And I couldn't tell him how worried I was about my job and that the post office might be on the list for closure, because he already had more than enough on his plate."

They'd reached the end of the track and stood in companionable silence gazing out over the bog. The late gorse glowed golden in the last rays of the reddening sun; vivid colour against the black earth. The dogs bounced happily across the wide, open land, darting in and out of patches of scrubby bushes, and jumping back and forth across the narrow ditches that crisscrossed the landscape. Every now and then, one of them would disappear from sight, only to pop up like a Jack-in-the-box a moment later.

"Look! Buzzards!" Jess pointed into the distance where three of the majestic birds circled lazily over the treetops.

"A wake," Sheelagh murmured, watching them swoop and soar.

Jess threw her a quizzical glance.

"A group of buzzards. That's what they're called. I wonder why…"

Jess shrugged. "Dunno. It's beautiful, though, isn't it?"

Sheelagh sighed in agreement. "I love it here. I can't bear the idea of having to move away. But one of us had to be realistic. If we sell the land, at least we'd be able to keep the house. Mike has struggled to see that. He's just buried his head, ignored it." Hands on her hips, she spat out the words like a burst of gunfire. "It was as if he could just ignore it and it would all be fine. Then when he couldn't ignore it any longer, he still couldn't face up to it. Doesn't want to fail us, he said. Stupid fool." She turned away from the open vista and started back along the track, not checking whether Jess or the dogs were following. "So I started confiding in James. And then I was crying on his shoulder one evening, and he was comforting me, and—well, long story short, we kissed. It was so nice to feel wanted and free from my problems and comforted and cared for. And … Well, you know how it goes? One thing led to another. And we should've stopped it, but we didn't because it was so *nice*. He made me feel as if things weren't so awful." She stopped abruptly and turned to face Jess. "Of course, it was making everything much worse. And I do love Mike, really I do. He was just … just so *draining*. And I needed someone to give *me* something for a change."

"Ah, Sheelagh." The poor woman.

Sheelagh walked on, Jess falling into step alongside her and the dogs gambolling ahead. "It gets worse. Mike found out."

"Ah."

"Yes. He was furious. And you know how he gets. And then he started saying things like he'd kill him, and I told him to calm down. Well, that was a red rag, of course." Her laugh was a hollow, bitter sound that fell like a stone onto the hard earth. "So I told him I'd go out to my mam's for the night, give him time to think things through, he could call me if he wanted me to come back, and I would, of course. Of course, I'd go back, if only I thought he really wanted me. He told me to get out, though, so I left." She threw Jess a sidelong glance. "But I went to see James first, to tell him; to warn him. To tell him to watch out for Mike, and to tell him we had to end it, right then."

Jess opened her mouth, closed it again without speaking. Had *Mike* killed Tractor?

"But when I got to James's, he got angry too. He was so furious at Mike, and said he didn't deserve me, and that I should leave Mike, and I said what for? Because it wasn't like he—James—would ever give anyone any security and we both knew I was just his latest plaything. Plaything! I'm nearly forty, for goodness sake, and I said 'plaything'!" A stifled laugh evolved into sobs. She swiped at her eyes with her fists but as she marched along the farm track towards the village, tears streamed down her cheeks.

Jess's mind whirled. She put her hand out to Sheelagh, to reassure her, but the other woman shrugged it off, wiped her face with a tissue, and swallowed with an audible gulp as she sniffed back her tears and continued speaking.

"And his gun was there on the table, and I picked it up and waved it at him, because I wanted him to calm down, and he told me not to be so stupid, and that it was loaded, because he'd been about to go out and try to find the fox that'd been causing trouble, and then ... and then ..."

Jess stopped so abruptly that Fletcher bumped into her legs. *Not Mike. Sheelagh. Sheelagh had shot Tractor.* She stared, open-mouthed. Sheelagh had continued walking so Jess's stupefied expression met only the other woman's back. She strode to catch up, grabbing Sheelagh roughly by the arm.

"So, let's get this straight? You'd been seeing Tractor for—how long? Six months? Not even? And then Mike found out, so what then? You went and shot him? Oh my God, Sheelagh!"

This time it was Sheelagh who came to a sudden halt. "No!" She glared through a sheen of glassy tears, but Jess wasn't finished.

"I don't see how that would solve the problem? Especially when you needed him to buy your land. It doesn't make sense." She groped in her pocket, searching for her phone, hoping she could find it without being too obvious. "You killed him," she said, stunned and disbelieving. "You killed him."

Chapter Thirty-Nine

"You shot Tractor O'Sullivan," Jess said quietly, more to herself than to her companion, trying to convince herself of what Sheelagh had done. She had her hand wrapped around her phone now but didn't remove it from her pocket. Was that really what Sheelagh was telling her? No, Sheelagh couldn't have shot Tractor. Not this slight, innocent, friendly postmistress. Not this woman Jess was walking alone on a deserted lane with, as the sun went down. Not Sheelagh. "Are you seriously telling me you shot Tractor?"

Sheelagh sniffed noisily, and wiped her nose with the sleeve of her cardigan. She nodded. "It was an *accident*," she said, through hiccupping sobs.

Jess was glad they were already heading back towards the village. She called Fletcher closer, hoping the tremor in her voice didn't betray her discomfort—her panic—at Sheelagh's confession. She began to walk a little quicker, her steps longer and her eyes on the path ahead. She'd keep Sheelagh talking; try to keep her calm, until they got back to the village and proximity to other people. She breathed in slowly through her nose, holding the breath in for a count of five before slowly releasing it. *Stay calm, Jess; stay calm.*

"So what happened? How do you accidentally shoot someone in their own kitchen? And where did Viktor come into it?"

"James tried to take the gun off me, make me put it down. I was only trying to make him listen to me. I didn't know it would go off. I put my fingers on the trigger, like he'd shown me how, when—and anyway ... It did; it went off. And then there was so much blood, and oh my God, oh my God, what had I done? And I panicked, worried that someone would have heard the shot, one of the farm lads, or someone from the houses on the lane. I didn't know what to do, so I ran across the fields. And there was that fisherman, and I was sure he'd heard something, and he saw me running out of the woods, and he took a step towards me, and I was frightened, and I shoved him, and he must have tripped over the rough ground because even though I didn't think I could shove him hard enough to get him back from me, he fell ... well, you know what happened, don't you, you found him."

"So—" Jess had steadily increased her stride, trying to breathe slowly despite the faster pace. Every step brought them closer to the busier road and away from this quiet dead-end farm track. Surely Sheelagh wasn't likely to hurt her, especially with no weapon to hand, but she'd rather not be alone with this woman any longer than she had to, and longed for the relative safety of the village centre. *Keep her talking, keep her talking ...* "How did you get him into the river?"

"No—no, he fell. He was on the riverbank!"

"So you had time to get through the woods, out from the trees, across the path, and push him, and he didn't move away from the riverbank even though you just said he was coming towards you in a manner that made you scared of him?"

Sheelagh was silent for a moment. "Yes ... No ... I—"

Jess forced her voice to remain level and low. "So, you'd been seeing him for a while, and then Mike found out, so you went to warn Tractor, and the two of you had a fight and his gun was just there, fully loaded, and you accidentally shot him? And then you ran across the fields and saw poor Viktor there and thought he'd heard the gun, so you shoved him in the river because he saw you?" She glanced at Sheelagh. "I don't buy that either. You'd have had to take him by surprise for that to work, and I doubt anyone could get that close without being heard ... He wasn't exactly a delicate man either. You'd need to have given him a damn good clout ..."

"He had earphones in. And I was quiet."

"You just said he was coming towards you, threatening you?"

"I didn't ... I ... He ... Okay, no, he wasn't, he wasn't threatening me ... I was in a panic, okay? I don't know what happened."

"But if he'd heard the shot, or seen you there, he would've been alert, listening ..."

"I wasn't going to take the chance, was I? What if he *had* seen me?"

"So, what did you do?"

"I hit him on the head, and he stepped backward, lost his balance, he tumbled down the bank, was in the water before I had time to think about what I'd done. Sank in under the water quick as ..." She tailed off, wiped her streaming nose on her sleeve, and gave a loud juddering sigh.

Jess shivered. "And what if I'd been there an hour or so earlier that day too? On the same patch of riverbank? Would you have killed me too?" She pulled Fletcher closer to her, resting her hand on the back of his neck. *Stay close, Fletch,* she urged silently.

Sheelagh stopped and grabbed Jess's forearm. "Of course not."

Jess shook her off. *Stay calm Jess. Stay calm.* Despite repeating the words to herself as they walked, Jess was feeling anything but calm as she imagined what might have happened if she had been on the river path only an hour or two sooner that evening. "If you'd thought I'd seen something ..." She couldn't finish the question.

Fletcher had manoeuvred himself to walk between the two women, and Jess entwined her fingers into his silky fur, looping her thumb under his collar to keep him close.

"No! I ... I ..." Sheelagh closed her mouth. Tears ran down her face, and she wiped uselessly at them with her sleeve.

Jess could hear passing cars; they were almost at the road. She turned the phone around in her pocket, twisting it into position so she could locate the side button she needed to hold down to bring the screen to life. *What next?* She used her index finger to swipe up, repeating the movement a couple of times in case it hadn't worked the first time. Thank goodness she'd never bothered to put a password or pin onto it. *Now what?* She closed her eyes for a second, trying to picture exactly where the call button was on the screen. *Bottom left? Bottom right? Dammit, Jess, think! Bottom left.* She forced her hand to relax, shifting the phone a little until it felt more natural in her hand, then tapped the screen with her thumb in the position she hoped would activate the call button. Thank goodness it was Marcus she'd called last. Now, if only it would work. She strained her ears to listen for the distant ringing sound, half hoping she'd hear it, and half worried that if it did connect, Sheelagh would hear it too.

Keep her talking, keep her talking...

Fletch had clearly sensed Jess's panic, as he was being unusually sensible, staying at her side and nuzzling his cold nose against her leg. She bent to clip his lead on; a natural enough action as they neared the road. With the road in sight, the panic eased a little. Besides, she was easily a match for Sheelagh; it wasn't as if the other woman had a weapon to hand, and Fletcher was a big, strong ally.

Also ... Something about Sheelagh's story wasn't adding up; she didn't seem to know exactly what had happened to Tractor and Viktor that night, so had she really done as she said, or was she spinning a lie? Why would she do that, though? Was she confused? If she *had* killed them, she'd have been in a blind panic, so no wonder she couldn't remember the details ... Just keep her talking, get back to the road, worry about the rest once they were back at the corner, in yelling distance of the pub, near to houses ... If Sheelagh did try anything, Fletcher would, Jess hoped, leap to her defence. He was bigger than the other two dogs, and stronger, surely.

But if Fletcher showed any threat towards Sheelagh, how might the two springer spaniels react? Would the dogs turn on each other if they felt threatened? She shook this thought from her mind. It wouldn't come to that; they were so close to the road now. *Almost there, almost there.*

Her breath was uneven as she raggedly gasped for air; her heart thudding so hard she wasn't sure she'd hear if her phone was ringing, or had been answered. She'd get it out of her pocket as soon as they reached the road, anyway.

Sheelagh, also panting a little, was talking again, tears still flowing. "I never meant to hurt anyone, but when Mike found out I was seeing James behind his back, I had to stop it, and when I told James we had to stop, he was angry and we fought and in the heat of the moment I grabbed his gun, because it was *there*. Just to calm him down, that's all, but it ... it just went off. It was all a terrible accident. My prints are all over the gun; they only need to check."

They were just a few strides away from the main village road now, with the final cottages on one side and the pub on the other. The low babble of voices drifted over a garden wall, and somewhere further away, a lawnmower buzzed.

Jess inhaled deeply, catching her breath as her heart rate began to steady. She slowed her stride to allow her breathing to even out, and, with the road only a few hundred yards ahead, her logical brain caught up with her panicked brain. "Foxes?" she said, as she realised that Sheelagh really was lying. There was simply too much that didn't add up. None of what Sheelagh had said made sense. Tractor had nothing on his farm that foxes would be bothering. Especially at this time of year. He only had cows. No sheep, and even if he did have sheep, lambing season was well over. All the lambs around were almost full-grown by this time of year. Foxes wouldn't be picking them off this late in the summer. No hens, either. *Nothing* foxes would be after. "You said he had fox trouble? Little buggers. What were they after?"

Sheelagh didn't answer.

A car rushed by. The breeze it created ruffled Fletcher's hair and lifted Jess's ponytail. They had reached the road.

Safely within shouting—or barking—distance of other people, Jess relaxed her grip on Fletcher's ruff and stroked the soft hair along his back. Sheelagh was lying. She was absolutely certain of it. All she needed to do now was to keep her talking until Marcus arrived and took over.

"Sheelagh?" she said, as they stopped on the pavement at the corner, regarding the chattering huddle of people seated on the picnic benches outside the pub, just a stone's throw away. "I don't think that's all true. Is it?" She turned to face the other woman, unwavering in her gaze. "Oh, excuse me... my phone." She finally pulled her phone from her pocket and looked at the screen, hoping Sheelagh wouldn't pick up on the lie—the phone had made no noise, nor was it vibrating.

But it *had* connected.

Marcus.

Thank goodness. She couldn't quite believe that her frantic pocket-swiping had worked. She stared at the lit-up screen for another second or two, maintaining the pretence, then glanced at Sheelagh. "Sorry, it's Mum. I'll just answer it and put her off—if I don't answer, she'll keep trying."

Sheelagh gave the tiniest incline of her head, a small, crumpled gesture that indicated that Jess's hunch was right.

"Mum, hi, I'm just at the pub in the village with a friend, I'll call you back in a bit, okay?" She spoke quickly, and disconnected the call before Marcus had time to speak.

If Sheelagh heard a man on the other end of the phone, she'd know it wasn't Jess's mother. *Please let Marcus have heard enough already. Please let the Gardaí be on the way.* At least now, with this last clue to their location, he'd know exactly where they were, and rush to the rescue. She slipped the phone back into her pocket.

"Let's have a drink? Inside? It's a bit chilly out here now." She pushed the door open then stood back, gesturing Sheelagh and her dogs to enter first. As Sheelagh stepped over the threshold, Jess moved in behind her, not giving space for Sheelagh to change her mind and back out. She pointed to an empty table in a quiet corner, away from the huddle of locals at the bar and a small group of younger villagers, probably not even old enough to be in here. "Go on, sit down, what'll I get you?"

Chapter Forty

Jess set a half-pint of lager on the table in front of Sheelagh, took a sip from her own condensation-smeared glass, and perched herself on a low stool opposite Sheelagh.

Fletcher lay beside her, his large bulk blocking Sheelagh's exit path. The two spaniels, tired out from charging around on the bog, also settled quietly under the table.

"So, shall we try again?" Jess looked directly at the postmistress, challenging her to tell the truth this time. "What really happened?"

Before Sheelagh could answer, a strong, familiar, and immensely reassuring hand squeezed Jess's shoulder. She looked up into Marcus's deep mahogany eyes.

"You okay?" His expression was laden with concern; his hand warm and heavy.

Her stomach flipped with relief and she leaned into the weight of his palm. "I am now."

Marcus slid onto the bench beside Sheelagh, pinning her into the corner.

Fletcher sat up, thumping his tail against the table leg as he wagged a greeting. He shifted position to lay his large black head on Marcus's knee.

Marcus stroked his silky ears, eyes still on Jess, searching her face. "Good boy, Fletcher. You are a good boy." Hand resting on Fletcher's head, Marcus turned his attention to Sheelagh.

"Sheelagh Flannery?" She nodded. "I'm Marcus Woo. There is a Garda vehicle on route. It sounds like we need to bring you in to the station? I believe you may be able to help us answer some questions relating to the deaths of James O'Sullivan and Viktor Dąbrowski?"

Sheelagh nodded again, staring into her untouched drink. After a long silence, she finally spoke. "What about these guys?" She gestured to the dogs, who had got up and were sniffing curiously at Marcus's legs.

Marcus looked under the table, as if noticing the extra dogs for the first time. "Er, hello fellas. I'd better get the dog handler out. She can drop them with your husband. Is he home?"

Sheelagh nodded. "I think so."

"Otherwise, they'll spend the night in the police kennels or the pound. They'll be looked after, don't worry. I think you have more to concern yourself with than these two." Marcus held out a hand for the spaniels to sniff, then rubbed their heads in turn. "We'll see they're looked after." He reached for his phone and spoke quietly into it, instructing the dog handler.

Outside, the sound of a siren filled the air and the room pulsed with the blue light that leaked in through the smeary pub windows.

"Jess and I will wait here with them, until the dog handler arrives. That okay, Jess? We'll look after them?" He threw the question at Jess with a flick of his eyes.

"Of course."

Marcus stood, held out his arm to gesture to Sheelagh to go ahead of him, and escorted her out to the Garda car.

Left alone with the three dogs, Jess shivered, despite the warmth in the cosy pub. She picked up her lager and swallowed it down in a few rapid gulps, then picked up Sheelagh's untouched glass and took a slurp from that, too.

Forty minutes after Sheelagh had been dispatched to Lambskillen in the back of the Garda car, Jess sat in Marcus's conservatory, idly watching Fletcher and Snowflake charge around the garden as if nothing unusual had happened all day.

Marcus pushed a mug of steaming tea into her hands and sat on the edge of the battered wicker chair across from her, elbows on knees, leaning towards her, searching her face with undisguised worry etched on his own.

"You okay, love?" His voice was soft and full of care, and Jess warmed at the endearment. Funny how it sounded so different coming from Marcus compared with how it sounded tripping naturally off Linda's tongue.

She smiled faintly at him.

"Oh Jess. You really do have an unfortunate habit of getting tangled up with the wrong people." Marcus leaned closer and patted her leg. "Drink that. You'll feel better. I put some sugar in it."

Jess, having just realised that, grimaced and spat her mouthful back into the cup. "I know. Yuk. Shock or no shock, I'm not drinking that, thanks all the same." She passed the mug back to him. "I guess I feel better already. I'll go make a proper cup." Her smile was firmer this time, and she started to push herself up from the small wicker sofa.

Marcus was quicker, and already on his feet. He held his hands up, palms towards her, gesturing her to sit. "Sit. Stay there. I'll do it."

Jess listened as he sloshed her sugary tea into the sink, and waited for the sound of the kettle to re-boil.

Instead, Marcus reappeared only seconds after he'd gone into the kitchen, with a different mug steaming in his hands. "I guessed you wouldn't drink it. I made this one too." He smirked at her and dropped a gentle kiss on her forehead as he bent to give her the fresh cup of tea. "You're nothing if not predictable."

Drained from the afternoon's events, Jess couldn't summon the energy to respond, so she sufficed with shooting what she hoped was filthy look, spoiled only by the smile that she knew was threatening to escape. *Oh Marcus. You know me so well.*

She took a large swig of the new tea. "I don't think I'm in shock anyway. I mean, there was a moment back there on the farm track where I was quite worried, but once we were back into the village ..." She tailed off, reliving the panic she'd felt as Sheelagh told her she'd killed two men. "Thing is, I think she was lying." She looked at Marcus, who raised his eyebrows questioningly.

"Go on."

"Well, not everything she said made sense. At first, I was ... well, yeah, I *was* a little bit scared if I'm honest, so I wasn't paying full attention to what she was saying, but then ..." Jess relayed her thoughts about the foxes, and how that had started the wheels turning about the rest of what Sheelagh had said. "If she'd just shot a man with a shotgun, wouldn't she be in quite a state? I mean, blood splattered, for starters, perhaps? I don't know, but aside from that, I can't imagine she'd be completely calm. And then, well, I don't know much about shotguns, but surely they have a safety catch?" She studied Marcus's face, seeking affirmation.

He nodded almost imperceptibly. "Yes, should do, unless it's been rigged. And yes, you'd expect a lot of blood from a shotgun attack. Go on."

"Well, also, there's the distance. I mean, if she shot Tractor, and Viktor had seen something, he'd hardly have stood around waiting while she walked across the fields to him? It doesn't add up."

Marcus massaged his chin with his thumb and forefinger. "Hmm." He got to his feet and stood in the doorway, staring out across his garden. "I wonder what she's said so far." He pulled his phone from his pocket and dialled a number, before stepping outside onto the concrete path. He paced in the garden for a few minutes while Jess strained without success to hear what was being said. He slipped the phone back into his pocket, wiped grass clippings from his shoes on the mat inside the doorway, and sat beside Jess on the small sofa.

"They haven't got to her yet. Waiting for a solicitor. She's due in the next twenty minutes or so. Sheelagh refused an on-duty one and requested her own, so there's a small delay. I said I'll go in, if you're okay for me to leave you?"

"I'm fine. You go."

"Do you want to wait here? Or shall I run you home?"

"Drop me here," Jess said as they approached the park. "I'll walk the rest, you get on. Be quick; I want to know what she says." She climbed out of the car, let Fletcher and Snowflake out of the back, and waved Marcus off as he proceeded towards Lambskillen Garda Station to interrogate Sheelagh.

"C'mon boys, Let's run round the park first. Well, you can run; I'll think and walk." She crossed the car park, unclipped the dogs' leads under the bright beam of a floodlight, and watched them charge off across the empty playing fields, silhouetted against a rapidly darkening sky, chasing birds and sniffing at goalposts.

The day's events spooled in her mind as she lapped the park. *Why* would Sheelagh lie? What possible benefit would it be to her? Why admit to killing someone if she hadn't? Why would anyone do that? She recalled other conversations she'd had with Sheelagh; the time they'd met in the woods at the weekend, and the casual chats in the post office. Hoping to visualise the conversations, and recall specific words, she stopped at one of the benches on the perimeter of the playing fields, sat down, leaned back and closed her eyes.

Something was niggling just at the edges of her memory. Something about the conversation in the post office on the day of Viktor's funeral. Whatever was it? She jerked her eyes open as the thump of heavy paws hit her lap and a wet nose touched her leg. "Ouch! Damn you dogs!" She shoved Fletcher off and nudged Snowflake away with her foot. "You little buggers. All right, I'm coming. Let's go home."

Marcus had little to report when he returned to collect Snowflake a little after ten o'clock that night.

Jess spooned hurriedly thrown-together pasta into two dishes, handed one to Marcus, then sat opposite him at the kitchen table. "You must be starving. I didn't eat earlier either." She fended off his protest about her having cooked for him again. "It's only now that my appetite has caught up with me."

"She's sticking to the story she told you," Marcus told her between mouthfuls. "There are plenty of holes, that's for sure, but she's not giving much away. We'll keep her overnight and see how she feels tomorrow."

Jess frowned. "Weird though." She picked up a chunk of garlic bread and crunched into it, butter running down her fingers and dripping onto the table. "This is so damn messy." She licked her fingers and swung around on her chair to grab the kitchen roll from the work surface behind her. "Here."

Marcus wiped his own buttery fingers. "Tasty though. Thank you. I still owe you a thousand meals. Would you like to come down over the weekend and I'll cook for you? Or we could even go out, if you prefer …"

"What, so you still don't have to cook!" Jess laughed, happy for the diversion of their teasing. "Sounds lovely actually. I haven't been out for ages." A flash of guilt popped into her mind as she recalled Shay's suggestion last week that they go out for a meal, but she brushed the thoughts aside. She'd made the right decision, being honest with him, she was sure of it.

"Tomorrow? Saturday? Either is good … both, if you like—we could go out one night and I can cook the other … if you've no plans? You're probably seeing that fellow from the garden centre though?" Marcus tailed off as he realised erroneously that Jess may, in fact, have had a social life.

Jess smiled. "I didn't tell you, did I? We decided we're just friends. It was a momentary distraction from all the shite and trauma that's been going on—me finding dead people, for example. I appreciated his attention, and he's lovely, but …" She tailed off, stopping the train of thought from emerging irretrievably, and concentrated on shovelling a well-loaded forkful of pasta into her mouth to avoid not only spilling out any potentially embarrassing or awkward words but also the weight of Marcus's curious gaze.

Swallowing the mouthful, she changed the subject back to the more pressing events of the evening. "So, what else did

Sheelagh say? Surely she must have said something to try to convince you?"

Marcus chewed thoughtfully. "She did say one thing. She said it would be easy to prove, as her prints would be all over O'Sullivan's gun. She was adamant about that."

Jess raised an eyebrow, a forkful of pasta hovering partway to her mouth. "Huh? And are they?"

"We're checking but—"

"Oh my God! I remember what was nagging at me earlier—she had a sore shoulder. When I saw her in the post office on the day of Viktor's funeral, she was rubbing her shoulder. Exactly where the kick of a gun would have bruised! I bet that was why it was sore. You should ask—"

"Even if that's true, and even if her prints are on the gun, it's irrelevant to that particular argument. It wasn't O'Sullivan's gun that killed him. His gun was in the hall, not the kitchen, and it definitely wasn't the one that was fired that night. It was loaded all right, but the safety was on and it hadn't been fired. We don't have the gun that was used. That she didn't know that was yet another hole in her confession."

Chapter Forty-One

Jess was almost ready to leave for work on Friday when a text from Marcus buzzed into her phone.
Just home, why not leave F with me, then come for dinner after you finish? IOU food and update x

Oh yes please! That would make her day so much easier. No cooking, no stress over leaving Fletcher alone for the afternoon, and not too many unfilled hours to juggle murders and motives around in her mind. She called Fletcher, grabbed his lead, opened the back door of the car for him to jump in, and texted a reply: *Perfect. Lovely, thanks, see you in 5 x*

The garden centre was a good deal calmer than the previous few days. Ella had recovered from her fall, so Jess wasn't needed in the shop. She wandered out to the polytunnels, knowing that she couldn't avoid Shay forever and might as well get it over with.

She found him in the middle tunnel, bent over a workbench laden with newly emerging brassica shoots. Immediately, she recognised what needed doing, and set to work opposite him. The events of yesterday gave her plenty to talk about, and the discomfort and awkwardness she'd expected didn't materialise.

Shay was, as ever, friendly, funny, and reassuring as they worked harmoniously and systematically along one of the benches in the polytunnel, albeit always at least two feet apart, and usually remaining determinedly on opposite sides of the table, to avoid accidental contact. He listened in silence, save for occasional interjections such as "Jess!" and "mm-hmm," until she got to the part about the dog handler arriving and her finishing Sheelagh's drink along with her own before going home with Marcus to decompress.

"I have to admit, Jess, you are better off with that policeman, if you will insist on hanging out with murderers all the time."

She looked at him across the greening pots and the smile they exchanged was warm and genuine. "It's going to be okay, isn't it? Us, I mean?" she said, meeting his eyes.

"Yes. Yes, I think it is."

Back at Marcus's, tired but happy and relieved that things with Shay seemed to be uncomplicated, and also feeling somewhat over-stuffed from a very satisfactory meal, Jess kicked off her shoes and swung her legs up onto the wicker sofa in his conservatory, still bright even as the sun lowered in the sky.

Marcus busied himself in the kitchen, clearing the dishes. Every now and then he called through a question or comment but mostly left her uninterrupted and enjoying the silence.

"Marcus!" Jess jumped up.

Alerted by her shout, they collided in the kitchen doorway, drinks slopping in his hands. "Ouch. Hang on." He backed up into the kitchen and put the drinks down on the table. "What?"

"It was nothing, I thought, but now I'm not so sure ..."

"Jessica! Get to the point."

"Sorry, thinking aloud ... well, on Wednesday, when I upset Mike, he said, 'I'm not sorry,' and I thought he just meant he wasn't sorry Tractor was dead, because, well, why would he be? Tractor had caused him enough trouble, what with taking his land and carrying on with his wife too ..."

"Jess," Marcus warned, in his firmest policeman manner. "If you have something to say, would you please just get on and say it before these drinks get cold." He took a dishcloth from the sink and wiped the wet bases of the mugs, before passing one of them to her. "Go back into the conservatory and sit down, and tell me whatever it is you are trying to tell me in a way that even I can follow." He gave her a gentle shove, shooing her back into the conservatory, now bathed in an orange glow as the sun sank lower on the horizon.

"Okay, so, what I think now is that he—Mike—didn't actually mean he wasn't sorry that Tractor is dead—well, I think he did mean that too ... All right! Sorry." She fended off Marcus's impatient glare with a flap of her hand. "I think perhaps he meant he wasn't sorry he'd killed him." She stopped and looked at Marcus, letting the weight of her words sink in.

He nodded, indicating that he was at least considering her comment. "Go on."

"Well, firstly, I know Mike has a shotgun. He's mentioned shooting crows, so you should definitely check that out, because here's what I think might have happened: I think Mike went looking for Tractor, to confront him, more about having it away with Sheelagh than about the land, but he was already angry about the land too, so that wouldn't have helped. He has a fair bit of anger in him at the best of times, that man. And maybe he had his gun in the car anyway, or maybe he took it deliberately ... I don't suppose he planned to actually shoot him, but maybe he wanted to give him a scare, I don't know ... I really can't see that he'd actually set out to shoot someone, but—" She broke off and rubbed her arm, suddenly remembering the bruise Mike's hand had left when he'd stopped her fainting the day after she found Viktor. "He's strong, and he's rough, and he's *very* short-tempered. Sheelagh's said that herself enough times, but I've seen signs of it now and then over the past few months at the gardening classes. He's a pretty angry man. So, maybe they got heated and the gun went off ... I don't know, maybe Tractor picked up his own gun, in defence, or as a warning to try to stop Mike doing anything silly? But maybe that was enough to make Mike shoot? And, then if Viktor was close by, fishing, he'd have certainly heard the shot, wouldn't he? I mean gunshot sound carries for miles, right?"

Marcus nodded. "We have questioned Mike, but more about the land connection. We didn't know his wife was seeing O'Sullivan until yesterday, so that hadn't been a line of questioning we'd followed, until now. And I don't think it's occurred to anyone to check Mike's gun. We've a register of gun owners in the area, of course, but it would take ages to work through every farmer in the radius, especially without knowing how wide an area we're talking about." He crossed the room and grabbed his phone from the hall table, dialling into it as he continued speaking. "I'll get someone to check that now."

"And, then if he went after Vik—"

Marcus held up a hand to silence her as a tinny voice answered the station phone.

Jess strained towards him, trying to catch both sides of the conversation, but Marcus paced as he spoke and the movement made it impossible to hear the other voice.

"—thanks. Let me know." He put the phone down. "They'll send someone out now. Get the gun checked out. You could be onto something." He looked at her appraisingly. "You are, sometimes. Onto something. I'm beginning to realise it's quicker to listen to your instincts than argue with you, Jessica O'Malley. You should re-consider this gardening idea and come and work with me."

Jess fluttered her eyes in pretence of sweetness and compliance. "I don't think I could work with a tyrant like you; I've heard you bossing your people around. Look how bossy you are to me already, telling me to sit down and not ramble." She smiled angelically at him. "Besides, if we worked together, who would look after your dog?"

"Hmm, good point. You're not easy to boss around anyway. You don't exactly take orders well."

She swatted at him with a cushion, knocking over his mug and spilling the drink across the glass top of the little wicker table. "Oh bugger. I'm sorry!" She leaped to her feet rushed to the kitchen, as he chuckled behind her.

"And you're clumsy too, I take it back. I couldn't cope with you on my work team." He grabbed her arms, spun her around, dropped a kiss on her head, and pushed her gently back to the sofa she'd just vacated. "Go and sit down, keep still, don't touch anything. I will clear this up and then you can expand more on your theory. Sit. And sit still."

She did as she was told. They'd have to discuss these growing feelings of ... of what? Attraction? Was that it? She let her mind drift to how his eyes creased into those cute little crow's feet whenever he laughed at her, and how easy they were in each other's company, and how he'd just kissed her forehead, and ...

Alice was right. She really did like Marcus. A lot. And she was beginning to suspect that he felt the same way about her after all.

He tossed the wet cloth into the kitchen sink from the doorway, breaking her reverie as it landed with a soft splat.

"Good shot, Woo. Guess I'm the only clumsy one around here. Okay, sorry about that, but now you sit down, too, and let me tell you the rest."

"Do you have a theory about why Sheelagh would confess to it, if it wasn't her?"

"I'm getting to that." Jess nodded slowly, thinking. "I think she does love Mike. They've been together for so long, and have had some hard times recently. I would guess she's been feeling a bit guilty—very guilty—about everything. Her own job being under threat has put even more pressure on him. She knows she's made him feel inadequate—financially, but also as a farmer. He can't sustain the farm; it's not been viable for a long time now. He was feeling pretty low about that, already—has been for ages, I saw that in him way back when we first started the gardening course back in the spring. He never wanted to be there, never enjoyed it, but he had to show willing. She thought maybe he could venture out; do something new with his land. And meanwhile, she was also plotting to sell up, in case he couldn't turn it around, and he was devastated. He felt such a failure. And then, icing on cake; his wife then had a fling with the very same man who was taking his land from him."

Marcus got up and stood gazing silently out across the garden, his back to her, in a stance she'd come to recognise as a sure sign he was listening, thinking, analysing.

"He must have felt such a fool. He hated Tractor, of course, but I think when Tractor died, Sheelagh realised just how far she'd pushed poor Mike. I think she knew he'd killed Tractor, and was prepared to take the blame for it. Her way of showing Mike she was sorry."

Jess paused, waiting for Marcus to turn so she could read his face.

He swivelled slowly and nodded, his face serious and thoughtful as he stroked his chin with his thumb.

"Or... maybe she just thought that without Tractor, she might as well go to prison," Jess said, shaking her head even as she uttered the thought. "No, that doesn't work. If she felt like that, she'd have been only too happy to point the finger at Mike ... I think I'm right with the first idea—that she knew he'd done it, but didn't want him to suffer anymore because of her actions. She felt she'd driven him to it ..." Jess tailed off, running out of conviction. "I'm not sure—something still doesn't quite ring true, does it. I can't get from her being involved with Tractor to her instantly forgiving Mike for killing him ... that doesn't seem right. And then there's still Viktor. Where does he come in?"

Marcus kneaded his stubbled face, deep in thought. When Jess said nothing to fill the silence, he looked up. "I agree. It almost works, but not quite. I think I'll have to bring him in and question him, see if we get anything out of him. Perhaps the knowledge they're both being interviewed at the same time will either get them to say something useful, or at least trip each other up."

He called the station again, and gave instructions for Mike to be brought in. "I guess I'll need to go to work." He sighed heavily. "I'm sorry Jess, but I really should go in, see if we can get this sorted out. You've been quite helpful." He said this so deadpan that she picked up the other cushion, ready to swing it at him. He held up his hands, blocking the action. "Put down the cushion and put your hands where I can see them."

She did as he instructed, laughed, and got to her feet. "Okay, but you'd better fill me in later. I'll get off home. Want me to bring Snow with me, in case it gets late?"

Chapter Forty-Two

By Saturday, Sheelagh had been released pending further questions.

Marcus hadn't been able to give Jess much of an update when he'd called early that morning to ask if Snowflake could stay with her for a bit longer. He sounded tired, yawning into the phone as he spoke. "I'm still at the station, and will be here for a while yet. We've let Sheelagh go for now—can't continue to hold her, when we know her story doesn't make sense. We'll hit her with wasting police time, if nothing else, but for now, she's home. We're keeping Mike in for now. I can't tell you more right now."

Jess, aware that her cupboards were running low and, more crucially, that she was out of both wine and chocolate, needed to shop. She hated shopping on Saturdays almost as much as she detested slugs, yet, if she left it till much later in the day, the supermarket shelves would be as empty as her cupboards and she'd be even more bad-tempered about it. She scrawled out an extensive shopping list, jumping up from her breakfast every few minutes to check the cupboards for something else she suddenly thought she might be low on. List made, she swigged down another cup of tea, and pulled on her trainers to give the dogs a quick walk before she went into town.

She half-jogged, half-panted around the park with Fletcher and Snowflake, stopping occasionally to bend over, heaving for breath, pretending to any passers-by that she was stretching. Luckily it was still quiet enough at that time of the morning. Even Patricia and Ann, two of her neighbours from Orchard Close, only passed her twice, as they jogged effortlessly around the path, their Lycra glowing and their trainers pounding a rhythm that almost drowned out the sound of Jess's pounding heart.

After one lap, she walked slowly home, still puffing. She stepped in far enough to fool the dogs into thinking she was going right into the house, pulling the door to, while she lunged forwards to grab her car keys from the hall table.

She squeezed back out through the barely-open door, blocking the gap to contain the dogs. "Back soon lads, gotta shop. I'll bring you both a bone. Be good." She shut the door on their dejected faces, glad they couldn't really understand her promise. She had absolutely no intention of queuing at the butcher on a Saturday morning for a pair of stinking bones that they would first fight over and then would drag up onto the sofa and slobber on.

Maybe she'd remember to throw a pack of dog treats into her trolley instead. Maybe.

By the time she was in the car, two mournful faces were pressed against the living room window. She gave them a cheery wave, blew them a kiss, and drove away. As she rounded the bend, she flicked on the radio, adjusted the mirror, and swore loudly. Dammit. The list. She'd left it on the kitchen counter. Bugger. Ah well, she'd have to manage. She wasn't going to go back in now and upset Fletcher all over again.

She swerved around Linda's cat as he sauntered across the road. He'd not only put on weight since Linda had tamed him, but he now treated Orchard Close as if he owned it. Other cats might dart across quickly, wary of other road users and the neighbourhood dogs, mindful that in return for food and occasional petting, they had to respect the street. Not Maigret. When Jess's father had tossed him the odd scrap and pitied the stray just enough to keep him fed but not tamed, he'd been wary, feral, and a nuisance who howled at night and tormented the girl cats. Now, after a few months of Linda's tinned salmon, he was a very different cat. So different, that even though Jess still thought of him as Maigret—the name her father had given him—Linda had renamed the tabby tomcat Hansel, in honour of him having followed a trail of tinned fish to her doorstep in the manner of a small boy following breadcrumbs in a storybook forest.

As she drove, she tried to recollect the items on her shopping list. She zoned out the sports commentary on the radio, her interest in local kids' Gaelic games absolutely zero, and recited a new version of an old childhood game. "Jess O'Malley went to the shop, and in her trolley she put wine. In her trolley she put wine and milk. In her trolley she put wine and milk and bread..."

By the time she'd driven past the lake, the refrain had settled into a repeating loop of wine, bread, milk, cheese, with various random items appearing occasionally, only to be forgotten again by the next loop of the chant.

In the supermarket car park, she reversed her little car neatly into a handy space beside the trolley park and rummaged in the glovebox for paper and pen, finding only a crumpled till receipt from the post office and a pen that didn't work. She shook the pen, licked its end, and scribbled it on the paper until a faint blue line emerged.

The pen gave up again after she'd only managed to write *bread, milk, wine, carrots,* and *rice*. Right. She'd just have to wing it, so.

With a carton of milk in one hand and a pot of cream in the other, Jess stared into a fridge, trying to decide whether to get a large tub of natural yogurt or a six-pack of fruit corners.

"Jess?"

She swung around, the cream almost slipping from her hand, caught with a nifty block from the milk carton. "Sheelagh! Hello! I didn't ..."

"Yes, well ... I ..." Sheelagh looked away, not meeting Jess's eyes, and leaving Jess wondering why she'd spoken to her in the first place.

"You know I didn't believe you anyway." Jess dropped the milk and cream into her trolley and turned back to the yogurt selection. "So I don't know why I'm surprised to see you."

Sheelagh gave a quiet half-laugh that didn't quite sound happy. "They let me go. 'Don't leave the country, blah-di-blah.' As if I had anywhere to go. 'Stay around for further questions,' they said. Like on TV, except with more disdain and less drama. I'll get hit with wasting their time, probably."

Jess didn't tell the woman that Marcus had already told her the same thing that morning, but concentrated on wedging a pack of fruit corners in her trolley between the milk and cornflakes. Yogurts stashed, she looked up. "But why? Why would you lie about something like that?" She grabbed a pot of Greek yogurt and added that to her load. "That's what I don't understand."

Sheelagh sighed, and glanced at her phone. "Have you time for a coffee?"

"Now?" Jess gestured to her trolley, then curiosity won out. "Oh, why not. I guess this can wait. I haven't got far." She shoved the milk, yogurts, and cream haphazardly back onto the yogurt shelf, before abandoning the trolley and cornflakes at the side of the aisle.

Sheelagh put back her own carton of milk and dropped her still-empty shopping basket into Jess's trolley and the two women walked out of the shop and into the small independent café across the precinct.

Its glass-fronted counter displayed a limited, but attractive, assortment of homemade cakes, and its teas and coffees were listed simply as 'Tea' and 'Coffee' on a simple blackboard behind the till, rather than the complicated array of lattes and soya-skinny-half-mediums or whatever pretentiousness the coffee shops in town scrawled across their fancy chalkboard menus in four different colours of chalk and swirling borders.

Jess liked this little café. She liked the ease of asking for a cup of tea, without frills or complication, and having it brought to her at the table in a proper china cup, with proper milk in a proper jug, that she could add to her tea exactly as she liked it. She ordered tea and a slice of coffee cake, and left Sheelagh dithering at the counter over carrot cake or Victoria sponge, while she chose where to sit.

The café was about half-full. Gaggles of elderly ladies spilled over three tables, their wheeled bags cluttering the space between the chairs. A clutch of young parents and their children took up a few other tables. In one corner a solitary man with ruffled hair frowned into a laptop and stirred coffee. Occasionally he sighed, then typed frantically for a couple of seconds, before resuming the thoughtful stirring. A pair of flies buzzed against the window.

Jess usually preferred a window seat, so she could watch the people go by in the precinct, but today, she chose a quiet spot, along the back wall. She'd have liked the laptop man's corner, but settled for the table next-but-one to him, leaving an empty table between them to buffer the conversation. He seemed the type who'd eavesdrop. A writer, she'd bet. She glared in futility at the huddle of old dears in the other corner. They'd clearly taken up residence for the day, judging by the number of crumb-filled plates and cups on the table already.

Would Sheelagh talk freely in the midst of all these people, mingling here for a brief escape from the drudgery of the rest of their Saturday? Hopefully the hubbub that filled the room like the buzz of a cloud of insects would ensure no one would be able to overhear their conversation. Not even laptop-man.

Sheelagh slid into the seat opposite, her back to the room. "I chose fruitcake," she said, unnecessarily, as the waitress was already behind her, unloading a tray of exactly that, plus Jess's coffee cake, a large pot of tea, and two pretty china cups.

Jess sloshed milk into one of the cups and slid the jug across the table to Sheelagh. "So, how are you? What did you want to talk about that had me abandoning my trolley and having to eat cake instead of speed-shopping and getting home to the quiet of Ballyfortnum?" Jess smiled at Sheelagh, stirred her tea, shook the drips from the teaspoon and chopped into her cake with the same spoon.

Sheelagh frowned. "I'll get another spoon."

"It's fine—this one is fine. So, what's up?"

Sheelagh broke a corner off her fruit cake with her fingers, dainty and careful, in the same precise manner Jess had seen her attach stamps to letters in the post office.

Jess fiddled with her cup, twirling it in the saucer, and wishing she had got another spoon after all. The laptop man was stirring his cup far too loudly, and her fingers itched to stir her own cup to the beat of her own thoughts instead.

"They're keeping Mike in," Sheelagh said, after a long pause while she crumbled pieces of fruit cake into miniscule bites.

Jess washed down a mouthful of cake with a slurp of tea, and nodded. "I know. Marcus told me."

"Mm, I guessed as much. What else did he tell you?"

"Nothing he's not allowed to say; just that Mike was being held for further questioning, and you weren't. That's all."

Sheelagh refilled her cup, then gestured with the teapot towards Jess's half-empty cup.

"Yes please." The absurdity of the situation overtook her and she tried to smother the giggle that burst from her throat. *Just drinking tea with a murderer, Laptop man; nothing to see here.* Cake crumbs caught where the laugh had not. She coughed, trying to clear her throat, but the damage was done. Hot-faced and coughing in uncontrollable, ugly chokes, she wriggled out from behind the table and stumbled to the ladies, feeling all the eyes in the coffee shop following her. Shite.

She leaned over the hand basin and splashed water on her face, still coughing and spluttering.

Behind her, a toilet flushed and one of the elderly ladies emerged from the cubicle. As she squeezed soap from the wall dispenser, she clucked at Jess sympathetically. "Do you need a slap on the back, dear?" she asked, in a voice as soft and crumpled as an old tissue.

Jess, tears streaming now, shook her head and let out a small burp. "Excuse me. I'm so sorry. I'll be all right in a minute."

Still red-faced, but from embarrassment more than coughing, she returned to the table, where Sheelagh had conjured up a fresh pot of tea. Head down, Jess slid back into her seat.

"Oops," Sheelagh said. "That was a big reaction from someone who wasn't surprised? Are you okay now?"

Jess managed a feeble smile. "It wasn't that; it was that it suddenly seemed so funny—the two of us sitting here like little old ladies, calmly discussing a murder—two, even—and sipping tea and eating cake. It seems so bizarre. Right out of an Agatha Christie book. It made me laugh and that caught me by surprise. Sorry." Aware that admitting to laughing at Sheelagh's situation suddenly didn't seem like the best idea, she looked into her cup and muttered, "Sorry," into the tea.

Sheelagh said nothing, sipping slowly at her own steaming tea.

"I'm sorry," Jess said again. "Tell me what's happened?"

Sheelagh's shoulders drooped; her body appearing to shrink as she slumped over the tea. "Jess—" Her words seemed laced with ice and Jess could have sworn the temperature in the room dropped by about ten degrees as Sheelagh gave her a look that could have frozen a lake. "You may find this amusing, but I can assure you that *nothing* about it is funny."

Jess held out her hands, placating. "Sheelagh, I know. I know that none of this is funny—"

"—hear me out—"

"—I will never lose the image of Viktor's body—"

"Will you shut up? I'm going to tell you, and if you keep interrupting, I won't be able to get it out. Just listen." Sheelagh's voice, still cold, left no room for argument.

Jess shut up.

Chapter Forty-Three

"Well, like I said, Mike had somehow found out about James and me. I needed to give James a heads up. I was up at James's on that Tuesday evening. I'd told Mike I was going to my mam's. All that was true—like I told you before. But I went to see James. I was going to try to break things off, but I wasn't sure how that was going to go, to be honest. He was so ... exciting, you know?"

Jess nodded fractionally, to indicate that Sheelagh should continue, not to show any level of agreement. She didn't know; couldn't relate to Sheelagh's experience. It had been stressful enough for her when she'd realised that her feelings for Marcus were stronger than her feelings for Shay. She'd felt so guilty, even without cheating on anyone. She couldn't begin to imagine what Sheelagh had been feeling. She gave her head a small shake to clear the thoughts. *Concentrate*, Jess. *She's telling you something important.* "Go on."

Sheelagh took a sip of her tea. "When I got to James's, well, we did argue a bit, like I said, but it was more about James being worried that I wasn't happy with Mike. He said that whatever the future held for the two of us, he thought I should seriously consider leaving Mike anyway. He—James—was quick to admit that he wasn't offering me a long-term relationship. We all know he's not one for settling down. I knew that, honestly I did. I couldn't imagine a future with him, not really, but even more than that, I don't think I could picture a future *without* Mike. We've been together so long and he's like a pair of old slippers. The passion is gone, for sure, but he's ... well, he's *there.* If you know what I mean?"

No, not really. She'd never had that with anyone, but again, she gave a non-committal nod, not wanting to interrupt by asking for relationship advice.

"And then suddenly we heard a car on the drive, and James jumped up in a panic because he could see the driveway from where he was sat, and his face drained of all its colour and I guessed it was Mike. I heard a car door slam, and then James told me go, before Mike came storming in, and I ... I ... well, I thought he just meant for me to get out of the way so Mike wouldn't know I was there—"

"But surely he'd see your car?" Jess mentally kicked herself for interrupting, but the words had emerged before her brain had reminded her to hold them in.

Sheelagh looked surprised for a fleeting second, but her expression immediately changed to embarrassed. "No, I always parked it round the back, tucked between the sheds. We were careful."

Not careful enough, Jess thought. His brother was onto you. She bit her tongue this time, allowing Sheelagh to carry on.

"Then James said again that I should go, and he sounded really panicked this time. He told me to go off across the fields towards the river, to go *now*, wait in the woods on the edge of the field. Stay out of sight, he said. He almost shoved me out of the back door. I didn't realise at the time, but now I know he was really worried. He sounded so urgent that I didn't argue with him. I thought he was protecting me. I mean ..." She faltered, and took another loud gulp of her tea.

"He was, wasn't he. I guess he saw that Mike had his gun with him. I didn't know, until the Garda told me last night it was Mike's gun ... It was Mike's gun, Jess." She looked so stricken Jess almost felt sorry for her.

She reached out to place her hand on Sheelagh's for a moment, before pulling it away as if it burned. *Mike's gun. Sheelagh running for the woods. Tractor caught in his own kitchen ...*

Sheelagh carried on as if Jess hadn't moved. "—and to think it was only a few days before that I'd been begging James to show me how to use his. I'd never used a gun, and it was one of those bucket-list things, and we didn't see any harm in it. He'd let me shoot at some cans in the field, where the hay is stacked. Said I couldn't come to much harm with the hay there to stop the spray of lead. He showed me how, helped me hold it right." She stopped for breath, looking at Jess with tears brimming in her eyes.

"So that's why you knew your prints were on the gun." Jess joined the dots as Sheelagh composed herself, loudly blowing her nose into a crumpled napkin. "And, you'd hurt your shoulder, hadn't you?"

"How did you know that? Yes. I only fired four shots—double barrels, twice. That was enough. It kind of hurt, and James said I'd be sore if I did too much, and people would question the bruising on my face."

"But your face wasn't bruised?" Had she been wearing thick makeup that day in the post office when Jess noticed her massaging her shoulder? Not that Jess could recall, anyway.

"Exactly! But it would've been, he said, if I'd carried on. My shoulder was bruised for a week. It wasn't sore, as such, but it was tender to touch and when I rubbed it, it reminded me of the fun we'd had. His arms around mine, guiding my sight, reaching round to knock the safety off ..." Sheelagh's eyes glazed at the memory, her voice dropped so low Jess had to lean closer to hear. "His amusement at how excited I was when I fired the first shot! I was hopeless, of course; didn't hit a single can. I kept the cartridges in my pocket for days, but I was worried Mike would find them, so I threw them away in the end. Mike would never let me use his gun. He was always so careful with it."

"Go on." Jess leaned towards the other woman, urging her silently to get to the point. "Tractor—James, I mean, saw Mike coming and told you to go. What did you do? Did you go?"

"Yes."

New tears spilled from Sheelagh's eyes, and Jess almost felt bad for pressing her. Almost, but not quite. She poured more tea into Sheelagh's cup, stirred in a sugar lump, and pushed it into her hands.

"So ..." Sheelagh took the cup and brought it to her lips.

Jess topped up her own, although the pot was cool. "Go on. What happened?"

"I did as he suggested, and ran across the field to the pines. I would have been nervous of the cows, but luckily, they were well over the far side of the field, and I stayed next to the hedge, to keep as much out of sight as I could. I don't know what I'd have done if the cows had been closer ..." Sheelagh shuddered, her face pale and blotchy.

Alternative scenarios spooled in Jess's mind. Sheelagh, too scared to run, gunned down by her husband. Sheelagh, chased by a herd of cows, whether in attack or curiosity, either way ... *eugh*. Jess shuddered too, albeit more in sympathy of the what ifs than the real story.

"It only took me a few minutes to cross the field. As I ducked under the electric fence into the trees, two things happened almost at once." She took a gulp of tea and met Jess's eyes. "There was a man there. And I heard a gunshot."

Sheelagh explained that she froze on the edge of the treeline, still in view of the house, and the man reacted by grabbing her arm. "He yanked me into the trees. I nearly wet myself. Talk about out of the pan and into the fire." She gave a dry, humourless chuckle. "But once I was amongst the trees, he let me go, stepped back. He apologised for pulling me, said he saw me running, heard the shot, and instinctively pulled me out of sight. He'd just nipped into the trees for a pee, he said, but then he caught the glimpse of colour moving in the field and was curious. He was still zipping his fly when he saw me, he said. He even gestured to his crotch to tell me this when he saw me!" She laughed again, a bitter sound that penetrated the babble of the room. "I guess he was trying to reassure me. Foreign, he was, so his words were a bit off. He waved his arms a lot when he spoke." Her face clouded. "I did a terrible, terrible thing to a lovely young man who only tried to help me. He was so kind to me. Oh my God." She lay her head on her arms and sobbed quietly, her whole body heaving and lurching.

Jess didn't know what to say. She still had questions, but Sheelagh was in no state to continue until the crying subsided.

The waitress, sensing drama, approached, but Jess shook her head and waved her away.

Sheelagh took a shuddering, jagged breath, and lifted her head slightly to speak again, her voice barely audible. "I told him everything, as we picked our way through the trees. I told him my name, and Mike's name and that I thought he might have shot James. He was shocked, but calm. And so kind. He said he'd walk me to the road, get us some help, and then ... and then I suddenly thought it would be all over for me if he told anyone what I'd said, because if Mike had shot James, or if James had shot Mike—and I still didn't know, I didn't know why a gun had gone off, but they were both so angry, and I knew, I just knew—" She blew her nose again. "—that gunshot was not anything good, and one of them ... one of them ..." Sheelagh's voice was high and shrill, and the buzz of the café had fallen silent as faces turned towards them, soaking up the unfolding drama.

Behind Sheelagh, the alarmed waitress approached again, cautiously, slowly, but holding out a wodge of napkins and making telephone gestures with her other hand.

Jess took the napkins, and shook her head, a tiny, subtle gesture that she hoped the waitress would interpret as "not yet."

The man on the laptop had gone, unnoticed by Jess, and in his place a pair of middle-aged women gawked at the scene, one openly holding her phone towards Sheelagh, filming, presumably. No doubt they'd be starring on social media even before Sheelagh got to the end of her story.

Sheelagh dabbed her eyes, seemingly oblivious to the quiet in the café and every customer watching her. "And if James had killed Mike, or if Mike had killed James, then, then, all I would be left with was whichever one remained, and if they went to jail, and ... and I love Mike, I really do, and in my gut, I wanted to believe that neither of them could do it, but at the same time, I already knew that Mike's temper was fierce and if one had shot the other, well, it was likely to be him ... Mike, I mean, and all these thoughts were running through my head, that one of them was shot and I'd told this fisherman their names, and it was as if I could see my whole life unravelling, even though it must've have only been a few moments because the man was reeling in his fishing line, and saying he'd just gather his things, and as he leaned over to pull up his net, I picked up his flask to help." She took another shuddering breath, and said, quietly, so quietly, "And then I realised that if he didn't say anything, then Mike or James at least would be safe and I'd still have one of them, so I ... I swung it as hard as I could and cracked him on the head with it and he didn't even cry out." She slumped onto her elbows, head bent over her hands as she ripped her napkin into tiny shreds and made a small pile from the debris.

Behind her, by the counter, the cashier was speaking quietly into a mobile phone, while the waitress ushered a few of the gathering onlookers to back off.

Sheelagh seemed not to notice she was the centre of the scene. She didn't look up as she spoke again. "He didn't even make a sound. There was a horrible, horrible crack and he toppled slowly in, like in slow motion, and I tried to undo it, I really did, I tried to grab him, pull him back up, tell him I didn't mean it, but it was too late, he had fallen in, and I ... I couldn't get him out." She stopped abruptly and stared at Jess.

"Well, now you know ... so you'd better call that policeman of yours again, and tell him that I may not have killed Tractor, but I did kill Viktor, even though it was a terrible, terrible mistake and I am going to have to live with that for the rest of my life." She straightened up, took a series of deep breaths, and looked steadily at Jess, slowly nodding her head: *Go on, Jess, do it now; I'm ready.*

Jess met her eyes, nodded, picked up her phone, and dialled Marcus. "Marcus, send a car ..." She told him where they were, and that there were enough people around for them to stay put. "She's going nowhere, and if she does ..." she let the sentence tail off, glancing around the café and mentally adding up those who could detain Sheelagh if necessary. Not many, realistically, but Sheelagh nodded again, her fight drained.

"It's okay. You can tell him I'm not going to cause a fuss. I've done enough."

Jess hung up the phone. "Why didn't you say all this the first time?" she asked as they waited.

"I knew that I was responsible for both their deaths, whatever anyone said about Mike shooting James. I love Mike, and I knew he's been eaten up by what he's done—I guessed, of course, as soon as I knew Mike was unhurt and I hadn't heard from James. I guessed that Mike had fired the shot and James was ... and then, later, hours later, Mike called me, over and over until I turned off my phone ... I never answered him because I didn't want to hear him say anything ... I walked back through the trees, but slowly, in case he was still there. I waited in the woods until it was almost dark, and then, when I saw no lights come on, I crept back across the fields. I wanted to look; to see if James was there, but I couldn't. The door was closed, the lights off, the house quiet ... so quiet. I told myself if I didn't look, it would be okay, he'd just gone away. Mike's car was gone. I got into my own, and I drove away. Not home, not that night. I drove up to the lake, and parked in a secluded spot, out of sight, and stayed there, trying to decide what to do. As the sun rose, I called Mike. I couldn't go home because I didn't know what state he'd be in. But when I called he answered straight away and I could hear in his voice how awful it was and how distraught he was. So I told him someone had seen him, but I'd dealt with it, and I was coming home and we'd make it okay ... And he said come home. So I did. I went home to my husband."

A new hush fell over the café as a pair of uniformed Gardaí entered the room. Jess recognised one as John, who'd been kind to her at the river that day that seemed so long ago now, yet was only a couple of weeks ago. She raised an arm to get their attention, and the Gardaí crossed the room in a few strides as customers pulled in shopping bags and baby buggies to clear the way.

"Here," she said weakly. "We're here."

John put his hand on Sheelagh's shoulder. His colleague produced handcuffs, and Sheelagh held out her arms meekly. The Garda snapped the handcuffs on, and gestured to

Sheelagh to stand, taking her gently by the arm to lead her away.

"Marcus said wait here. He'll be here in a few minutes." John told Jess, as she gathered her bag, rummaging for the right change to pay for the extra pot of tea she'd shared with Sheelagh.

The girl behind the counter waved the money away. "On the house, hun, don't worry."

Jess didn't argue, but followed the little party out of the café and across the precinct. "I'll call him from my car," she told John. "I can't wait here with all these people looking at me."

John looked her up and down. "If you're sure? Marcus said—"

She held a hand up to stop him. "I'll be okay. I'll make sure he knows you tried." She stood a little distance from the Garda car as they opened the door for Sheelagh, and watched as John's colleague put a firm hand on Sheelagh's head to guide her into the back seat. Once the Garda slammed the door and got himself into the front seat, Jess turned away and crossed the tarmac to her own car.

She fumbled in her bag for her keys, slid into the driver's seat, turned the key in the ignition and switched on the radio. The lunchtime news filled the car, the newsreader's rhythmic voice a reassuring presence making her feel as if she was not quite alone, as she fired off a text to Marcus to tell him where to find her.

At the sound of tapping on her window, Jess jerked her eyes open, the leap in her chest telling her she was, after all, a bit unnerved by the morning's developments. She hit the button to deactivate the central locking and Marcus pulled open the door. "Hang on, I'll get out."

He held his arms out, and she stepped into them. He wrapped her into a tight hug, holding her close for a very long time.

At last, she pulled away.

"Are you all right?" Marcus said softly. "How about I take you home? We'll collect the car tomorrow. I think you've had enough excitement for one Saturday. Come on." He held out his hand to lead her to his car.

She started to follow, then stopped, in the middle of the driving lane. "Wait! I've no food in the house. I abandoned my shopping. I haven't even got milk."

"Oh, Jess!" The look he gave her was pure exasperation. "I told you it was time I repaid some of your cooking. This was a somewhat extreme way to make me keep my promise. We'll go to your house and get Fletcher and Snow, then back to mine for lunch. We can decide later whether you can cope with more of my cooking, and if you can't, I'll take you out for dinner?" He took her hand again, led her to his car, and opened the passenger door for her.

Before she could duck into the seat, he pulled her close for a second hug, kissed her gently on the top of her head, and whispered into her hair: "Please, Jess, no more murderers, I really would prefer you to stay safe."

She looked up into his deep, kind eyes, full of concern for her, and tilted her face to his.

His lips met hers, just for an instant, as soft and delicate as dandelion seeds on the breeze, and she knew she was safe. "Come on, O'Malley," he said. "Let's go home."

Acknowledgements

The first thanks, as always, must go to you, the reader. It's one thing to write; it's quite another to know someone reads my work! You make me very happy.

There are many people I need to credit for help with creating this story. Some years back, after I finished writing *A Diet of Death*, I put a post on Facebook asking for ideas. My post said: *Looking for plot ideas for a new story: Why would someone kill a man? Give me your reasons please. (Specifically, the dead man was killed whilst fishing on the river bank, but that doesn't have to influence the motive.)*

This story actually began life not as a sequel to *A Diet of Death*, but as an idea for a short story for a competition. On that Facebook thread, I wrote: *[...] for an anthology based on collective nouns for groups of animals, genre is cosy mystery, so I'm using the characters from my novel and giving the MC another murder to solve.*

I never finished that short story or entered the contest; I was too busy growing it into a full-length novel, which became this second Jess O'Malley mystery. The theme of the contest also gave me the idea for the book's title, *A Hover of Trout,* and some of the subsequent titles in the series.

A LOT of people responded to my Facebook post; it seems we all have ideas about how or why to kill someone! One friend—that will be you Ian O—wrote this:

Maybe he asked for story ideas on Facebook, wrote a bestseller off them, but didn't credit anyone or share the profits...

So here are the credits: Thank you to Stephen M, Ellen K, Nazzarena C, Clodagh D, Joy S, Edel W, Octavia T, Arlene E-VO, Elizabeth C, Ian O, Malcolm R, Maria C, Ani B, Tracy H, Jill S, Scott B, Margaret M, Alec F, Mia F, Stephanie W, Sally R, Tammy W, all of whom commented with ideas and confessionals on the original post. I'm particularly grateful to Octavia, who commented that she saw me snooping about down by the river that day and *didn't* call the Gardaí. Thank you also to Kris T who gave me insight into what she does (as a police officer) when she finds a body in the river. This story belongs to all of you, although many of your ideas were more serial killer/thriller-worthy than cosy mystery and I'm worried about you all! I don't think I used *any* of your ideas for the actual motive in *A Hover of Trout*, although my sister's suggestion did get paraphrased by Jess's brother Eric: *chip shop owner sold some dodgy fish ... ratings are down and he blames the fisherman!* Did you spot it?

I also want to give a special mention to a guy named Seb, who gets a cameo in the story. He's a real-live (hopefully!) fisherman I met while walking by the river one day, who gave me inspiration for many of Viktor's characteristics and cemented his nationality. In Chapter Twenty-Three, Viktor shows Jess the fish he just caught. I have some great photos of the real Seb showing me a fish he'd just caught. Thanks for chatting, real-Seb!

My work as an ESL (English as a Second Language) teacher has helped me with Viktor's family's dialogue, aiming for a realistic representation of how well ESL speakers use English without any need to perfect 'Queen's English'. I have so much respect for everyone who learns another language.

So, big thanks to all of the above, who were there from the inception of the story. I hope you read this and remember that thread.

Thank you also to Rebekah T, from my MA, who helped me get to grips with publishing this series in a different way. Thank you to my cover designer, Shayne at WickedGoodBookCovers.com, who has been a great help with advice as well as creating these awesome covers. Thank you to the Cozy Crime Collective for inviting me in, and to Indie Authors Ireland for opening up a new support network. I'm sure there are people I've forgotten, so get out your pencils and add your names to this page.

Thank you to my husband and family, and my dogs who enjoy long river work walks. We've never found a body, but we keep exploring areas where Jess O'Malley might find another one, in another book.

About the Author

Jinny was first published in Horse and Pony magazine at the age of ten. She's striving to achieve equal accolades now she's (allegedly) a grown-up. Jinny has had some publishing success with short story and flash competitions and has been placed in the prestigious Bath Flash Fiction Award, Flash 500 and Writer's Playground contests, published in MsLexia Magazine and Writing Magazine, among other publishing credits. Jinny has recently completed an MA in Creative Writing with the University of Hull, for which she was awarded a Distinction.

Jinny also teaches English as a foreign language to people all over the world and finds her students a constant source of inspiration, for both life and stories. Her home, for now, is in rural Ireland, which she shares with her husband and far too many animals. Her two children have grown and flown, but return across the Irish Sea when they can. She quite likes to shut the door on them all and write.

For up-to-date news and exclusive content including your own map of Ballyfortnum and extra stories about the characters in this series, please sign up for Jinny's newsletter by popping over to her website:
www.jinnyalexander.com
Say hello at facebook.com/JinnyAlexanderAuthor

If you enjoyed the book, please take a moment to leave a review on Amazon and Goodreads. Thank you.

Also by Jinny Alexander

Book 3 in the Jess O'Malley Irish village mystery series, *A Wake of Buzzards*, and Book 4, *A Deathbed of Roses* are out now. Book 5, *A Snapshot of Murder*, will be coming soon.

Jinny is currently working on more sequels in the Jess O'Malley Irish village mystery series, as well as the next book in her second cozy mystery series: Mrs Smith's Suspects. Book 1, *Claude, Gord, Alice, and Maud*, was released in summer 2024.

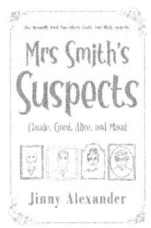

Jinny also has stories and flash fiction in anthologies and magazines, and a more comprehensive list can be found on her website at www.JinnyAlexander.com

Dear Isobel (March 2022, Creative James Media) is currently out of print following Jinny's reversion of rights.

Printed in Dunstable, United Kingdom